W9-DEV-811

To Tyler—
Thanks for the .. Publicity

JOHN RAVEN BEAU

O'Neil de Noux

O'Neil De Noux

for Harlan Ellison – *forever, man*

JOHN RAVEN BEAU is a work of fiction. The incidents and characters described herein are a product of the author's imagination and are used fictitiously. Any resemblance to actual persons living or dead, business establishments, events, or locales is entirely coincidental.

PUBLISHED BY

BIG KISS PRODUCTIONS

NEW ORLEANS

FIRST PRINTING MARCH 2011

CHAPTERS

Introduction of John Raven Beau

from the short story collection
NEW ORLEANS NOCTURNAL
Big Kiss Productions, 2010

John Raven Beau came to life when my first recurring character, NOPD Homicide Detective Dino LaStanza, decided to become a private eye. I had more to say about homicide work in New Orleans through the end of the 20th Century and into the 21st.

I needed fresh blood. I also needed someone with some of LaStanza's traits (a relentless pursuer with a killer instinct). Since LaStanza tapped my Sicilian half, I decided I needed a French-American character, so I went to my paternal grandmother's side – Cajun. Wait, Cajuns are not known for the relentless pursuit of anything except life. My Cajun relatives celebrate life. They are gregarious, happy people who are better known to *laissez le bon temps roulé* (let the good times roll) than meticulously hunting killers. Not that hunting is foreign to Cajuns, who stalk the swamps and great floating prairie of south Louisiana to hunt and trap every creature present.

An inspiration came from the work of my friend John Edward Ames as I was reading his *Cheyenne* series of novels about a tall white boy called Touch the Sky who was raised by the Cheyenne. In the Cheyenne and their cousins the Lakota (Sioux to most of us), I found the traits I needed. The stoic plains warrior - tenacious, loyal, determined and tough. Obviously, the Sioux are some of the finest humans who ever existed.

Wow – I thought. An automatic conflict within the man. Happy-go-lucky Cajun mated with indomitable warrior, indefatigable at work. Grinning and frowning simultaneously.

'Beau' came from one of my favorite movies, *Beau Geste* (the Gary Cooper version). It means 'beautiful' in French and my character would be good looking. The first name 'John' is in homage to John Edward Ames and 'Raven' from my favorite poem by my favorite writer Edgar Allan Poe.

Beau is different from LaStanza. He's taller at 6'2" and is clean shaven, although he has a persistent five o'clock shadow. He is unattached, as women float in and out of his life. Like LaStanza, Beau has killed men in the line of duty. Beau is more aloof, quieter and more brooding. He grew up poor, living a solitary life with his parents in a Cajun *daubed* house (a wooden structure with inner walls filled with swamp mud to keep the place warm in winter and cool in summer) off Vermilion Bay in Southwest Louisiana. Beau didn't know he was poor until he went to Catholic school (tuition paid by the Catholic charities) and was promptly informed by the other children. A standout athlete, star quarterback in high school, he was still unable to get a date to his senior prom as no girl would go with a 'swamp rat'. His heart was broken when the girl he thought was the love of his life left him shortly after he injured his knee playing football at LSU.

Coming to the big city, the Paris of French Louisiana it – New Orleans – John Raven Beau found a houseboat on Lake Pontchartrain and a vocation with the NOPD. He's made good friends and done good work, yet his penchant for shooting people, people who give him no other choice, has made him stand out. He is a killer, blindly admired by rookies, avoided by veterans who have been on the job long enough to know a police officer who kills, especially who kill more than once, is an aberration.

Homicide Detective John Raven Beau is a relentless pursuer, a man who will track a killer across miles of dark streets, through swamps, wastelands, over rivers and bayous. He will never give up. And he's an excellent marksman who also carries an obsidian hunting knife. Claims that he's scalped a few murderers is a persistent rumor.

Chapter 1
THEY USED TO TEACH DUELING HERE

Just as the hard rain lets up, a loud beep tone blares on my portable police radio followed by an excited voice – "Headquarters - any unit. Signal 34-S on police. Officer down. Five hundred block, Chartres Street. Units respond."

I step from under the covered walkway in front of the old Cabildo and look up Chartres past yellow streetlights and hulking black balconies suspended over the narrow street. A blue police light flashes three blocks up. I switch the radio to my left hand and bolt up the street, leaping two rain puddles and dodging an oncoming minivan. Bouncing off a parked Chevy, I barely lose a step. The driver of the minivan leans on his horn behind me.

That's what I get for wearing blackout – a black tee-shirt with black jeans and black Reeboks. The dress shirt I wear over my tee-shirt is charcoal gray. Unbuttoned and untucked, it covers the star-and-crescent badge clipped to my belt above the front left pocket of my jeans as well as my nine-millimeter Glock model 19 in its black canvas holster on my right hip.

Pumping hard, I cross Toulouse Street and the scene comes into view, a short block away. Inaudible voices yell on my radio. The blue light I'd spotted flashes atop one of the Yamaha motor-scooters used by the uniformed division to navigate the French Quarter. A small group of people are crowded next to the Yamaha in front of the Napoleon House Café, while two couples stand across Chartres at the rear of Royal Orleans Hotel. Tourists. The couples across the street have cameras around their necks, the men wearing mismatched shirts with baggy shorts. They stand mesmerized by the scene. Locals would have scattered by now.

I run up on the banquette alongside the Napoleon House. A short, blond patrolman takes a step toward me and raises his hand. I open my shirt to show the badge and say, "Homicide."

The patrolman puts his hand down. I point across the street at the tourists.

"Go over and get their IDs."

As I pass the patrolman, I add, "Now."

The front door of the Napoleon House faces the corner of Chartres and St. Louis Streets, separated from the corner by a ten foot slate banquette, known everywhere outside New Orleans as a sidewalk. Two feet from the open door lies police officer Cassandra Smith, her head propped in the arms of another officer. Andy Knight, his light blue police shirt covered with blood, looks up at me with red eyes. Motionless, Cassandra lies on her back, the front of her police shirt saturated with dark blood, her legs straight out, her arms opened wide. Even in the dim yellow light I can see she's dead, her face glossy with the unmistakable waxen look of death. Her mahogany complexion is gray and ashen, the color of burned leaves. I feel my heart stammer in my chest.

Leaning against the masonry wall of the three-story Napoleon House, perspiration rolling down the sides of my face, I try to catch my breath. I suck in hot, humid night air, thick with the odor of gunpowder and the sharp scent of blood. I spot a roach working its way up the wall next to my hand, up to where the masonry has fallen away to reveal the Creole brick-between-cypress log construction of the ancient building. I pull away and run my hands through my hair. It's damp.

Sirens echo down the narrow street, reverberating off the lacework balconies and masonry walls. Brakes squeal and a voice calls out, "Detective!" It's the blond patrolman waving at me from across Chartres. An ambulance brakes sharply as it slides to a stop in the center of the intersection. Two marked police cars stop behind it along Chartres.

I cross Chartres and the patrolman, whose name plate reads 'S. Stone', points to the heavy-set tourist in a yellow striped shirt and baggy plaid shorts.

"He says a cop chased the killer that way." Stone points his chin up Chartres.

Turning up my radio, I put it to my ear, in case there is something audible on the air, but have to turn down the screaming voices immediately.

I point the radio at the heavy-set tourist and say, "Describe the killer!"

"He's white. About six feet tall . . ."

I begin backpedaling up Chartres. "What's he wearing?"

"Oh, an orange shirt." The man points up the street and says, "A oop ran after him!"

Backing away quickly, I yell to Stone, "Keep them here. And get someone to write down the license plates of every car parked in a three block radius."

Stone nods as I turn and race up Chartres, past two more oncoming patrol cars. The Wildlife and Fisheries Building is on my right and I run along the six foot page fence surrounding it where the renovations continue to convert the old white marble building into the state supreme court. If the killer climbed this fence he could easily hide in the huge, white marble building. I dodge another oncoming patrol car, look across Chartres at the crowd lined up outside K-Paul's Kitchen and yell to them, "See anyone wearing an orange shirt run this way?"

Two sharp gunshots echo in front of me. I duck instinctively as two more shots ring out. Crouched, I shove my radio into the left rear pocket of my jeans and pull out the Glock. A heartbeat later, I run up to the corner just as three more shots echo from up Conti Street.

I turned the corner and spot a uniformed officer leaning over the hood of a white car. Arms extended, the officer fires three shots into Exchange Alley, then ducks as his shots are returned, blowing out a window of the white car. The return fire echoes.

Magnums.

I cross Conti and approach the alley, the Glock cradled in both hands. I squeeze the rubber grips that feel tacky from my sweat. Perspiration drips from my chin. Stopping just before the alley, I call out to the cop behind the white car.

"Homicide! You O.K.?"

The cop doesn't answer.

"You hit?"

"No." He sounds pissed.

I smell the burnt odor of cordite from the gunfire and flinch as two more shots slam into the white car from Exchange Alley. Louder now, it's definitely a magnum. I move to the edge of the building at the entrance of the alley. I know the alley's layout – a double wide sidewalk between rows of party-wall buildings pressed against one another in a long line. Tunnel-like with second story black lacework balconies, the alley runs for three blocks all the way to Canal Street.

Three uniformed officers, two carrying shotguns, come running down the middle of Conti, probably from the Eighth District Station a half-block away. The two officers with shotguns are short and stocky and run with the shotguns raised.

I wave to them and yell, "Homicide!" Pointing to Exchange Alley now. "He's in the alley."

The cops with the shotguns are wearing black body armor and black army helmets and don't even slow down when they reach the alley. Leveling the scatter-guns, they race headlong into the alley, blasting away.

"Jesus!"

The third uniformed officer, a lanky blond without a helmet or body armor and carrying a Steyr, one of those Austrian-made NATO machine guns usually carried by SWAT, follows the shot-gunners into the alley. I step in behind him.

The two with shotguns are at either side of the alley, crouched and holding their fire while the machine-gunner sprays the alley, shattering glass windows, splintering two hundred year old doors, blowing up one of the old black wrought-iron streetlights that line the center of the alley.

The gun jams and the cop tries to eject the magazine. The two shot-gunners step away from the walls to cover him just as another magnum round slams into the wall two feet from my head. Something sharp hits my left cheek and I go down on one knee. Instantly, the shot-gunners blast away at the shooter, who's hiding behind a green dumpster. The dumpster bounces for several seconds. The shots stop simultaneously and both cops start reloading.

Still on one knee, I take in a deep breath, let half of it out and carefully aim at the corner of the dumpster. The gunman sticks his arm and face out and I squeeze off three quick rounds and he falls straight down and doesn't move. I walk slowly forward. Illuminated by the streetlights behind him, the man in the orange tee-shirt lies crumbled on his right side, a nickel-plated Colt Python .357 magnum next to his head, which rests in a pool of blood that looks as black as night.

"He dead?" A voice calls out behind me. It's the machine-gunner.

I go down on my haunches a foot from the man I just shot, the Glock still pointed at him. I look at the unshaved face and unblinking light eyes and neat entry wound just above the man's right eye. The exit wound at the back of the man's head is matted with brain tissue and blood. I slip the Glock back into its holster and wipe the sweat away from my face with my left hand.

"Damn," the machine-gunner says as the two shot-gunners join us.

I look at the three and snap. "Who the *fuck* are you guys?"

The three blink in unison.

I point back to the alley entrance. "And what the fuck was that? A banzai attack?"

The machine-gunner takes a step back, his eyes wide. The two shot-gunners, light-skinned black officers with faces only slightly darker than my Cajun face, both look down at their feet. The one on the left chuckles nervously. Jesus, they're young.

Two years in Homicide, and barely thirty myself, I remember how crazy-brave I was at twenty-two. Although I was never that fuckin' crazy.

I let out a long breath. "At least y'all didn't shoot each other." I look around. "You only killed one fuckin' streetlight, a dumpster, fourteen or fifteen windows and a handful of fuckin' doors."

Pulling my radio from my back pocket, I tell them, "Y'all better check those doors and make sure no bodies are behind any."

The patrolman who had used the white car as a shield comes walking up. Moving slowly on stiff legs, a tired smile on his black face, Sam Batiste puts his hand on my shoulder and says, "I knew it was you."

All I can do is shake my head. Then I turn up my radio. I hear the machine-gunner asking Batiste who I am.

"It's Beau, man." Batiste winks at me. "Detective John Raven Beau. Don't tell me y'all never heard 'a him."

The three stare at me while pretending not to stare. I speak into the radio with the trade-mark Homicide Division's flat radio voice. "3124 — Headquarters."

Someone cuts me out and then another voice cuts in. So I try again, "3124 — Headquarters. Code four. Code four."

The high-pitched voice of the radio dispatcher responds. "Go ahead, Code four."

"3124 — Headquarters. We need a homicide supervisor at Exchange Alley and Conti. Perpetrator down." A moment later I add, "We'll also need the crime lab and the coroner."

"Do you need an ambulance?"

"Naw. He's 10-7."

Batiste moves toward the body and asks me, "You think it's *him*?"

I shrug and move to the side of the alley. Leaning my back against the wall, I fold my arms and close my eyes. Slowly, the thunder of my heartbeat fades from my ears.

God, I hope it *is* him.

I remember the previous victims, the crumpled bodies of two police officers gunned down in the line of duty, the horror of seeing their bodies on the autopsy table, watching morgue attendants cutting off NOPD blue uniforms.

"If anybody was gonna get *him*," Batiste says loud enough for me to hear, "I knew it'd be John Raven Beau."

Brakes squeal on Conti Street and footsteps approach as more voices arrive, but I keep my eyes closed. Someone mumbles the word 'Sioux' and I know they're talking about me, about the half-Cajun, half-Sioux detective with a penchant for extreme violence. If they only knew how my stomach was churning now, how I wished one of the damn shot-gunners or even the machine-gunner would have taken the killer out, so I could do what homicide detectives are supposed to do – write a report. Instead I'm headed for another goddamn Grand Jury appearance.

A voice says, "Look, he had a box of ammo."

Without opening my eyes, I call out, "Don't fuck with the body!"

The voices die down.

A minute later someone moves up close and says, "All right. Talk to me."

I blink my eyes open and look at the sweaty, dark face of my commander, Lieutenant Dennis Merten. Two inches

14

shorter than me, Merten stands an even six-feet but looks larger. A linebacker build, skin as dark as burned wood, Merten's wide face carries a perpetual scowl, even when he smiles, which is as rare as snow uptown.

I shrug. "I had no choice."

"That's what you said the last time."

"And the time before that." Immediately, I wish I hadn't added that tidbit.

Merten snarls and lowers his voice. "Just tell me what the fuck happened."

I leave out the sarcasm as I tell him about waiting out the rain under the Cabildo, hearing the broadcast, finding Cassandra, the witness, following the sound of gunshots and then following the banzai attack into the alley.

"They shot and missed. He shot and missed. I didn't."

Merten raises his right hand and touches my chin, turning my head aside. "What's this blood?"

Huh?

"Your face is cut."

I touch my left cheek and it burns. "Probably brick from the wall." I point across the alley. "One of his shots just missed my head."

"Lucky you." Merten's voice is still angry but I can see a hint of relief in my lieutenant's eyes. Merten's shoulders sink for a moment. He looks back at the body and says, "I sure hope it's *him*."

"He's a cop killer, all right. Don't know if he's *the* cop killer."

Merten rubs his eyes with knuckles the size of walnuts. "He's got a magnum. A Colt fuckin' Python to boot."

I nod, although I know there are almost as many Pythons in the city as rosaries. For a revolver, it's one of the best. Before I switched to a semi-automatic, I carried a Python. Mine is stashed in a drawer at home now.

A crime lab technician, burdened with a camera and two black cases, moves slowly down the alley toward the body. A white coroner's van stops at the alley's entrance. Two attendants climb out of the meat wagon and pull out a gurney and a black body bag.

The blond banzai attacker steps around Merten and asks me, "How'd you get here so fast?"

Merten takes him by the arm and leads him away. No way Homicide was explaining how their roving stake-outs in the Quarter did not stop the killing of another cop. I spot a streak of blonde hair to my left and watch Sergeant Jodie Kintyre enter the alley, followed by her new partner. She walks straight for Merten.

I watch Jodie, the woman who broke me in Homicide, as she steps in front of Merten, plants her right fist on her hip, her page-boy blonde hair glowing in the dark alley. She seems taller than five-seven because of her slim build and habit of wearing snug-fitting, dark clothes. That evening she wears a brown blouse with a slim black skirt, her weapon dangling beneath her left arm in a canvas shoulder rig. Commanding the other homicide platoon that evening, Jodie would have to handle another Beau shooting.

I close my eyes again and let my hands fall to my sides. My arm pits are sweaty and my back, still pressed against the alley wall, is wet. A cool breeze filters into the alley, and I smell rain in the air again and know it's coming back tonight.

Jodie's high heels claps as she approaches and I wait until she speaks to open my eyes.

"You know the routine," she says. "Not a word to anyone until we get to the Bureau."

I look into her hazel, wide-set eyes. Expressionless, Jodie's cat eyes blink back as she points to the crime lab technician standing on her left.

I know the routine. I withdraw the Glock and pass it to the tech who hands it to Jodie's partner, Detective Mike Gonzales. A rookie, he goes by the numbers, holding the Glock for the tech to photograph, unloading it to show how many rounds were left in the magazine. He'll have a time picking up the casings, especially the ones from the Steyr.

Jodie takes a step back and waves to the front of the alley where a crowd has already gathered. "I need an EMT over here."

Merten's standing across the alley. The big lieutenant's looking at the wall where the bullet struck, the one that almost killed me. A white-jacketed emergency medical tech, carrying a gray metal case, hustles into the alley. Chubby and younger looking than the banzai attackers, the EMT asks Jodic to hold his flashlight as he quickly cleans the wound on my face.

Merten sticks his angry face in and growls at Jodie, "The fuckin' media's here. Get him outta here."

The EMT nods and says, "It's just a cut. I'll be finished in a second."

Merten turns to leave, turns back and snarls at me. "Gimme your car keys."

I dig them out of my pocket and toss them to Merten. "It's in the police zone on St. Peter, next to the Cabildo."

Merten storms off. Jodie looks around, then looks back at me. "Wanna hear something funny?" She says it without expression.

"I could use a chuckle."

The EMT dabs something on my cheek, then pulls a bandage out of his case.

Jodie points around the alley and says, "They used to teach dueling here."

"What?"

"Ever hear of the *Code Duello*? Dueling masters had fencing academies here on Exchange Alley back in the seventeen, eighteen hundreds. Affairs of honor and all that shit."

The EMT finishes and steps back to examine the bandage on my face, as if it's a fuckin' work of art.

"You finished?" Jodie asks. The EMT nods.

"Come on," she tells me and leads the way out, leaving Gonzales to process the scene with the crime lab and Merten.

Dueling, huh? I feel goose-bumps on my arms. Sometimes this city is un-fuckin-real.

Bright television lights bathe us as we move through the crowd. I spot a black hand reach for me and see Batiste leaning over to tell me something. So I stop. He leans close and says, "Cassandra didn't make it."

I fuckin' knew that.

Jodie turns and looks back just as a blonde reporter in a gold foil dress and spiked heels steps in front of me and sticks a microphone in my face.

"Detective Beau. Did you kill another one?"

I try moving around her so I don't run her down on live TV.

"Well, did you?" she asks.

I give her a good, long, expressionless stare as I move past her.

"How many is that, Detective Beau? Five?"

Her name is Abby Grange, investigative reporter for Channel 4's Eyewitness News. A pretty woman, Abby made her reputation by bursting into private offices with a camera crew and shoving a microphone in someone's face, demanding responses to pointed questions. After all, it's the people's right to know.

As I open the front passenger door of Jodie's unmarked LTD, Abby calls out behind me, "Detective Beau, did you give this one a chance to surrender? Or did you execute him, like the last one?"

I want to tell her she's wrong. I've only shot four. But I know if I open my mouth, I'd just get into a 'fuck you' contest with her on videotape. So I shoot her a cold smile and climb into the LTD.

I hear her say something to the camera about NOPD vigilante rule, so I roll the window down in time to hear her quote the old saying, "Kill a cop – you die." As she berates me, calling me "judge, jury and self-appointed executioner" I roll the window back up.

Jodie climbs behind the steering wheel and I tell her, "Know what that woman needs?"

"Actually, I do."

"She needs a sense of humor."

"Nope," Jodie says as she cranks up the engine. "She needs a good ass-whipping and I'm just the woman to do it."

Chapter 2
THEY CALL IT – THE FLOATING LAND

Jodie looks up and asks one last question. "Is there anything you wish to add or delete from your statement?"

"No."

She points to the wall clock behind me and says, "It is now 9:05 p.m. This statement is concluded." She stands and turns off the video camera.

"I sure hope it's *him*," she says.

"You and me both."

She opens the door of the cramped interview room. "Good, the crime lab's here." She scoops up her notebook. "After he swabs you, go home."

I stand and stretch, then pick up the empty coffee mugs and follow Jodie into the squad room. Cluttered with government-issue, gray metal desks and matching chairs, the room smells of stale coffee and pine oil. She waves the crime lab tech forward and tells him, "I want Beau out of here before the animals arrive."

I have to smile. She's right. All I need is the Detective Bureau circus ragging me. I put the coffee cups on the coffee table and stretch my hands out for the tech to swab. The tech, a wide-set man with horn-rimmed glasses, hands me my car keys. "Your lieutenant says it's in the garage."

The tech quickly swabs my hands for a neutron activation test to verify if I indeed fired a weapon that evening – even though the closed-breech Glock was unlikely to register any antimony or barium. It's standard operating procedure.

"I'll see you at the Superintendent's Hearing," Jodie says. "Nine sharp."

I toss my keys in the air and catch them without looking. "You think they'll serve donuts with the coffee this time?"

She blows a loose strand of hair from in front of her eyes and I know my lame joke is a dud.

"Is the firearms examiner coming in early?" I ask.

"No." Jodie brushes her hair back with both hands now. "He works the *day shift*." Her voice drawls out the words *day shift*, sarcastically.

"Call me soon as they check the Python.".

Jodie sighs wearily.

"From Exchange Alley. You remember?" I point to the bandage on my face.

She looks at me for a long moment and I see something in her wide-set eyes. She blinks and tries to hide it, but I'd seen the pain. She turns away and shifts her weight from one leg to the other.

"You better get outta here."

At thirty-seven, Jodie's face is still void of age lines. And her yellow-blonde hair, as always, looks as fresh as if she'd just blow-dried it. The most solid homicide detective I know, Jodie can handle murder after murder, death after death, even dead children, with the precision of a master sleuth. Yet, every time I get into shit, she's there and so is that look of pain in her hazel, cat eyes.

"Go," she says firmly, whirls and walks away and I catch a whiff of her perfume again.

"See ya' in the a.m.," I tell her on my way out of the squad room.

I manage to get my unmarked black Chevy Caprice out of the police garage, barely. The rain has returned with a vengeance. South White street is flooded again, so deep I have to creep up to Tulane Avenue, the water sloshing at the outside of my doors. Rain slams against the windshield.

After a left on Tulane, I turn on the civilian radio and search for the weather channel near the top of the FM dial. I find it and discover, as I cross semi-flooded Jefferson Davis Parkway, that most of the streets in New Orleans are mini-canals.

"Hey. Hey!" The weather man says, "Welcome to wetsville. New Orleans is under water – again." He sounds like a bad impersonation of George Carlin's hippie-dippie weatherman. Clearing his throat, the weatherman turns serious for a moment, listing the streets that are impassable.

As the rain pummels my windshield, I slow down and remember the New Orleans History class I'd taken at LSU. The professor explained how the city was built in a place God never intended a city to be built, six feet below sea level, in the middle of a swamp, between a giant river and a huge lake. The French called it *Le Flottant* – the floating land.

I stop for the red light at Carrollton Avenue. Two cars are flooded out to my left, sitting in the center of the street. The weatherman returns from a commercial with, "Hey. Hey! Welcome back to the *only* major American city built below sea level. Just look outside!"

Then he explains that I-10 – the city's major hurricane evacuation route – is closed at Metairie Road. The underpass beneath the railroad crossing is five feet under water and getting deeper. So I take a right on Carrollton and creep up to Canal Street where I take an illegal left turn. Canal Street is clear and I make good time up to City Park Avenue for a quick right followed by a quick left on Canal Boulevard, which is flooded. Hugging the left lane, nearest the high neutral ground, I move slowly all the way up to Robert E. Lee Boulevard, passing several more cars stalled in deep water.

My windshield wipers are on high, and I can barely see out the window as the torrent slams against the car. I feel the car float through the intersection of Canal and Robert E. Lee, then feel the tires rolling again. I barely make it over the West End hump to Hammond Highway, which is passable. So I punch the Caprice and hit the brakes several times to dry them on my way out of Orleans Parish.

Crossing the small concrete bridge over the Seventeenth Street Canal into Jefferson Parish, I take the first right on Orpheum Avenue and slip into Bucktown. The canal is understandably high and the rain sprays the sailboats and pleasure boats moored to my right. With only a light wind, the canal is surprisingly calm.

I look to the left. Flamingo's Cafe appears to be still open, its pink neon sign on, and I feel a pang of hunger as I drive past. The cars parked in the oyster shell parking lot of the cafe have water up to the top of their tires already. I continue on to the narrow point of Bucktown that juts into Lake Pontchartrain and stop next to my houseboat. I look out the passenger side window and see my houseboat is riding the storm well; so are the houseboats on either side.

Turning left, I drive the Caprice between two houses to the levee and gun the accelerator, sliding to a stop atop the tall earthen levee built to protect the city from the lake. The levee here on the Jefferson Parish side is much higher.

A bolt of white-hot lightning flashes overhead illuminating the wide lake. Ghostly gray clouds hover over the black water that shimmers momentarily and looks like obsidian glass peppered by a million raindrops. The roll of thunder that follows causes the Caprice to shudder.

Shoving my portable police radio into the back pocket of my jeans, I grab my keys and jump out. I'm drenched immediately, as if I'd fallen into a swimming pool. The rain is cold. I slip and nearly fall on my way down the grassy levee, but pick up a head of steam near the bottom and jog all the way to the gate of my houseboat.

I fumble with the keys but manage to unlock the dead-bolt of the tall wrought-iron gate of my dock, the rain slapping me unmercifully. I make sure to re-lock the dead-bolt before crossing the narrow, wooden dock to *Sad Lisa*, checking the mooring as best I can before climbing aboard.

As soon as I step on the covered deck, I wipe the rain from my face and arms, pull the radio from my back pocket and unlock the door to the main cabin. Two minutes later, I'm back on deck, a white towel wrapped around my waist, an ice-cold long neck Abita beer in my left hand, wet clothes in my right hand. I throw my jeans, tee-shirt and dress shirt over the deck chairs and prop the drenched Reeboks on the plastic seat of another chair. I take a deep swig of beer. It's so cold my throat aches, the beer tasting bitter and sweet and wonderful. The rain picks up even more, hammering the covered deck's tin roof. The air smells of grass and fish. A bolt of lightning flashes again, immediately followed by a loud clap of thunder that reverberates over the canal.

Turning to go back in, I hear something – a cry or a moan. No, it's a whimper coming from the dock. Peering through the rain, I'm about to go back in for a flashlight when lightning brightens the sky again. I see a small animal standing outside the wrought-iron gate for a moment, but the sky goes dark.

So I go back in the cabin, climb into a pair of gym shorts, grab a black umbrella and a flashlight and go out to the gate with my keys. I turn the flashlight on and a puppy, still whimpering, takes a step away from the gate and looks up at me. Shivering, the puppy cries louder as the rain pelts it. I unlock the dead-bolt and open the gate. The puppy takes another step back.

"Well, come on," I say, swinging the gate wide.

The puppy goes down on its belly and then rolls over in the wet grass.

"Jesus!" I shove the flashlight under my arm, step out and scoop up the puppy, shoving it under my other arm. Wiggling and trying its best to lick my face, the puppy cries loudly as I try to lock the gate and keep the umbrella overhead. I manage to get the puppy, umbrella and flashlight inside the main cabin without dropping anything. After toweling off again, I dig out another towel for the shivering canine.

I flip on Channel 4 to catch the ten o'clock news and sit with the puppy on the rug in front of the TV. The puppy squirms as I dry it. It nips at my hands when I lay it on its back on the rug to finish drying it, leaving it under the towel when I finish.

Channel 4 News opens with shots of flooded streets. The pretty face of its newest anchor, a black woman with a slim face, wide brown eyes and bushy eye-brows, announces that this May flood is already worse than the infamous May floods of 1978 and 1995. And it's *still* raining.

The puppy finally disentangles itself from the towel, rolls on its back again and flails its paws at me. It's a male. Under the bright living room lights I stand the puppy on its feet. It licks my hands frantically and I see it's a Catahoula hound dog.

"Son-of-gun. Where'd you come from, little guy?" It's only a month or two old but already has the clear markings of the Catahoula, mottled coat of brown, black and gray, big floppy ears and trademark sky blue eyes.

"I wonder if there are any coyotes out there, too." The puppy gives me a goofy-eyed look. I'm batting zero with my lame jokes today. I stand and stretch.

"You hungry?" I ask the puppy. "I'm hungry." As I stand, the TV switches to a rain-soaked reporter standing on the Claiborne Avenue neutral ground, surrounded by flooded cars and exasperated drivers.

I dig three frozen burgers out of the freezer, pop them into the microwave to defrost. Then I go into the bathroom to replace the wet bandage on my left cheek and run a brush though my thick, wet hair. I need a haircut again. So what's new?

The cut on my face is about an inch long in the center of my left cheek but not deep at all. It takes two Band-Aids to cover properly. When I step back into the kitchen, I find the puppy sitting in front of the microwave. Its little tail wags back and forth. I plop the three burgers into a frying pan and turn on the gas stove just as the TV switches to a scene in Metairie. Veterans Boulevard at Transcontinental is flooded. Streets in River Ridge are under three feet of water.

"Jesus," I tell the puppy. "River Ridge is high ground." As if to answer, the anchor comes back on to explain how a storm front has stalled over the city, right atop River Ridge. Outside the houseboat the rain picks up.

I pull two hamburger buns from the bread box and a fresh Abita beer from the refrigerator. As soon as the burgers are done, I break one up for the puppy and put it in a dish in front of the TV. I realize how hungry I am as soon as I start eating. The puppy wolfs down its burger with relish. Then I go grab a bag of tortilla chips out of the kitchen. Channel 4 takes a break from the great flood to report other news. They update the war.

Jesus Christ, more American casualties. Then, a new wrinkle on the old O. J. Simpson Case. Fuckin' lawyers. Finally, they report that a New Orleans police officer was shot and killed on Chartres Street earlier this evening. The alleged assailant was subsequently shot by police a short while later on Conti Street.

"Exchange Alley," I correct the T.V.

They show a picture of Cassandra in uniform. I put the beer down. Then they go back to the flood.

Abby Grange's face finally comes on the tube a half hour later. Reporting from Arabi where a tornado has set down, Abby is as drenched as the puppy was when I found it. And it occurs to me that Abby's cop-killer story, featuring John Raven Beau, has been buried under twenty inches of rain. I raise the Abita to her and finish it off.

The puppy curls up next to my feet. I pick up the remote and flip off the TV and lean back in the easy chair. The rain taps on the roof of *Sad Lisa* like the steady beat of distant drums. I close my eyes and try not to feel lonesome, try not to think of home. I try breathing steadily, to lull myself to sleep. I don't feel like climbing up into the loft to my bed, not with the weather like this outside.

My mind wanders and I wonder if it's raining back home in Cannes Bruleé. I remember watching the clouds build into huge gray mountains over the Gulf of Mexico and move in across Vermilion Bay, how the air would suddenly cool and the Spanish moss on the Cypress trees would dance in a southern wind that smelled of salt water and fish. Sheets of gray rain would sweep over the swamp to pound the land and drench the small villages like Cannes Bruleé and St. Justville and towns like Abbeville and New Iberia and even St. Martinville, where Evangeline is buried. Then the rain would go away. The coolness would vanish immediately and humidity, like steam from a pot of boiling rice, would bathe your face like a wet rag.

Cannes Bruleé echoes in my mind with the sound of cicadas droning on summer evenings – fire flies and mosquito hawks dancing on moon-filled nights. I remember the sharp taste of filé gumbo, crawfish etouffee and bisque – the sound of my dead Cajun father laughing at the *Dick Van Dyke Show* and reruns of *The Honeymooners* on our old black and white Zenith TV.

A clap of thunder shakes the houseboat. I open my eyes and the puppy looks up at me.

"You know," I tell the dog, "One day the water's gonna wash this city away."

He pants at me.

"I killed a man tonight." My chest feels suddenly heavy.

The Catahoula twists its head to the side and stares at me with clear, baby-blue eyes.

"I killed *another* man tonight."

The puppy twists its head the other way, then puts its head back down. I close my eyes and lean back in the recliner and force my mind to think of nothing, to go blank. I breathe deeply, steadily, hoping for sleep.

•

"All right, pipe down!"

Assistant Superintendent of Police Bob Kay, commanding the new and improved Cop Killer Task Force, stands at the front of the Detective Bureau squad room, his arms folded across his large chest. Kay waits patiently for the detectives to settle down. We've been talking about the great flood. One guy even brought fins and a snorkel. Sitting behind my gray metal desk, I look through the wall of windows to my left at the bright afternoon sun. The green tint, sprayed on the windows to filter the sun's rays, has peeled away over the years, giving the windows a ragged look.

Kay, wearing horn-rimmed glasses with an elastic band that holds the glasses close to his round face and cuts a perpetual line across the back of his close-cropped brown hair, stands six feet even, but appears bigger because he always wears a bullet-proof vest – always. Today it is clearly visible beneath his white dress shirt.

"I want y'all to know how proud I am to be commanding this Task Force."

Bob Kay isn't a boy scout, actually. He just sounds that way. The long-time commander of the Training Academy, Kay had personally trained every detective in the room. We were his pupils, his little brothers and sisters; and he cares for us more than his life. He'll tell you.

"For y'all that are new to this investigation I'll give you a run down."

For the next fifteen minutes Kay explains the random shootings of two police officers and the fruitless investigations into the killings. Then he takes a minute to explain about the shooting of Officer Cassandra Smith. It seems that her killer was a 107 – a suspicious person. As soon as she stepped off her Yamaha, he shot her four times.

"As you know, the killer was subsequently killed by Detective Beau in Exchange Alley."

Someone at the back of the room claps, but only for a moment. Kay shoots the clapper a harsh look.

"The Colt Python the man carried was *not* the murder weapon used to slay Officers Stevens and Cochran. Consequently the killer from Exchange Alley," Kay pauses to look at his notes again, "this Casey Jones, is not the man we've been looking for ."

"Fucker was named after a train?" someone at the back of the room calls out.

"Hey, Beau." Another voice from the back. "How'd your Superintendent's Hearing go?"

Kay answers for me. "As you can see, Detective Beau has his Glock back on his hip and he's here, isn't he?"

"All fuckin' right," a familiar voice says.

I turn and see it's my old partner, Tim Rothman. Tim grins back and nods furiously, his curly Harpo Marx hair bouncing, his eyes bulging.

Fuckin' lunatic.

I turn around just as another voice from the back congratulates me for another good shooting.

"Fires three shots. Three hits."

"Fuckin'A!"

"You're all right, Beau!" It's Rothman again. "Even if you are a lone-fuckin-eagle crazy Sioux Indian. You're all right."

I have to force back a smile. Rothman and I go way back. Straight out of the academy we were teamed together in the Second District, the Jew and the Sioux riding through the wild nights, like little boys with guns. He's the reason I'd given up correcting cops, telling them I'm Lakota and that our enemies called us Sioux, which means "snake in the grass." Sioux sounds fiercer anyway.

Kay finally raises a hand. "I promise y'all one thing." His voice gets deeper. "We *will* catch the man who killed Stevens and Cochran – no matter what it takes." He flips open his notebook and reads the roll call, running off the names of the assembled cast of four homicide detectives, two robbery detectives, two burglary detectives, two sex crimes investigators, and three general assignment dicks. When he finishes, Kay gives everyone their new assignments, dividing up the murders of the two officers for intensive follow-up.

Since each officer was shot while on duty, each in a different part of town, the areas around the crime scenes would be thoroughly investigated again for witnesses and or suspects. Kay assigns other detectives to follow-up any miscellaneous leads that come in.

Then he says, "Detectives Beau and Gonzales will work independently. Gonzales, because he speaks Spanish, will use that expertise in the Latin areas of town. Beau, because that's the only way he works, or so I hear."

"Fuckin' A," someone cries out.

"Track 'em. Shoot 'em. Scalp 'em!"

I raise my hand.

"You have a question, Detective Beau?" Kay likes to keep things formal.

I pull my wrap-around Ray Ban super-black sunglasses from the front pocket of my dress shirt and put them on and say, "We're not working this on the *day shift*, are we?"

"No way," Kay answers and raises a hand when another 'Fuckin' A' rings out. "And we're taking Lieutenant Merten's suggestion to end the surveillance work. We're working this case like a homicide should be worked. At night and on the street." Kay sticks his jaw out and pounds his chest. "No more sitting around, waiting to react. We're using pro-active homicide investigating."

Good. My kinda ball game.

Chapter 3
IT'S TIME TO GO PLAY SHOOT 'EM UP

I rub my chin and feel my perpetual five o'clock shadow. Standing with my back against the rear wall of The Blue Note Bar, I scan the crowded room. The driving sound of a reggae band reverberates in my ears. Couples gyrate on the hardwood dance floor. Women, mostly brunettes in miniskirts, move hypnotically to the music with well-dressed partners, young men wearing baggy pants and open-collared shirts.

I'm wearing a blue, linen tee-shirt, black pleated pants, and a short-sleeved, navy blue dress shirt, unbuttoned and hanging out of my pants to hide my badge, Glock and the handcuffs I'd tucked into my belt at the small of my back. I have an Abita beer long neck in my left hand. A whiff of cigarette smoke wafts across my face and I wave it away just as the crowd on the dance floor opens and a dark-haired couple, doing the Lambada, dry-hump each other to the rising cheers of the crowd.

I continue scanning the bar, looking for red hair. The Blue Note's young crowd is a true melting-pot of whites and blacks and various shades in between, like me. The band of Caribbean blacks, their shirtless skin shimmering under the band lights, sound so much like Bob Marley and The Wailers, I did a double take earlier. The lead singer's hair is braided Rastafarian-style, and he looks a little like the late Bob Marley.

Just to the left of the steel drummer, I spot a familiar face also scanning the crowd. I smile to myself and slip away from the wall to worm my way through the crowd and ease up next to Mike Gonzales. I wait until Gonzales looks my way, raise the Abita and call out over the music, "Óla, amigo!"

Gonzales closes his eyes and shakes his head.

A blonde in a silver minidress pushes past me, her perfume strong and sweet. She gives me a wicked wink and continues on. I take a swig of beer.

Gonzales opens his eyes and shouts, "Your cologne stinks."

I point to the swaying hips of the retreating blonde.

Gonzales shoots her a look, cups his left hand next to his mouth and says, "What are you doing here?"

"Working? I thought you were hanging out in the Latin areas?"

Gonzales' brown eyes widen. "*This* is a Latino bar."

"It is?" I look around at the people and shrug.

Gonzales throws his head back and laughs. He points to the front door and shouts, "Outside!"

I lead the way through the people and the sound of driving guitars, a hollow steel drum and a singer moaning about waiting in vain for love. Outside the heat and humidity wash across my face like an oven door opening. A bus moves along Magazine Street, puffing acidic exhaust fumes over us. Gonzales coughs.

I wait to catch my breath, then say, "I'm looking for a red-headed girl."

"So who isn't?" Gonzales wears his hair slicked back tonight, á la Andy Garcia, along with a nice two-piece black suit. His shoes are two-tone black and white.

"Her name's Sandie. She's a hooker." I take a hit of Abita, then say, "Half-a-hooker, actually. Semi-pro."

Gonzales laughs so hard he starts coughing.

I look up and then down narrow Magazine Street. Most of the shops are closed at night. Cars are parked back to back on either side of the two-lane street. Most of the small businesses have apartments to rent upstairs, wood frame buildings painted loud colors in this lower-middle class part of town.

When Gonzales recovers, I add, "She only works weekends. This is Tuesday. She'll be out catting."

The door opens behind us and I turn in time to see the blonde in the silver minidress slink out. I step aside and she breezes between us, her strong perfume ridding the air of exhaust fumes. We watch her pass and watch her turn around.

She purses her lips at us and says, "You're wanted in the car." Lifting her right hand, she points to a white Ford Taurus parked against the curb a half block down Magazine.

"Yeah. Right!" I take another hit of Abita.

"You," the blond calls out. "Tall boy. I'm talking to you." She waves her finger at me.

Gonzales leans a hand against the wall to keep from collapsing from laughter.

I give the blond the look my Sioux grandfather taught me, the stern look of the plains warrior – a hard glint to the eyes, a face completely void of expression.

Just then a head sticks out of the Taurus, a red-head. "Beau. Get your Cajun ass over here."

"Come on," I tell Gonzales. "Better back me up. The blond looks dangerous."

"No. I'm looking for someone too." Gonzales rolls his eyes. "Only my snitch ain't as nasty-looking as yours." He goes back into the bar.

The blond leans against the side of the Taurus and sucks on a cigarette.

I move around her as Sandie leans across the front seat to the passenger side window of the car. She wears a red minidress so low-cut I can see her left nipple. She smiles at me and purrs, "Sorry I'm late."

I look at the blond again and she blows smoke up in my face.

"You know," I tell the blond. "You look a lot better from a distance."

"Yeah! Well fuck you!" She pushes away from the car. "Fuckin' cop." Then she swishes back into the bar.

Sandie pulls her long curly hair away from her face and shrugs. "She's got a temper, that one." She runs her tongue lightly over her lips which shine with bright red lipstick.

"So." I lean into the car. "You come up with anything?"

Sandie twists her head to one side and says, "Not a goddamn thing."

"Come on. There's not one word on the street? Not even a rumor?"

"I hear you got men working the projects pretty hard. You know I can't help you there."

"You slummin' on me, young lady?" I shake my head.

She recoils as if I'd slapped her.

"You know better than that." She bats her light brown eyes and gives me a hurt look. A long-time snitch ever since I helped her get away from a boyfriend who liked to beat her,

Sandie is as good as she is naughty. I check my watch. It's ten sharp.

"All right," she says. "I told you I'd come up with something and I will. It just isn't easy." She leans over further, her minidress rising. She touches my arm. "We're talking about cop killers, for Chrissake. They ain't easy to catch."

I back away from the car and her hand falls away. I pull out a business card and jot my home phone number on the back and pass it to her. "Call me when you come up with something. Call headquarters or this number." I point my right index finger at her pretty nose. "Call me."

As I walk away, she says, "How about a hum job? On the house."

I'd parked the Caprice a block down from Magazine on Milan Street beneath the twisted branches of a magnolia tree. Cranking up the engine, I put the AC on frosty and take Milan straight down to Annunciation. The AC hasn't had time to even cool me before I pull over in front of a white shotgun house sandwiched between two camel-backs. I step through the front gate of the page fence in front of the house. Three steps later I'm up on the narrow front gallery knocking on the screen door. Across the street, three wary black faces watch me.

The door opens and Reverend Chester Holliday's face beams at me.

"Well," Holliday says, opening the screen door. "Come on in John." One of the few who call me by my first name. I step in and the reverend pats me on the shoulder. "Good to see you, my boy."

The house smells of lemon cleaner and popcorn and is thankfully cool. I fan my dress shirt . The reverend waves me to an easy chair next to the sofa.

"Popcorn?" The reverend lifts a huge orange plastic bowl from the coffee table.

"No thanks."

"How about a cold one?"

"A soft drink'd be nice."

The reverend puts the popcorn bowl down and goes back to the kitchen. He's back in less than a minute with two icy Coca-Colas and passes one to me. He sits on the sofa and scoops up the popcorn bowl with his free hand.

I take a sip of Coke. "I'm working on the murders of those police officers."

"I figured." The reverend leans back and shoves a handful of popcorn into his mouth. A former New Orleans Saint now in his mid-fifties, he's a big man with a massive frame and a wide face as muddy brown as Mississippi River water.

"You got a real problem don't you?" The reverend's brow furrows.

I nod and take another drink of Coke.

"I'm familiar with the case, of course." The reverend takes a drink of his Coke. "I'm concerned, since one of the murders happened not far from here."

Cochran was killed not six blocks from here on Tchoupitoulas Street. I watch the big man's eyes.

"I've been checking on my own."

"I figured you would."

I wait while the reverend stuffs another handful of popcorn into his mouth. We'd met five years earlier, when I was a patrolman. Reverend Chester Holliday called police when he saw four teen-aged boys park a car in front of his house and start to strip it. When my patrol car made the corner, the teens bolted like jack rabbits. I recovered the stolen car. When the reverend said he didn't know the names of any of the teens, I didn't push the issue. The reverend seemed to appreciate it and over the years always talked straight to me, as straight as any man could.

"I was worried at first. So I talked with the kids around here. They know everything that happens in a neighborhood."

I couldn't agree more.

The reverend goes, "I'm pretty sure it's nobody from around here. I hear it's a street thing."

"What?"

"Just a rumor. A street thing between some hard-ass white boys and the police." The reverend blinks his dark eyes at me. "Thank God, it's white boys."

I make sure my eyes don't reveal my thoughts. A witness had seen a white man running away from one of the murders.

"I appreciate your help," I tell him. "If there's any way you can find anyone who saw anything, or who *hears* anything – "

"I got my ear to the ground."

"Thanks." I stand up and finish the Coke.

Before leaving I ask to use the bathroom.

"Remember what Lyndon Johnson said?" Smiling, the reverend points the way to the bathroom. "He said never pass up a free meal or the chance to use the bathroom."

•

I make a quick stop at the A&P on Robert E. Lee Boulevard before heading for Bucktown. As I pass Flamingo's, I look at my watch. Ten-forty. I have time for a good supper after I check on the puppy. I park the Caprice next to my gate and grab the grocery bag. The puppy starts yipping before I unlock the gate. As I step onto *Sad Lisa*, the puppy bounces up and down, then spins around in circles, yipping louder.

"So how's it going, little buddy?"

The puppy rolls on its back and kicks its paws at me. I put the bag down, lean over and rub the puppy's belly. It licks my hand furiously. I reach in the bag with my free hand and pull out a can.

"See what I bought you?" I show him the can of puppy chow. So excited, the puppy pees on my hand.

"Great!"

I get up and move to the outside sink and wash my hands. We go into the main cabin and fix the puppy's supper, mixing dry food with a half can of puppy chow. I put it out on deck and the puppy attacks the food. After making sure the puppy has fresh water, I go back in and wash my hands thoroughly in the bathroom and check the answer machine. No messages.

Stepping back on deck, I catch a whiff of urine. I turn on the main lights and see yellow spots on deck, as well as a couple puppy turds. I pick up the puppy and his food dish and put them on a chair, then grab the hose and wash off the deck. Putting the puppy and dish back down, he doesn't seem to notice he's been moved. He keeps eating. I refill his water bowl.

"See 'ya later," I tell the dog on my way off the boat and remind myself I need a good name for the little sucker.

•

Flamingo's Cafe is an old-fashioned diner with a long counter running from the register next to the front door to the bathrooms at the rear. A center aisle divides the counter's stools from the five booths against the wall of windows that face the oyster shell parking lot and Orpheum Avenue. With pink walls and a turquoise Formica counter that matches the table-tops of the booths, Flamingo's is straight out of the Fifties.

As usual, the cash register is manned by owner Cecilia Henderson, white female, fifty-five, five feet-five inches tall, weighing in at around two hundred. Cecilia wears her light brown hair up in a bun in back and the sleeves of her white waitress uniform rolled up her beefy arms. Her spectacles dangle around her neck on a silver chain. The grill, behind the counter, is manned by a short, wiry black man named Joe whose perpetual smile is as much a fixture as his great cooking.

When I enter, Cecilia looks up at me and her mouth makes a little 'O'. She waves me to my usual booth at the rear of the diner and follows me with a short glass of water and a napkin wrapped around two spoons, a fork and a butter knife. The strong smell of fried burgers and onions causes my belly to rumble.

"How it's going Joe?" I call out as I pass.

"OK, how you doing?" Joe waves a metal spatula at me.

"Fine." I put my radio on the table and settle in my booth, my back against the rear wall so I can watch the front door like a good cop.

Cecilia puts the utensils and water in front of me, leans over and says, "Are you really OK?"

"Sure why not?"

It takes a second for me to realize she's shook.

"What is it?"

"The paper said – "

I let out a long breath, then tell her, as nicely as I can, that whatever the newspaper says is bullshit. "The paper has more fantasy in it than a *Star Trek* script."

"Then you're not in trouble?"

"No. Just hungry."

I'm so glad I don't read the paper.

The door of the storeroom between the bathrooms opens, and to my surprise, another waitress steps out and moves up the aisle to the only other customer in the place, a bald man wearing a green polo shirt.

Cecilia clears her throat and says, "She started the night of the flood and we all almost drowned trying to get out of here."

"What's her name?"

"That's for you to find out," Cecilia whispers. On her way back to the cash register, she taps the new waitress on the shoulder and points to me.

Turning my way, the new waitress pulls a pencil from the top pocket of her uniform. She's very pretty and has a nice, petite shape that looks damn good in white. Her dark brown hair is cut in a long page boy. She looks like Marisa Tomei, a lot like Marisa Tomei.

She doesn't look at me until she reaches my booth. When she does, she focuses a pair of large blue-green eyes at me – aquamarine eyes. I feel my chest tighten a moment, but it fades into a sinking feeling. She's young, too young. Twenty maybe.

I look around her at the menu on the wall above the counter, as if I need to look at it. "I'd like a cheese-burger. Fries. And a Barq's, please."

Nodding, she writes my order on her pad then looks back at me.

"Anything else, officer?" The way she calls me "officer" makes me sound old. She has a nice mouth, a little too large for her small face. Her lips are delicate and sculptured. She is fuckin' beautiful.

I shake my head and she pirouettes and walks away. I look out at the dark night. I'd don't want to look at her backside again. When she came out of the supply room, I'd more than noticed how nice it was.

She returns with the Barq's and smiles shyly at me. I reach for the icy bottle of root beer, expecting her to leave, only she doesn't. I look up at the aquamarines. She tilts her head to the side, her hair falling away from her face on one side and across her neck on the other. She says, "Why is your houseboat called *Sad Lisa*?"

I sit back and smile slightly and tell her the previous owner named it. "Probably after the Cat Stevens song."

"Who?"

Too young to know Cat Stevens. I feel old.

"Why didn't you change the name?" Her voice is deep and sounds very sexy, like Lauren Bacall back when she was about twenty, spinning Bogie's head around.

I shrug. "I had a cousin named Lisa who died a long time ago. Leukemia. So I figured, why change the name?"

"Oh." She looks over her shoulder at the bald-headed man, then looks back at me and says, "What's it like to kill someone?"

It's like a stab in my belly. I narrow my eyes and look deep into the aquamarines. I want to say something cute, like asking if she's writing a book or maybe working for the FBI, but I don't feel cute, so I say, "It's different each time."

Her mouth makes an 'O'.

Joe puts my plate on the counter and calls out, "Ready."

She backs away and I look out at the night again.

When she returns with my burger and fries, she leaves a bottle of ketchup. I watch her go to the front and sit on the stool next to Cecilia at the register. She has an easy, smooth walk and her legs look extra nice when crossed.

I pick up the burger and take a bite and it's spicy-delicious, just the way I like it. I wave to Joe who grins at me. I look out at the night once more as I eat the burger and the fries, washing them down with the cold Barq's. Cecilia starts talking to the bald customer about the great flood, how Flamingo's would have bought it if it wasn't elevated several feet. The new waitress waits until I finish before bringing me a second Barq's without me asking. I like that. I thank her and take a swig.

She puts her knee up on the bench on the other side of my booth and puts her right hand on her hip, the aquamarines staring at me again. I stare back for long seconds before she finally blinks and says, "What kind of accent is that?"

"Cajun, I guess."

Her head tilts again. "Cecilia said you're Sioux Indian."

"My mother is Oglala Sioux, my father was pure Boogaleé."

She looks over her shoulder at the front door, then looks back and says, "Boogaleé?"

"A polite term for Coon-Ass." Which is slang for Cajun.

She looks at the front door again, then asks, "What happened to your face?" She points at the my left cheek.

"Cut myself shaving."

She looks back at the front door just as it opens. A burly man with curly salt-and-pepper hair steps in. Wearing a plaid shirt and jeans, he waves to the waitress, who turns back to me and pulls her note pad from her pocket. She puts my check next to my plate. She looks again at the burly man who's leaning an elbow on the counter now.

I dig out a twenty and tell her to keep the change.

"Thanks." She smiles for the first time and her face brightens. She shoves the money and ticket into her pocket, grabs my dish and utensils in one scoop and moves away.

I get up and go to the bathroom. When I step back out, I see her leaving with the burly man. They climb into a Yellow Cab and drive off down Orpheum. I grab my radio and move to the front of the cafe and sit on the first stool next to Cecilia, who's preparing to close the cafe at midnight.

"Coffee?" Cecilia asks.

"Sure."

She pours me a mug and puts it in front of me.

I laugh at myself and say aloud, "Didn't even get her name."

"Angie," Cecilia says. "Angie Calogne. She's twenty-two. Goes to UNO. That was her daddy. He drops her off and picks her up. Pretty ain't she?"

I take a sip of coffee. "Do you know anyone around here missing a puppy? A catahoula."

45

Cecilia shakes her head the way the nuns used to when they wanted me to say something and I said something else instead. She folds her arms and says, "I saw a pregnant dog around here about a month ago. It looked wild."

"Well, I found a Catahoula puppy the night of the flood. If anyone comes here looking for it, let me know, OK?"

Then I hear my call number on my radio. It sounds like Bob Kay. I pick up the radio and say, "3124 - go ahead."

Kay asks me to return to the office. He sounds excited.

"We got something working?" I ask.

"10-4. We have a name." His voice is more than excited.

I step off the stool, stretch and thank Joe for the burger.

Cecilia points to the radio and says, "What did that mean?"

"It means it's time to go play shoot 'em up."

Her mouth makes that little 'O' again.

For the next six hours, Kay and I and the boys race around the streets like Keystone Cops, trying to locate a man whose name has been given as a hot tip to the Task Force, a man who shot and wounded a Jefferson Parish Deputy several years ago.

At exactly six a.m., Tim Rothman calls Kay on the radio to say the man we've been looking for has been in parish prison for the last four months. And again, I'm reminded of one of the first lessons Jodie taught me.

Use the damn police computer.

Chapter 4
A GOOD SNITCH IS WORTH A HUNDRED NIGHTS ON THE STREET

As soon as I enter the Magnolia Funeral Home, everyone looks as me as if my zipper's down. The sickly-sweet aroma of chilled roses, mixed with cigar smoke, is almost nauseating. I move to the guest register and sign in. A small picture of Cassandra Smith wearing a pink dress sits in a frame next to the register. Before I'm finished signing, they descend on me, like vultures.

A couple guys from my old platoon in the Second District shake my hand. I remember when one of them once complained to my sergeant that I sometimes slept on the midnight watch. The next evening I brought a pillow to roll call. Moving through the crowded parlor, I shake many hands and try, with no success, to blend in.

"That's him," somebody whispers behind me.

"The one who got him."

"That's Beau."

I turn in time to see three young patrolman staring as me with a reverence that is more than bothersome. It takes me a while to find Cassandra's mother. Chief Kay points her out to me. Sitting in a small easy chair, half hidden behind the police honor guards next to the coffin, Mrs. Smith is about ninety pounds, with white hair and a sunken, almost cadaverous face.

I lean down in front of her to say, "Excuse me, Mrs. Smith. You don't remember me, but I was in the academy with Cassandra."

She blinks her large brown eyes at me. The white part of her eyes are yellow. "I remember you," she says suddenly, "you gave a speech at the graduation."

I nod. President of my academy class, I gave a brief, awkward speech at graduation. Mrs. Smith takes my hand and says, "You're Beau, aren't you?"

I nod again and she thanks me for getting the man who killed her daughter.

"You a hero," the old woman says.

And suddenly, all the things I wanted to tell her go out of my head. I wanted to tell her how Cassandra tutored me as I struggled, trying to memorize the parts of the criminal code book. How I returned the favor at the pistol range, helping Cassandra become a marksman. I wanted to tell her how terrible I feel, but I know she feels worse. I realize I'm shaking my head.

"What is it?" she asks.

"Cassandra was a hero. I . . . . I was just too late."

A hand touches my back and I stand to face a tall, male version of Cassandra. He introduces himself as her brother and introduces his wife and two aunts. I move aside as the family gathers around Mrs. Smith.

The line to the casket is shorter now so I stand in it, with my head bowed. Cassandra is in uniform, a medal of valor pinned to her chest. I touch her cold hand and say an Our Father and turn away.

It takes me the next forty-five minutes to get back to the foyer. Shaking hands and greeting comrades in NOPD powder blue shirts, I meet cops from Kenner and Jefferson Parish and St. Bernard, St. Charles, St. John, St. James, Baton Rouge and a host of cities. Of course there are also representatives of the Harbor Police, Levee Board Police and even cops from Mississippi.

Finally, I spot Merten standing next to the signing book and wave to him. He comes to my rescue by making a hole, a big hole in the crowd that I slip through. Stepping into the hot, early evening air, I take in a deep breath.

"You might want to skip the burial tomorrow," Merten says. "It's gonna be brutal." Merten wears brown shoes with his black suit. He's the only man I'd never tell it didn't match. No fuckin' way. I can't wait to get out of my dark gray suit, get back home and slip into my usual black-out tee-shirt, jeans and dark dress shirt.

"I paid my respects to her mother," I tell Merten. He's right, I think I'll pass on the procession tomorrow, with its hundreds of police cars and long blue line to the cemetery. I've heard Taps enough times recently.

Four plainclothesmen move toward us, Tim Rothman leading the way.

"Join us for a beer?" one of them says.

I shake my head as they pass, heading toward the bar across the street. In New Orleans, there's always a bar across the street from a funeral home. Probably that way in every American city. I know I'm not imagining it, but I see the same look in their eyes as they pass, the curious stares, the attraction to someone, something dangerous.

"I've got work to do," I tell Rothman when he grabs my sleeve. He lets go. And as I walk away, I know what they're thinking. I'm a lone wolf, a misfit, not really one of the boys. Not a new feeling for me. When I think about it, it's hard to remember a time in my life when I did fit in. OK, once, only once – when I was on the bayous with my daddy. But I was little boy then.

As I move to the Caprice, I loosen my tie and remember something Jodie Kintyre told me on my first case. "The solution to every murder is out there on the street. The hard part is finding it."

•

There's a message waiting for me when I arrive at the office. The pink slip taped on my desk is marked 'urgent' and reads: "A prisoner at the HOD named Felice called three times for you. She said it's important."

I sit at my desk, pick up the phone and call the House of Detention and learn Felice Marquee had been booked the previous night on nine counts of simple burglary.

"Who's the arresting officer?"

"Matt Sinclair."

"Thanks." I hang up and walk across the squad room to the Burglary Division side and catch Matt Sinclair just as the red-headed detective is walking out.

"Matt!"

Sinclair turns around.

"I need a favor."

•

I stand in the corner of a gray interview room, my back against a cinder block wall. Matt Sinclair sits behind a small green table to my left. He's thumbing his fingers on the table top. I can't recognize the smell in the tiny room, but it isn't pleasant.

"So," Sinclair says, "this Felice a good snitch?"

"She used to be when I worked the street."

Sinclair looks at his watch and says, impatiently, "Well, she better have something good for you."

The door finally opens and a matron appears with Felice Marquee. Felice, her corn-rowed hair frazzled, is decked out in an Orleans Parish Prison orange jumpsuit. She's barefoot. The matron passes Felice in and locks the door from the outside.

Felice folds her arms across her chest, looks at me and says, "Why'd you bring him?"

"He brought me. It's his case."

Felice shakes her head "I don't wanna talk to him. I wanna talk to you." Light-skinned, Felice once told me she had Spanish blood way back, from the days of the Quadroon Balls.

Sinclair raises his hand and says, "You have something to sell, you have to go through me."

Felice is street-wise enough to know the score, but has to play her hand. She tells me, "I never broke in no houses. It was my old man."

Sinclair answers for our side. "You drove him. Waited for him in the car and drove him away with the loot. You're as guilty as he is."

She leans back against the door. "I'm an accessory."

"You're a principal to the crime," Sinclair says. "You took part in every phase of nine burglaries and it looks like more. Come on." His voice rises. "I didn't come here to waste my time. You got something for us or what?"

She shoots me a pleading look with her light brown eyes.

I shrug. We both know the game, and know I have to play hardball with her. So I wait.

"She also violated her parole." It's Sinclair again.

She takes in a deep breath, wipes a tear away from her left eye and says, "I can't stay in jail."

I like the tear. It's a nice touch. Actually, I feel for her, but make sure it doesn't show on my face. She stares at me for a time, then says, "Let me back on the street and I'll get a line on those cop killers."

"Yeah?" I say. "What have you heard about them?"

"They're white boys. Everybody knows that." She gives me the black woman's head bob, chin jutting out as she bobs. Even under the harsh white light and after the years of abuse, she's still a pretty woman. Then again, she's barely nineteen.

"Everybody knows it, huh?" I say.

"You know I hang out in white joints, sometimes. To make a buck. I heard it was some bad-ass white boys doing this."

"Which joints?" I finally recognize the room's smell as old vomit.

Felice pulls the folding chair from the table and sits across from Sinclair. She looks at Sinclair, cocks her head to the left and says, "We gonna have to make a deal. About these burglaries first."

It takes a while. Sinclair has to call the D.A.'s Office. I keep Felice talking, trying my best to get as much information as possible, in case the D.A. doesn't want to play ball. Finally, someone in authority at the D.A.'s Office tells Sinclair, "Sure, OK, make a deal. Just quit calling us after hours."

Sinclair comes back and tells me. Then I tell Felice, "This is going to be a long night, young lady."

We sign her out and bring her, still in her orange jumpsuit, to the Detective Bureau where she sits cuffed to the chair next to Sinclair's desk. I make a fresh pot of coffee, its strong aroma finally ridding my nose of the vomit smell. Felice signs two dozen confessions, implicating her old man in each.

Sinclair clears so many burglaries he almost loses count. Stretching as Felice signs her last confession, Sinclair yawns and says, "Only good thing about this is that I get to book your old man tomorrow with a shitload more counts."

"Just keep him in jail," Felice's voice is low. "He's bad news."

Sinclair leaves and I'm alone with Felice. I unfasten the handcuffs and tell her, "OK, so how are we gonna work this?"

First, I have to get Felice some front money from a reluctant Bob Kay, who insists on meeting Felice and delivering a lecture on citizenship and helping the police. Felice listens, her eyes ovaled and unbelieving. I hold back a smile. Kay *is* a boy scout.

Then I take Felice back to the House of Detention to get her released. She comes out a half hour later in a green halter top and cut-off jeans, no shoes. I take her to where she stays to pick up her clothes. I wait outside in the Caprice.

Felice comes out in a white crew neck tee shirt and designer jeans and black high heels. She'd made up her face a little and looks pretty nice. I almost tell her, but don't want to go in that direction. I drive her to her auntie's house on Congress Street.

Sitting out front of her auntie's small wood frame house, in the semi-darkness of the Caprice, I tell her to be careful. The yellow streetlight filters in through the windshield and Felice gives me a strange look.

"You beginning to sound like that other guy." She means Kay.

I look at her eyes and say, "Don't get your ass in a crack you can't get out of, understand?"

"Why? You gonna worry 'bout me?" Her voice sounds brave but I can see a hint of emotion in her eyes. I reach into my pocket and pull out a business card, jot my home number on the back, just as I had with Sandie, and give it to Felice.

"Call me."

She opens the door. "I'll keep in touch."

Before closing the door, she leans back in and looks at me. Her mouth turns up in a sad smile as she says, "Thanks."

"Don't mention it."

Then she walks away, as smooth as a cat.

•

I dream of my daddy that night. In my sleep I can actually feel my chest aching as I dream. I see the sun shimmering off the dark green water of Vermilion Bay as my dad guides our pirogue around Cypremort Point. A bass jumps out of the water to our left and freezes in mid-jump.

"Shoulda brought de cane poles," my dad says, his face grinning at me. Then the old man's face freezes into a snapshot as the pirogue continues gliding across the water. I study my father's craggy face.

Skin nearly as dark as cypress bark, the old man's cheeks are taut and lean, his chin square and his nose wide. His hair is as black as a raven's feathers and his thick moustache droops over a mouth that seems to smile all of the time. A perpetual cigarette dangles from his lips. I swear, I can smell the cigarette in my dream. He smokes Picayune cigarettes, no filters, so strong the smoke is never white, it's as gray as angry rain clouds.

Unlike my mother, who's as serious as her Sioux warrior ancestors, Calixte Lucien Beau found humor in nearly everything. Once, when my dad and I were caught in a sudden Gulf storm in Southwest Pass, the old man laughed as the waves tossed the pirogue around like so much flotsam.

"Hold on, boy," Calixte called out and then laughed again as the flat bottom boat plunged over another white cap.

I remember my father's arms, muscles flexed as he paddled the pirogue into the safety of the great Marsh Island. We crashed against cypress knees and had to weather the rest of the storm in the open, sandwiched between cypress trees and the alligator marsh, cold rain stinging hot against our faces. Calixte railed against the rain, calling it dirty names in Cajun French and in English.

My dad's face un-freezes in my dream and the bass slaps back into the water.

"If I had a scoop net, I could have caught it," I say.

"Mais yeah." My dad laughs and rubs his chin

"What, you don't think I can catch it?"

My dad continues to paddle and shakes his head. "You sho' a funny kid."

Then he starts coughing a hacking cough. The cigarette still dangles from his lips as he convulses. They'll kill him one day, when I'm in high school on the saddest day of my life.

In my dream, I'm nine years old.

When my dad finally stops coughing, I ask him, "How funny was I, when I was little?"

I like this part the best because my dad always tells me funny things I'd done when I was too young to remember. Like the time I chased a coon out of the yard with a wooden spoon. Barely two, I managed to swat the coon a good one on its flank as it scampered over our wooden fence. Then there was the story about how much I liked to play hide-and-seek in our old house, how I always hid in the same place, behind the kitchen door next to the refrigerator.

Once, when we were supposed to be going somewhere, I insisted on hiding. As usual, my dad pretended he couldn't find me. So he went into my room and brought out my stuffed monkey, Zip. He walked Zip through the house, letting Zip sniff for me. My dad pretended Zip was talking, making high-pitched monkey noises as he led my dad straight to where I was hiding. Zip pointed behind the kitchen door and my dad found me.

I stepped out angrily and kicked Zip in the belly and said, "Stupid Zip." I never liked that damn monkey after that. I tried to feed it to the raccoons.

The dream slips away and I roll over and realize I'm in my bed in the loft at the rear of *Sad Lisa*. I look at the digital clock on the night stand and it's four a.m. I sit up and look around the houseboat. It looks secure, so I lay back down, readjusting the sheet. I hear the puppy moving around at the foot of the stairs down on the main deck. Then it's quiet again and I drift back to sleep.

And dream again. This time it's like a movie. It's as if I'm behind a camera panning an open prairie. Suddenly, over a slight rise directly in front of the camera, four warriors ride toward the camera, their long black hair unrestrained and streaming behind them.

Crows.

The warriors ride furiously. One looks back over his shoulder just as four more warriors crest the rise behind them. These warriors wear white feathers. They are Sioux. The lead warrior, tall and lean, has painted white spots on his body. As a boy, his name was Curly. After he lead his famous wild charge against the Arapahos, he is known as Crazy Horse.

Cresting another rise, the Crows race headlong down to a river and crash into the water, each rider falling off his horse. When the Sioux warriors reach the crest overlooking the river, they stop and look down at the Crows struggling and gasping in the water. Crazy Horse lifts his battle lance and laughs and the Sioux warriors laugh with him as the Crows are washed down river. One by one the Crows make it to the other side of the swollen river and one by one they stumble away, coughing up river water, with the echo of Sioux laughter ringing in their ears.

I had that dream before and it's as familiar as the creases in my daddy's face. I roll over again and feel a slight movement of the houseboat beneath me as it rolls gently in the canal. I fall asleep again and see the worn face of my snowy-headed Sioux grandfather. Sitting in the old rocking chair on the back porch of his South Dakota home, my grandfather tells me how the Sioux fears no one, fears nothing on the earth, except drowning.

"If a Sioux drowns, his spirit remains trapped in the water forever and cannot fly up into the Land of the Ghosts."

It was at that moment, at age nine, I realized my grandfather would never visit us in Cannes Bruleé. There was too much water. My grandfather's gravely voice echoes in my ears. I'm six years old now, sitting on that same back porch. My grandfather has just commented on the excellent vision of my light brown eyes. Leaning forward, conspiratorially, the ancient warrior says, "I will tell you something now, John Raven Beau. Tuck this secret next to your heart, little one. Your secret Lakota name is . . . Sharp Eyes. Tell no white man this name, not even your father. And don't let the white man say your name because the more it is spoken, the more your strength is taken from you."

Sitting back in the rocker, my grandfather says, "Remember always, you are Lakota. You are Oglala Sioux, the fiercest warriors of the great plains."

"Yeah," I say, "but I'm half Cajun, too."

"Only from the waist down."

There's a twinkle in the old man's eyes.

•

The phone wakes me. It's still dark. The digital clock reads five-twenty. I pick up the receiver and grunt into the mouthpiece.

"Hey, good lookin'. You busy?"

Recognizing the voice, I roll over on my back and say, "What is it?" I close my eyes. My mouth feels cottony from the three beers it took to put me to sleep after dropping Felice off.

Sandie lets out a long sigh on the other end of the line, then says, "Those dead cops. Were they missing anything?"

My eyes snap open. I sit up in bed and tell her to go on.

"Were they missing something shiny?"

I feel my heart racing.

"Go on." I try to keep my voice level.

"I heard the killers took their badges."

"Where are you?"

"Right now?"

"Where *are* you?" It's no use, my voice is excited.

"I'm at the pay phone outside Café Du Monde." Her voice has a teasing quality to it, like she's playing a game.

"Go inside and wait there for me."

"It's an out door cafe."

"Go *inside*. By the cash register and wait for me!"

"All right. All right."

"Do it now." I hang up and jump out of bed.

I dig a gray tee-shirt from my dresser drawer and climb into a fresh pair of jeans, pulling on my white Nike running shoes, not bothering with socks. I scoop my Glock and two magazines loaded with hollow point rounds from atop the night stand and clip my badge to my belt as I descend the stairs.

The puppy is up and doing circles at the bottom of the small staircase. I bend over and pet it a moment before grabbing a light-weight black jacket from the downstairs closet to hide the Glock now tucked in the jeans at the small of my back. I shove the clips into the jacket's pockets and snatch my radio on my way out. Setting the dead-bolt, I steady my hands.

"Jesus!"

She knows about the badges. I feel myself breathing heavily as I hurry off the boat. Only the killers and a handful of homicide detectives know about the missing badges. I feel myself smile nervously. Sandie sure did good.

And I remember the old police saying that a good snitch is worth a hundred nights on the street.

Chapter 5
THEY'LL HAVE SOMETHING ON YOU

I don't spot Sandie as I cross Decatur Street to the high banquette running alongside Café Du Monde. A dozen or more people dot the outside tables of the open air cafe. Mostly alone, they are typical New Orleans all-nighters. A line of white clad waiters sit next to the windows outside the closed part of the cafe. I still can't see Sandie.

Scents of powdered sugar and coffee fill my nostrils as I move through the narrow double doors and step into the well-lit cafe. Sandie sits in the far corner, in a nice blind spot that can't be seen from the street. Her long red hair fluffed like a lion's mane, she wears an iridescent blue top and pink miniskirt. She uncrosses her legs to give me a view of her white panties as I approach. She opens her knees and grins at me. As I sit, a waiter hurries over.

"Two coffees," I tell him.

The waiter lingers a moment, leering at Sandie's crotch before backing away. Sandie leans back in her chair and opens her knees wider. Her dark pubic hair is plainly visible through the sheer panties.

"And I wasn't going to wear panties tonight," she says in a slurred voice. Her eyes are bleary.

I reach for the cup of coffee already in front of her and raise it toward her bright red lips. "Come on, Babe. Drink some of this."

"Oh?" She raises an eyebrow. "I'm *Babe* now, huh? The other night you wouldn't even let me suck your dick, now I'm your Babe?"

I lean close and ask her to keep her voice down. "You'll scare the straights. OK?"

She leans over and kisses my neck, then pulls back giggling. I lift the coffee to her lips and she takes a sip, then another. The waiter returns with our cups of fresh cafe-au-lait and I pay him. As he leaves, he checks out Sandie's panties again on his way back to a group of waiters who have now gathered behind me. Sandie giggles again and crosses her legs, tugging her skirt down.

"Enough for now," she says.

I pour sugar in my coffee and two spoonfuls into hers and stir both. She bats her bleary eyes at me as we take a sip.

Smiling broadly, she says, "I did good, didn't I?"

I nod and tell her to drink more coffee. She does and it isn't until we start our second cup that I get down to business. Sandie is still drunk and it takes a while to get the story out of her. I take notes.

She was in a bar in the Ninth Ward. Can't remember the name. Some bikers came in, greasy-looking men wearing leather vests and tattoos on their hairy arms. Talking loudly among themselves, they were rowdy from the start and sidled up to Sandie who was sitting at the bar in her hot outfit. *Jesus*. She went to a Ninth Ward Bar dressed like this.

Sandie's eyes brighten for a moment as she taps a finger against her temple. "I foxed them. I been telling people my ex is a cop. A real son-of-a-bitch of a cop. Most bar-roomers don't like cops."

She goes on to explain how one of the bikers said something derogatory about cops and Sandie keyed in, telling her story. A tirade of loud talk ensued. Some time later, one of the bikers said something about the murdered cops. Then another said something else. Eventually one of them said he heard the cops were missing something. The bikers laughed even louder.

"Then I turned on the charm," Sandie says. "I got the big one to tell me what was missing. I let him feel up my tits. He said it was their badges."

I press her for details, descriptions, exactly what was said. I put more coffee into her, but I can see in her eyes, it's no use. She's floating in a liquid heaven.

"Come on." I help her stand and lead her to the ladies room.

She wants me to come in with her, but I stand outside the door. She comes out and hands me her panties. I shove them into my pocket and put my arm around her and lead her out back to Decatur and around Jackson Square to where I parked my car in the police zone next to the Cabildo. I glance momentarily up Chartres Street to where Cassandra died before I climb into the Caprice.

"You taking me home?" Sandie curls up against the passenger side door.

I take her into the Ninth Ward, to the side streets running off St. Claude Avenue, pass bar after bar through the dark, narrow neighborhood known as Bywater. I look for motorcycles and I ask her if each is the bar. It's no use. She has no idea.

"How'd you get to Café Du Monde?"

She's confused and finally laughs, "The big fucker."

"What?"

"The big fucker from the bar. I promised him a hum job, but I bailed on him when we stopped for a light on Decatur."

"Where's your car?"

"At home. I took a cab to St. Claude Avenue and started walking."

"Jesus!"

As we reach Poland Avenue and the Industrial Canal, I stop and look around at the faint dawn light. "Did you cross the canal?"

Sandie is asleep. Her skirt hiked up nearly to her waist, her reddish brown bush exposed and pointing toward me. She has no purse and I realize I don't know where she lives, exactly. Somewhere on Jackson Avenue, I think.

I turn the Caprice around and head for *Sad Lisa*. Readjusting my dick, I punch the accelerator. I have a diamond-cutter hard-on. All I fuckin' need. I remind myself of what LaStanza once told me. The man who broke Jodie into Homicide, the best Homicide cop I ever knew, once told me – "Never fuck an informant. If you do they'll have something on you. They got a piece of you and I'm not talking about a little dick either."

•

"Hey!"

Sandie's voice wakes me. The clock reads eleven-thirty. *Sad Lisa* is bright with sunlight.

"Hey! Where the fuck am I?"

I climb out of bed and peek down from the loft. Sandie sits up in the daybed downstairs, her head in both hands. My puppy comes out from the kitchen area and yips at her.

"Bucktown," I tell her.

She looks at me and squints.

"Beau?" She's surprised.

I run my hands through my hair and stretch. Sandie sinks back on the daybed. I go down and start a pot of coffee, then take a quick shower and shave. She's sitting back up when I step out, a towel around my waist.

"What the fuck happened to me last night?"

"You don't remember?"

She shrugs and climbs off the daybed. Her skirt is up to her waist again. She doesn't bother pushing it down. The puppy scampers out of her way, then follows her.

"Where's the bathroom?"

I point over my shoulder, then head back up to the loft to climb into my gray suit. Sandie comes out as I'm pouring two cups of extra strong coffee and chicory. Her skirt is finally down and she's run a brush through her hair. She sits on the stool and crosses her legs.

"Your dog have a name?"

And it comes to me in a flash – *The Call of the Wild* – so I tell her his name is Buck.

"He's cute," she says. "Likes to lick my ankles when I'm peeing."

"He's a charmer."

She stares at me for a moment then asks why the shirt and tie.

"I've got Grand Jury at two o'clock."

"Did we fuck last night?" Her eyes are still bleary.

"What the fuck were you drinking?"

She nods and says, "Jagermeister, I think. That's my usual, lately."

"You remember the bars in the Ninth Ward?"

"Bars?"

It's no use. Even after more coffee, her memory's fried. I cook up some bacon and eggs and she picks at it. I let Buck go out on deck, filling his food dish with fresh food and the leftover bacon, which he devours. I make sure I have Sandie's new phone number before taking her home. She directs me back downtown to a converted warehouse on Jackson Avenue. As we pull up in front, she tells me her apartment is on the second floor, tucked along the back of the building. I tell her what she did last night, about where she'd gone and what she'd told me and then warn her about doing it again – without me covering her.

"Especially dressed like this."

She laughs.

"I'm serious. It's a fuckin' miracle you weren't gang raped." As she climbs out, I add, "I need you to go back, but not without me covering you."

She says, "Yeah. Yeah." And gets out and doesn't look back.

"I mean it!"

She wiggles her butt at me as she goes through the door.

•

Assistant District Attorney Alan Olson turns to me and asks, "How many times did you fire your weapon, Detective Beau?" A prissy looking man in a baby blue seersucker suit, a pink tie to go along with his white shirt, Olson looks about fifty years old.

"Three times."

Olson looks at the Grand Jury and explains that the body of Casey Jones had three entry wounds, one in the sternum, one below the right nipple and one above the right eye.

I watch the jury members, middle-aged citizens who stare at me with owl eyes as Olson describes the destructiveness of my hollow-point bullets. The jurors are almost innocent in their curiosity, like children staring at someone dangerous, someone downright lethal. Olson goes on about the shooting then asks a question I almost miss.

"Oh, I had no choice," I explain. "In the exchange of gunfire, I aimed and saw him and fired. We all fired."

"Detective Beau was the only one to hit what he fired at." Olson then goes on about the nick on my face. If this wasn't justifiable homicide he says, if this wasn't self-defense, he's never seen it. A half hour later, as I sit in the waiting room, Olson comes out and waves me forward. He puts a friendly hand on my shoulder as he leads me out into the hall.

"I've never indicted a cop," Olson brags, then explains that the shooting in Exchange Alley has been classified as *justifiable homicide*. I'm off the hook. Olson goes on, like a typical lawyer, to explain I can still be sued by the family of Casey Jones. "If anyone comes forward to claim the body," he adds.

Of course, and when that happens, a school of lawyers, like sharks, will encircle the family and convince them to file suit. What have they got to lose?

"I handled the Algiers Shooting," Olson says with a swagger.

Algiers? I'm confused. Cops were indicted in that case. So I ask.

"No one was indicted for shooting anyone. Later some went to federal prison for beating witnesses." Olson smiles and says he has to go and leaves me at the door at the end of the hall.

I step out of the Criminal Courts Building and look back at the hulking cement structure. Covering a city block, it's a monument to the 1930s, a brooding municipal courthouse that looks as if it was carved from a single block of gray stone.

I remember reading about the Algiers case. Back in 1980s, a patrolman was murdered in Algiers. An intense investigation followed, leading to the killer and his confederates who lived in a shotgun house in a lower-class arca of Algiers. Detectives stormed the house around four a.m. Everyone inside was killed, including a woman who climbed out of a tub and armed herself with a pistol. The man who killed the patrolman was among those killed. His street name was Comanche, I think. No, he wasn't a blood brother.

What saved the cops, when the fuckin' FBI and everyone else investigated the shooting, was the fact that a few minutes earlier, the detectives had kicked in the wrong door of a house a short distance away. Rushing inside, they shot no one in the wrong house. None of those occupants had guns. Damn good thing for everyone. Algiers was a good shooting, just like Exchange Alley.

As I put on my dark sunglasses, the bright sun warming the top of my head, I know I'm lucky. Four shootings in my career and all good shootings. I'm an aberration, an abnormality. Most cops never fire their weapon at anyone in a twenty-year career. I'm an oddity, a curiosity to normal people who go about their lives and never injure anyone. I've sent four men to their graves. A police officer with a penchant for extreme violence, I don't fit in.

So what else is new?

I walk around the corner, past the old parish prison with its high cement wall painted a faded white, and over to headquarters. The Homicide squad room, which the Task Force is using, is deserted. My government-issue, gray metal desk is next to the wall of windows facing South Broad Avenue. I check my "In" box and find three memos from Bob Kay. One is about a gang fight at a local high school in which several boys bragged about being involved in the cop killings. The second memo involves a psychic from Mississippi who's coming in today with important information. The third is about the Manson Family. Seems the captain of the Intelligence Division, watching the re-run of that made-for-TV movie staring Steve Railsback as Manson, surmises that an off-shoot of the Manson Family, known to be hanging around the grunge people in the French Quarter, just may be involved in the killings.

Jesus Christ!

I pull out my pen and write on each memo – *Bullshit* across the memo about the high schoolers. I write *Yeah. Right. What about the Hole In The Wall Gang or the Dalton Gang?* across the Manson memo. Across the memo about the Mississippi psychic, I write, *This sounds promising. We should have this wrapped up in no time. Suggest you assign my old partner, Tim Rothman. He's somewhat of a psychic himself.*

I toss the memos into Kay's 'In' box on my way to the coffee pot. The coffee's cold and I don't feel like making a new pot. Glancing up at the clock above the unofficial logo of the Homicide Division – an art deco drawing of a vulture perched atop a gold NOPD star-and-crescent badge – I see it's pushing five o'clock. I wonder where everyone is. I know. They're lining the Interstate, awaiting the fuckin' psychic. Ha. I scoop up my phone and punch in Sandie's number. She answers on the second ring.

"You going out tonight?"

"Who's this?"

"Bill Clinton. Who do you think it is?"

She sighs and tells me she's going out tomorrow night. She sounds tired. "I've got a class tonight," she says and I hear her yawn.

"Class?"

"Yeah. I model for an art class at UNO Nude. Wanna come?"

Son-of-a-bitch. Whores modeling for college art classes. I love this city.

"What time?"

"Six-thirty to eight."

"I'll take you to dinner after."

"Why?"

Sitting at my desk, I feel a headache coming on. I kick my feet up on the desk and explain as best I can. I don't want what happened last night to happen again. It's too fuckin' dangerous, her going out like that. I don't tell her I don't want her getting so loaded when she stumbles on a lead, she can't fuckin' remember shit. I have to be subtle.

"You wanna catch those cop killers, don't you?" She asks sarcastically. "I have my own way of doing things."

"We're not going to catch anyone if you're fuckin' dead." So I tell her I'm backing her up and that's it.

"Do I have to eat with you?" She's being cute now.

The squad room door opens and Bob Kay lumbers in, stops and motions behind him. His suit coat seems tight with the bullet proof vest beneath his white shirt. A mousy woman with red Bozo-the-clown hair takes a step into the room, looks around and waves her hands in a wide circle. Something tells me our psychic has arrived.

"So you coming to see me pose?"

"Wouldn't miss it."

Kay shuffles across the office, mousy woman in toe. She wears a long, dark blue chiffon dress and white tennis shoes. A foot shorter and fifty pounds heavier than Kay, she stares intently at me as she approaches. I tell Sandie I have to go and she tells me the class is in the Art Building at the rear of the campus.

"You know where that's at?"

Kay stops at my desk and folds his arms. His eyes bulge. I have to look away so I don't laugh in his face. Sandie repeats her question and I tell her I know the building and hang up.

Kay clears his throat. "Um. This is Ruthie Grundermann."

"The psychic from Mississippi," I say as I stand and reach to shake Ruthie's hand.

She takes a step back, narrows her beady eyes and croaks, "How'd you know?"

"Tim Rothman told me. He described you perfectly."

Ruthie tugs on Kay's coat. "Who is this Tim Rothman?"

I answer for Kay. "He's another detective. He's also psychic."

Ruthie gives me a disbelieving look as Kay leans forward and picks a tablet off my desk. He jots something on it.

"Really," I tell Ruthie. "Tim Rothman predicted Global Warming. Back in the eighties. He also predicts Jerry Lewis

70

will finally win that elusive Nobel Peace Prize, if the French have anything to say about it."

She's confused. I like that in a psychic. Kay hands me the tablet. In large letters he's written *Help! Call the Police!* I pick up my portable radio and call Rothman. I ask if he can join us. He says he's in the garage and on his way up.

"Rothman's coming to help," I tell Kay as I move away from my desk for the door. "You'll love him," I call back to Ruthie. "Just don't mention Hitler, Cajun fritters or women romance writers."

I run into Rothman at the *Police Only* elevator. I point over my shoulder. "Kay's looking for you."

He gives me a distrustful look. I shoot back the most innocent look I have. "Seriously," I say. "He wants you to find out if the women in there is really Anne Rice's half-sister."

"What woman?"

I step into the elevator and push 'one' – several times.

•

Buck races down the levee to the boulders at the water's edge, bounces twice, then runs back up to me, his big ears flailing in the air. The little tike sure loves to run. His mottled spots stand out dramatically in the fading sunlight The boulders, placed at the bottom of the levee, serve as a breakwater.

I go down on my haunches and he licks my hand, then scampers away again, back toward the brown-gray lake water. He stumbles over his feet, which seem too big. I sit on the thick grass atop the levee and shield my eyes from the sun setting in the western sky. In the distance several sailboats glide past, one with a baby blue sail.

All right, I should have written a daily about what Sandie discovered, right? Have every swinging dick go down to the Ninth Ward, rousting every biker, a headlong cavalry charge, right? No way. I can't even be sure Sandie was even in the Ninth Ward. She could have been in Bywater, Marigny, or even the Quarter.

I do know one thing – somebody knows about the badges. And I realize it's imperative I talk to Sandie again, tonight. My daddy's voice echoes in my mind. "Any excuse to see a naked woman," he would say.

"Right, Pop. Any excuse."

Buck comes back up for a lick, yips twice at me and then spots several sea gulls on the rocks below. He takes off after them. They let him get within a dozen feet, then soar off. Buck stops, spreads his legs and looks up at them as if they are magic beings. Then he yips at them and bounces, then goes off to check something at the edge of the rocks.

My stomach rumbles and I call for the little tike. He looks back at me but doesn't come. I have to go down and get him. He has a crawfish cornered between two boulders. Sniffing it, he yips and growls. The crawfish has its claws raised in defiance and I remember my daddy once saying it should be the state mascot, instead of the pelican.

"Crawfish are more like people," my daddy said. "Onry. Put one on de railroad track and when de train come, what do de crawfish do? It raise its claws in defiance. It wants a piece o' dat train, yeah."

I pick Buck up and carry him back to *Sad Lisa*. He licks my hands all the way.

•

Angie Calogne wears a white dress shirt and faded jeans today, tight jeans. She seats me at my usual table and asks if I'll have my usual – cheeseburger, fries and a Barq's.

"Yep."

Cecilia calls out, "I made Blackberry pie."

I tell Angie I'll have a slice for dessert and watch her hips as she moves away, lithely. She checks on the only other customers, two construction workers in the first booth. Joe slaps my burger on the grill and the smell immediately wafts my way. Cecilia hands Angie my Barq's, and she heads back. She puts the root beer down, but doesn't leave. Again.

I look up at the Marisa Tomei face and those aquamarine eyes staring back at me.

"I looked up Oglala." The Lauren Bacall voice again. "It's the sect that produced Crazy Horse, isn't it?"

Never heard us called a sect before.

"My grandfather claims to be descended from Crazy Horse's brother, who also fought at the Little Bighorn."

Angie blinks and stares at me as if I said something in Greek. She blinks again and puts her knee up on the bench on the other side of my table.

"Then you're related to Crazy Horse." She says it flatly.

"That what my grandfather claims."

"No wonder." She looks out the picture window.

"No wonder what?" My stomach tightens.

"No wonder you're so good at what you do."

It's my turn to look out the window. A minute or two later, Joe slides my plate on the counter and rings the bell. Angie gets my food and I take a sip of the icy Barq's.

"Enjoy," she says as she puts my plate down and moves back up to help the construction workers, who want some of that blackberry pie too. As I take my first bite of spicy burger, I feel that tightness in my belly again. Hunger, I tell myself, although I know better. It's the Marisa Tomei face and those aquamarine eyes. It's this young woman – a woman I'll never know except in passing, here at Flamingo's.

At thirty I thought I was beyond this kind of yearning, this kind of desire for a pretty girl I'll never have. But the heartaches a boy feels growing up in a Cajun *daubed* house, most people would call a shack, and seeing the pretty girls passing on the way to the Cajun dance hall's *Fais Do Do*, still lingers in my heart. Nights spent listing to the driving sounds of a Cajun band and hearing the high-pitched laugher of pretty girls while I sat between cypress trees to stare at the still water of Vermilion Bay – days spent at school stealing looks at the pretty girls who were always beyond my reach, still haunt me. I guess it always will for a boy who never fit in.

I chuckle at feeling sorry for myself and wonder when I'll grow out of it. I don't look at up when Angie brings my slice of pie. She puts it down and says, "You didn't cut yourself shaving."

She reaches over and touches my cheek next to the cut that's almost healed now. I almost flinch and look up at her. She pulls her hand back and points a finger at my nose.

"Don't patronize me. The paper said you were nicked by concrete from the killer's bullet. Is that true?"

"It was a piece of brick."

"I'm serious." Her voice lowers, more Bacall-like. "Don't patronize me. I'm not a little girl."

She walks off and I sit here wondering – why is my heart racing?

Chapter 6
PRETEND YOU HAVE AN ASSIGNMENT

Standing on a small podium, illuminated by spotlights from the high ceiling above, Sandie has her hands cupped behind her head and her eyes closed as she poses naked for the two dozen students. A middle-aged woman in a baggy pink jumpsuit hurries over to me as I enter the room.

"May I help you?" She has a school teacher's voice.

I pull my credentials from my coat pocket and open them.

"Police." I nod toward Sandie. "Do you have a license for this?"

"Huh?"

"Just kidding. I'm Sandie's cousin. I've seen her like this before."

I walk past the woman and sit on one of the stools at the back of the class, as if I own the place. The woman watches me for a few moments before going back to her drawing. The clock on the far wall reads a quarter to eight. I lean back against the wall and fold my arms across my chest. I've shed the suit for a black tee-shirt, jeans and light-weight gray sport coat. Reaching back, I readjust my Glock, pressing against my backbone.

Sandie moves, bringing her arms down for a moment, rotating her hips slightly before resuming her position. Her light eyes seem golden as she stares at me, a slight smile coming to her mouth.

I spend the next minutes trying not to stare at Sandie. I look at walls covered with amateurish paintings and charcoal drawings. I look at the backs of the students heads and parts of their drawings of Sandie. I look at the tile floor, then at the high ceiling before giving up and stare at Sandie as she repositions herself, sitting on the stuffed chair. She drapes one leg over the chair's arm, giving the students in front of her a view of pink.

Her hair is curled and falls past her shoulders. Her face is made up like a fashion model, her lips a bright crimson. Sandie's full breasts are perfectly round with small nipples and delicate pink areolas. Her thick mat of public hair stands fluffy. I'm sure she brushed it out. Her legs are long and slim, sculptured, like a dancer's legs.

Repositioning myself, I try to cross my legs but can't with my jeans. I try to subtly readjust my crotch, but Sandie notices and grins at me. My watch reads 7:57.

Why was Angie angry? I just met her when she asks about the bandage on my cheek. What was I supposed to say? The truth? I got nicked in a shootout. Sounds like a pick-up line. Like I'm trying to impress her. Hell, I don't want to impress anyone. Especially her. Especially when she focuses those aquamarines on me. She's too damn young and too damn pretty.

"Thank you," the woman in pink tells Sandie as everyone starts packing up their stuff. Sandie gets up, twists and turns to work out kinks in her back. Grinning, she strolls over and folds her arms under her breasts.

"Enjoy the show?" She winks at me.

"Shouldn't you be getting dressed?"

Two students, one blond and one Asian, check Sandie's ass as they pass.

"Wait here," Sandie says, touching my knee momentarily before bounding away to an oriental screen on the back side of the room. I almost laugh as she goes behind the screen to dress. A dark haired young man stands just inside the door and checks me out, only when I look back, he looks away. He switches his backpack from his right shoulder to his left and waits, staring at the screen now.

Sandie comes out brushing her hair. She's in a red minidress and white sandals. She hurries over to the dark haired guy, pecks him on the lips and takes his hand to pull him over to me. I climb off the stool as they arrive.

"This is Samuel," she tells me. We shake hands and his palm is damp.

"This is my cousin Beau. He's from the country."

The country. Cute.

I take Sandie by the wrist and tell Samuel we have to talk alone for a moment. Sandie follows me away, rolling her hips back at Samuel, who isn't pleased.

"Two things," I say when we're out of earshot.

"Isn't he scrumptious?"

"Yeah. Right. First – tell no one and I mean *no one* about the missing badges."

"OK." She bounces and looks back at Samuel. I catch a whiff of her strong perfume.

"Second – I'm backing you up tomorrow night. Understand?"

"OK." She starts to back away.

"I'll pick you up at nine p.m."

"OK!" And she's off, hurrying back to Samuel who puts his arm around her. On their way out he squeezes her ass and looks back at me with this bad-ass look and I have to laugh. Tough schoolboy. Maybe *he* should back her up tomorrow night. I find a pay phone outside the Education Building and call Felice's auntie.

"I'm looking for Felice."

"Well, she ain't here."

"Do you know where she is?"

"No and *ifin* I did I ain't tellin no body on no phone."

"Can you ask her to call me?"

"What your name?"

"Beau." I spell it.

She corrects my spelling and says it should be Bo.

"Wif one 'O'," she says. "*Ifin* it be with two 'Os' you'd be a ghost, right?"

"Yes ma'am."

She hangs up.

Eight fifteen and I've got nothing to do. As I walk back to the Caprice, I wonder if I should hunt for Felice, as futile as that sounds. If I find her, I couldn't talk to her anyway, not in any bar. I crank up the Caprice and head over to the Fifth District Station. Maybe some street cops can tell me about biker bars in the Ninth Ward.

•

At five the following evening, I'm back in the squad room, sitting at my desk watching Bob Kay go over the leads from yesterday and today.

Gonzales, in a black shark-skin suit, his hair slicked back, sits at his desk and seems to be listening intently to Kay's words. The other homicide detectives assigned to the Task Force sit at their desks with bored looks on their faces. Al Mercier, his light brown hair neatly trimmed, his tan suit neatly pressed, looks as if he stepped out of an ad for *Gentleman's Quarterly*. His partner, Sam Costanza sits reading a *Playboy*. His dark hair is messed and his pink tie clashes with his maroon jacket, but he's happy scanning the pictures in the mag. I fight off a yawn as Kay explains that the lead involving the braggart high school students has no merit. Big fuckin' surprise.

"Now, we still have no corroborative information about the former Manson family members who might be running around with the grunge people in the Quarter. We're still working on that."

I notice Tim Rothman for the first time today as he moves to the coffee pot. He's in a tan suit too. I, for a change, am not wearing black. I wear faded jeans, a dark green tee-shirt with a brown sport coat and white Nike running shoes. That's as colorful as I get.

"As for the psychic from Mississippi..." Kay has to pause as the cat calls break out. Someone lets out a loud fart sound behind me. I don't have to look. It's Tony Dunn, burglary detective with the annoying habit of providing sound effects at inopportune times.

"Detective Rothman," Kay continues, "worked through the night with the psychic..."

Someone in back hoots, while Sam Costanza laughs out loud. Tony Dunn makes a barfing sound. They must have seen Ruthie too.

As the tirade continues, Rothman shoots me a disgusted look and moves toward the back of the room. Dunn injects a loud "ping" and two "pops" followed by a "zowie." Rothman stops next to a stocky detective wearing a two-tone Baltimore Orioles baseball cap. Before Rothman can escape, he's in the middle of a Fudd.

The stocky detective, Elvis Channard, better known as Elmer Fudd, because of his striking resemblance to Bugs Bunny's nemesis, leans close to Rothman and starts talking.

The most long-winded of creatures, Channard's mouth moves rapidly as Rothman closes his eyes. I'm sure he's trying to ignore Channard but it's plain by the hangdog look on his face, Rothman is in the middle of a <u>Fudd</u> and can't get away.

"Detective Rothman," Kay's voice rises, "um, feels, um that this psychic has nothing relevant to add to this investigation."

"Big fuckin' revelation!" Al Mercier's voice booms, which causes everyone to pause. Usually quiet, it's not like Al. He shrugs and acknowledges the momentary glitch by looking down, like a schoolboy who said something out of place in class.

Sam Costanza turns to me and shows me the fold-out in his *Playboy*. It's another naked blond. I've seen her before, or her clone in any number of previous *Playboys*. Kay starts passing out leads for tonight. I look out at the darkness closing on the city. Reaching my desk Kay passes me a memo. I read it:

Det. Beau,

I'm giving you this piece of paper so the others will think I'm giving you an assignment. Pretend you have an assignment. And when you get a chance will you let me know *what the fuck you're doing!*

Assistant Superintendent Kay

As people start getting up to leave, Kay calls for everyone's attention one more time. He pulls a paper from his clipboard. I recognize it immediately as a National Broadcast from the FBI to all local agencies.

"Summary of law enforcement officer killed." Kay's voice booms. "Paris Texas Police Department advises officer, thirty-nine year old Hispanic male, shot and killed one a.m., this morning, while executing a narcotics warrant. As officers entered residence, white male, aged forty-two, barricaded himself in bedroom and fired upon officers with nine-millimeter semiautomatic handgun. Deceased officer shot in head, two other officers wounded and assailant justifiably killed."

Kay pulls another sheet of paper out and reads from it. "Over the last twelve months 161 police officers have been killed in the line of duty in the U.S. Of that number, only two cases are still unsolved." Kay folds the papers and looks over everyone's heads. "Both of those murders are here."

He takes in a deep breath. "There's never been an unsolved murder of a New Orleans Police Officer. I don't intend to rest until we erase this fucking blot!"

He's one of the few cops I know who puts the "g" and the end of fuckin'.

Sam Costanza puts the *Playboy* away. Mercier is his serious self again. Gonzales, standing now, pulls out his Beretta and checks it. Even Rothman's jaw is set in determination. I gotta hand it to Kay. He knows how to motivate.

As people shuffle out, I pour myself a fresh mug of coffee and head for the police computer. Pulling out the notes I took at the Fifth District Station, I start running addresses in the computer, addresses of Ninth Ward Bars. An hour and a half later, I stand and stretch. Before returning to my desk, I tear the print outs off the dot matrix printer. I have seventy-seven pages of arrests at various bars, incidents from disturbing the peace calls to knifings and shootings from the last twelve months. As I approach my desk I hear yelling on my portable radio.

Turning up the volume, the radio is suddenly silent. I drop the print outs on my desk as a faintly familiar voice calls in a Code four, then starts asking for a homicide team and the coroner. I recognize Mercier's voice and start packing my briefcase immediately.

Jodie answers headquarters and learns Mercier and Costanza are calling for a homicide team in the 1000 block of Gravier Street. The radio goes bananas again and I turn it down as I grab my sport coat and head for the door.

•

I park my Caprice around the corner on South Rampart just as Jodie arrives. She climbs out of her car, brushes her skirt down and spots me. I raise both hands and shout, "I didn't do it! Just got here."

She shoots me a weary smile, then reaches back in her car for her radio. I do the same, slipping mine into the back pocket of my jeans. I leave my coat in the car, readjusting my Glock's canvass holster at the small of my back. I'm getting used to wearing it back there, butt pointing to my right so I can easily reach around for it. Easier to hide. My star-and-crescent badge is clipped to the front of my belt.

Jodie waits for me at the corner. She looks especially nice this evening and I almost tell her. Her eyes look more cat-like than usual. Probably new eye-liner. Her blond hair looks freshly blow-dried as usual. She's in a gray skirt suit with a black blouse. She lets out a tired sigh and says, "You don't need to be here."

"Thought you could use a hand," I tell Jodie as she turns and leads the way around the corner. A squeal of brakes behind Jodie turns us both around as Bob Kay jumps from his car and rushes down Gravier Street.

Mercier leans against the side of his unmarked white Ford LTD, parked on the uptown side of the street. Costanza is on the other side of the vehicle, on the sidewalk. A uniformed sergeant stands next to him. Six feet away, next to a gray building, lies the crumpled body of a white male in dark clothes.

Costanza points at the body and starts blabbering to Bob Kay, who looks stunned. Jodie steps between them, separates Costanza and moves him away. I don't have to hear to know she's telling him to stop talking. Behind me a bright light comes on and I know a TV camera is firing up. Kay wheels and the uniformed sergeant moves immediately toward the camera.

"Hey," shouts Kay. "Keep those people outta here!"

Behind me two more uniformed men have arrived. It'll be their job to cordon off the area. Jodie waves me over and asks me to stay with Mercier. I step around to Mercier who stands looking up at the dark sky.

"You all right?"

He nods and looks at me. "Costanza shot him." Mercier's voice is low, for my ears only. He looks over his shoulder at his partner, then nods toward the body. "Stupid fuck came at us with a knife." Mercier holds up his left arm to show the neat slice in his sleeve of his nice tan suit coat.

"Fuckin' 107 call." Mercier closes his eyes again. A 107 is a suspicious person call, the same type of call that got Cassandra Smith killed.

The officers at the end of the street start yelling and Kay rushes over to help them fight off the media. I see two television cameras now. Jesus, they get here fast. It takes another twenty minutes for the crime lab to arrive. Mercier and I pass the time in silence as I watch Jodie take notes, watch her move around, like a feline predator, stalking out the crime scene. When the crime lab technician arrives, she snaps quick and precise orders.

Costanza passes his weapon to the tech. Jodie flags Kay over and asks if he can take Costanza to headquarters where another sergeant waits to take Costanza's statement.

She points to me. "You get Mercier out of here. We don't need the media circus."

"But I thought I'd canvass." I grin and Jodie shakes her head.

Kay waves me along and I turn and ask Mercier if he'd like a lift, knowing he can't ride or talk with Costanza until after they give their statements.

"Sure." He pushes off the car and we start back.

Only someone touches my shoulder and I turn to see Jodie leaning close to my ear.

"Look who's here." She points to a blond apparition at the end of the block. The blond wears a long red dress and spiked heels. Abby Grange, arms folded, glares at me. I wave and smile broadly.

"If I wasn't so fuckin' tired," Jodie says, "I'd kick her ass."

She leans her elbow up on my shoulder and I have to grab her waist to keep from falling off the edge of the sidewalk. Jodie has a nice, curvy waist. She pulls back and blows a strand of hair from her eyes.

"Get out of here."

And she turns and walks back into the crime scene.

As I start for the corner, I spot the Orioles baseball cap in the camera lights as Elvis Channard's unmistakable portly figure bobs through the lights, heading my way. I pick up my pace, leading Mercier forward.

"Wow!" Channard says as he arrives. "Is Jodie here?"

I point over my shoulder and suddenly remember Jodie mentioning how she thinks Elmer Fudd has a crush on her.

"Think she can use an extra hand?" Channard looks past me.

"Sure," I tell him. "I'm sure she could use some help."

"Goody!" And he bounces away.

He actually said *goody*. Ya' gotta love the guy.

I lead Mercier to the corner where Abby Grange waits with her cameraman. She positions herself in my way, her mike in hand. As we converge, Abby calls out, "Did you kill someone else, Detective Beau?"

I grin at her and ask, "Where's your corsage?"

"Detective Beau, were you involved in yet another shooting?"

I step closer to her as Mercier slips by, heading for my car.

"You have very pretty eyes," I tell Abby as I move around her. Actually she has beady blue eyes.

"Why won't you talk with us, Detective Beau? Do you have something to hide?"

I spread my arms, palms up, as I backpedal. "Women in red dresses intimidate me!"

I turn and unlock the passenger door for Mercier, go around and climb into the Caprice and drive away, the bright television light glimmering in my rearview mirror. Mercier and I do not speak all the way to headquarters. And it occurs to me that Kay sure knows how to motivate his troops, all right. How did he put it, " ... assailant justifiably killed."

Goddamn suspicious person call.

•

Sandie climbs out of the Caprice and wiggles away in her black spiked heels. She wears a low cut red blouse and tight black jeans. Crossing Port Street, she moves to the corner of North Rampart to Borman's Bar, a one story wooden neighborhood bar with two Harley Davidsons parked out front. It's the fifth bar we've visited and it's barely eleven p.m. I wait fifteen minutes and follow her in.

She's the only woman in the place. Bending over the pool table, she doesn't look up as I enter. A burly man with a full beard checks out her ass as Sandie shoots and misses. Giggling, she picks up her beer and passes the cue to a tall, skinny man wearing a vest but no shirt. The man has tattoos on both arms and hair in a long, greasy-looking pony tail.

I sit at the bar and order an Abita dark from a bartender who looks a lot like Brian Dennehey. And as I take a hit of the cold beer I try to remember what movie Brian Dennehey played a bartender in. I can't hear what Sandie and her pool partners are saying, but the men seem to be having a good time, brushing past Sandie, holding her waist as she bends over for a shot.

At eleven-thirty, a bored customer rises from the far end of the bar and plays the jukebox. Lord no. Country music. Still nursing my Abita, I have to endure the reverberations of a steel guitar as some hillbilly starts wailing about his woman who left him for an insurance salesman. What?

All right. I get it. It supposed to be funny. I smile at the bartender, who looks back stone-faced. The next song is funny too. Some woman complaining about how she shaved her legs for *this*. I finish the Abita and have a little buzz now, so maybe everything is going to be funny. I stop drinking and peek at Sandie, who's sandwiched between the two pool players. Flirting and yakking, I hope she comes up with something, besides hard-ons.

Round midnight, Sandie picks up her tiny purse and heads for the door, the tall skinny man following like an excited raccoon. I ease off my stool and beat them to the door. Without looking back, I walk around to the Caprice. As I pull around to the front of the bar, Sandie is in perfect position next to the street. Slim has his hands in the back pocket of his jeans as he throws his head back in laughter.

I slide the Caprice up and Sandie opens the door and climbs in and Slim gives us a good impersonation of Disney's Goofy caught in a big surprise as he watches us drive away.

"*Ten*." The name of the movie comes to me and I tell Sandie.

"What?"

"Brian Dennehey played a bartender in that movie with Dudley Moore and that naked girl. *Ten*. Remember?"

She squints at me so I tell her about the bartender looking like ... She gives me a bored look.

"Did you learn anything?" I ask.

"Nothing." She pulls off her heels and says this shit's getting old. "Bring me out to UNO"

"What?"

"That big dorm on Leon Simon. That's where Scrumptious stays. You know. *Samuel.*"

I drop her off a half block away and watch her prance into the dorm like she belongs. When she doesn't come right out, I drive off, back downtown.

A half hour later, I kill the lights as I ease the Caprice against the curb fifty feet from Felice's auntie's house on Congress Street. I roll down the driver's side window, hunker down and wait. Beneath the twisted branches of a huge magnolia, I'm sure no one can see me. The dim streetlights at the end of the block gives the dark street and eerie yellow glow.

At exactly three a.m., I spot Felice coming down the sidewalk from the direction of North Claiborne two blocks away. I climb out slowly and Felice stops. I move around into the street so she can see it's me. Shaking her head, she continues forward. She's in tight jeans too, baby-blue jeans with a black blouse. Her hair looks freshly corn-rowed.

"How about some coffee?" I ask as she arrives.

"How about some breakfast?"

One of the nice things about New Orleans – you can eat anytime.

I give Felice her choice of places and she picks Aleta's Cafe in the Monteleone Hotel.

"So what's up?" I ask, pulling onto Claiborne.

She looks out at the passing houses for a minute but finally answers. "Been getting my affairs in order. Got myself set up with some money for the future." I don't ask. I wait for her to continue, but her patience outlasts mine. As we cross Franklin Avenue, I re-start the conversation.

"You been hanging out at those white joints you mentioned in the House of D, or what?"

"Matter of fact, that's where I came from tonight."

"Yeah. What places?" I glance at her and she's still looking out the passenger window.

"I don't write down all the names, but I been to four places in the Quarter and four near the muses."

The muses – she's talking about the Sixth District, streets named for the Greek muses, Melpomene, Terpischore, Euterpe. I think there were eight originally before the city fathers started renaming them after dead New Orleanians.

"Learning anything?"

She shakes her head and says it ain't from lack of trying.

"What about bars around here? In the Ninth Ward."

She looks at me and furrows her brow.

"I don't fuck around by my auntie's." She looks straight ahead. "You know the old saying. Never shit where you eat." Before I can agree, she adds, "Men will do that, o'course."

I laugh and can't stop for several blocks. When I look back at her, she's smiling. I think it's the first time I've ever seen her smile. In that moment, she looks so young. Then again, she's still a teenager.

Chapter 7
OUR DAY BEGINS WHEN THEIR DAY ENDS

Bob Kay pulls off his sport coat, turns and drapes it over the back seat. His bullet proof vest is bulky beneath his shirt. Surprisingly, I don't see any boy scout merit badge. I check my watch. Sandie's been in the Hoodwink Bar seven minutes. We're parked in the next block, beneath another magnolia tree. It's only nine p.m. and there's only one motorbike parked outside the bar.

"Now, let me get this straight," Kay says. "You've been doing this for a week?"

"Nearly two weeks now."

Again, I apologize for not telling him about what Sandie heard. I explain I wasn't holding anything back. She was so lit that night, she couldn't remember who told her or even where she heard the story. Kay nods as he listens and tells me it's no problem. My penance for holding back – I get to ride with Kay tonight. Lucky me.

A car whizzes by and takes the corner so fast its wheels squeal.

"It's like fishing," I say.

Kay continues nodding.

"Put out your bait and hope for a strike." I don't believe I'm saying this, but it seems to be working. "We can go in like storm troopers, if you think that'll work. Raid all the bars."

"No." Kay shakes his head forcefully. "We've been doing that all over town. You heard about that warrant last night?"

It's my turn to nod. The previous evening nearly thirty officers stormed a house on Law Street, not far from St.

Augustine High. Looking for a parole violator who used a
.357 magnum in an armed robbery a week ago, the officers
succeeded in terrorizing an entire neighborhood, shooting
two dogs which attacked fence-jumping officers, without
locating the parole violator or his magnum.

"He surrendered this morning," Kay explains. I'd heard.
"Even brought the gun, which was a Smith and Wesson."

I look at my watch and it's been nearly ten minutes since
Sandie slithered out of the car.

"Come on," I say as I climb out. Kay follows and I have
to suggest he put his jacket back on.

"It's too hot."

I point to his vest and he looks at it and asks if it's that
obvious.

"Yep."

As we start for the bar, Sandie comes out. In another pair
of tight jeans, pink this time, she wears a low-cut white
blouse and red high heels. She waves at us, shaking her head.
We stop and wait.

"Goddamn ass-holes!" Sandie breezes by us for the car.
She turns and says, "Y'all comin', or what?"

Kay takes off his jacket as I head back to open the car.
Sandie climbs in the back seat. As soon as we're settled, she
says she's had enough tonight and is anyone hungry or just
her?

"I could eat," Kay says.

I crank up the engine. Kay passes Sandie his jacket and
she folds it across the back seat.

"What about that place by your houseboat?" Kay asks.
"The one you've been bragging about?"

Sandie leans forward and asks coyly, "You have a houseboat?" As if she doesn't fuckin' know.

"In Bucktown," Kay volunteers enthusiastically. "It's kinda old ..."

"The *Sad Lisa*," Sandie says as she sits back. "He sleeps in a loft and has a puppy named Buck."

"Huh?" The boy scout blinks at Sandie.

"I woke up there once with no panties and my skirt up to my waist."

Kay's mouth actually drops.

"I don't think we fucked, but I'm still not sure."

I pause a second for a red light at Elysian Fields, then drive through it. Kay clears his throat. I know. I know. Don't run red lights.

"Why don't we go to Jaegers or Fitzgeralds?" I suggest two nice seafood restaurants along West End. Sandie and Kay prefer to try out my place. So it's Flamingo's.

Parking the Caprice in the oyster shell lot, I spot Angie standing next to the counter. She's talking with Cecilia who waves at me as we approach. Joe is the only other person in the place. He grins at me from behind the grill.

Angie turns as I step in and hold the door for Sandie and Kay. Leaning against the counter in her white uniform, she looks at me from over her shoulder. With her body twisted, her hips look especially nice. She focuses those killer eyes at me for a moment, then looks at Sandie, then away. Her face remains expressionless as I introduce Assistant Chief Kay and Sandie to Cecilia, Joe and Angie, who curtly scoops three menus from the counter and leads us to my usual booth.

Sandie asks for the ladies room and Angie points to the door. Kay and I slip into opposite sides of the booth.

"I like this place," Kay says, tapping a knuckle on the Formica table top. "Reminds me of when I was a kid. The Woolworth Cafe on Canal Street."

Angie hands him a menu and drops the other two in front of me. I try not to watch her rear as she moves away, but it isn't easy. Kay stares and when Angie's out of earshot says, "Mighty pretty, ain't she?"

Sandie comes out and slides in the booth next to Kay, who moves closer to the window. She's got him pinned, sitting too close to him now. She picks up the menu and asks him what he ordering.

"What's good here?" he asks me.

"Best burgers in the city. The catfish is great. Chili's excellent."

Angie returns with water and set-ups. She doesn't look at me as she puts them down and pulls out her pad and pen.

"I'll take the usual," I say without picking up my menu. Sandie asks what that is and I tell her. She orders the same without the onions and Kay follows suit. Angie moves away without looking at me and I feel the frost.

As Sandie asks Kay about his bullet-proof vest and he starts in on the merits of police safety, I look out at the dark sky.

It's better, I tell myself, that Angie is a cold fish tonight. Better that she's keeping her distance, better that – then it hits me. *Why?* That elusive word most homicide detectives don't ask because *why* isn't the important question in a murder investigation. You start asking why and you jump to conclusions. In homicide, how is more important. Find out how someone is killed and that will lead to who.

But I ask myself why. Why is Angie like this tonight?

Sandie?

Naw. Sandie's all over Kay.

Angie returns with our three Barq's. I look at her but she doesn't look back and I remember that lingering look as I held the door and Sandie breezed in. I take a hit of the cold Barq's and wonder. Naw. It's something else. She's too young and too pretty and I'm too tired tonight.

I tune out Sandie's chattering, letting my mind drift and find myself in a pirogue, sitting between cypress trees as the red sun falls into Vermilion Bay. I smell the salty water, hear the screech of a hawk, feel the sun's warmth on my face.

Joe's burger is as good as ever – hot, spicy and juicy.

Sandie keeps the conversation going and Kay is more than eager to talk with her. I find myself looking at Angie again as she sits on a stool next to the counter. She's cut her hair. Only a little, but it's curled under and looks very nice. So does the line of her face in profile, her small nose and sculptured lips. I chuckle at myself and Sandie asks what I'm laughing at.

"Nothing."

She turns and looks at Angie, looks back and waves a finger at me.

"You're so obvious," she says. Smiling at Kay, she tells him all men are obvious. That's one of the things she likes about men. They're simple.

Yeah. Right.

Kay surprises me later, as we drop Sandie off. He gives me more money for Sandie and Felice. Sandie thanks me, turns and kisses Kay softly on the mouth before moving away into her apartments. He's so stunned, he sits like a stiff for the next five minutes.

Coming out of it, he finally speaks. "You're not really having sex with her, are you?"

I remind him of LaStanza's saying.

Kay approves, then goes on to tell me about how he apprehended a murderer once at a Schwegmann's Super Market and how LaStanza came and handled the case.

"Best detective we ever had," Kay concluded. "One reason why Jodie Kintyre's so good. He broke her in."

Then, as we pull into the police garage, Kay adds. "Of course Kintyre had the talent all along. He just pointed her the right way."

"And she broke me in," I remind Kay.

"Exactly." Kay lets out a long sigh. "You trouble me, Beau."

I know. No need to ask, he'll go on.

"LaStanza's problem was he went looking for trouble. And the fact he can kill with the best of the Sicilians." Kay pauses for effect. "You, on the other hand, seem to find trouble without looking for it."

"Just lucky," I tell him as I park the car.

Kay shakes his head and continues shaking it all the way up to the office.

•

The sun wakes me and I roll over on my back and just lie there. Golden sunlight streams through the open portholes, illuminating the cypress rafters above me. The afternoon light falls directly on the museum-quality print of Van Gogh's *Starry Night*, hanging on the wall above the night stand where my Glock rests. The dark blues and bright whites seem to shimmer in Van Gogh's yellow moonlight. The swirling night sky is luminescent.

I watch it as I listen to the water gurgling outside. A boat must have drifted pass on its way through the inlet, or maybe a speedboat on the lake sent a distant wave to shore that finally brushed against the hull of *Sad Lisa*.

The air smells of salt water, brackish water that's far less salty than it should be. Just before the recent flood, as if by divine knowledge, the Corps of Engineers opened the spillway above New Orleans to lower the river level, sending millions of gallons of muddy fresh water into Lake Pontchartrain. Pissed off the 'Save The Lake' folks, big time. Don't know why exactly, except when anyone fornicates with the lake, the 'Save The Lake' people get pissed off.

I stretch. It's nice under the sheet with a warm breeze flowing over me. And, for the hundredth time, I remind myself how much I like Bucktown. It's peaceful, even though we're still in the city. There's a different feel here, tucked into a small corner of the big city, with a wide lake at our back.

Buck yips downstairs. I stretch again and crawl out of bed. I peek down the ladder and Buck is at the bottom, looking up. Seeing me, he spins and yips louder, bouncing on his big feet. Time to let him out to do his business. Time to shave and shower and start mine, but only after feeding the little tike. Then I'll take him to the levee for a good run.

At four o'clock, I stop by Flamingo's for a late lunch. I'm the lone customer. Angie isn't there and Cecilia waits on me, as talkative as ever. Today the subject's the Audubon Zoo. She leads me to my booth, explaining how she liked the zoo better when it was free, back when it wasn't animal-friendly, back when it was people-friendly.

I watch Joe plop my burger patty on the grill and sprinkle generous slices of onion on it. The strong scent of sizzling beef drifts my way. Cecilia tells me how she used to go to the zoo all the time. *It was free.* You could walk in and walk out, have picnics there. Now it's a damn *zoological garden,* costs twelve bucks a head and you can't get anywhere near the animals. Cecilia used to like to play with the monkeys in their cages, back when they were within arm's reach.

Joe turns my patty over, sprinkling more onions and slices of garlic on it. Cecilia goes on to berate the damn uptowners, those money-grubbing 'Friends of the Zoo' who turned an admittedly inferior zoo into a Disneyesque theme park with all the personality of a shopping mall. When you got right down to it, Cecilia admits, what galls her the most is when things change.

The door opens and Angie rushes in, dropping her school books behind the counter. She's in a fitted pink tee-shirt and black jeans. Her hair is nicely windblown. Cecilia moves away as Joe slides my plate on the counter. Angie scoops it up on her way to my booth.

"Hi," she says in a breathless voice as she places my plate in front of me.

"You OK?"

She brushes her hair from her eyes. "Running late." Her lipstick is more faint than usual. She looks at my table again and goes back for my Barq's and a frosty mug. I thank her as she heads, purse in hand, for the bathroom.

When Angie comes out, she's less rushed. She puts her purse behind the counter next to Cecilia, turns and heads back for me. She puts a knee up on the seat across from me and lets out a long sigh. The sculptured lips are deep red now. Suddenly her face reddens as she asks who was that redhead. I want to say something smart-assed, but I opt for the truth.

"She's trying to help us."

"She's with the police?"

I lower my voice, the way Jodie taught me, because people listen more intently if they have to pay attention just to hear.

"She's working the street for us. Going places we can't go. It's dangerous work. Really."

Angie looks out the window and lets out sighs again

I change the subject. "Rough day in class?"

"Exams coming up."

"What are you majoring in?"

"American Lit. We're doing Nineteenth Century right now, you know Poe, Hawthorne, James Fenimore Cooper."

"I thought Cooper was earlier." I have a dim recollection of *The Deerslayer* taking place before the American Revolution.

"He wrote about earlier times, but *The Last of the Mohicans* was published in 1826." She stares hard at me, steps to the side and looks at my face in profile.

"What?" I ask.

"The more I look at you, the more you look like Indian." She moves back to the booth. "Um, Native American." She corrects herself.

"We're all native Americans. We were born here. But what can our tribes do, call ourselves Indigenous Americans?"

She nods. "I know. I know." She sounds as tired as I do of the politically correct things to say.

"What do you mean, the more I look like an Indian?"

She puts her knee back up on the seat.

"You have the look of a bird of prey," she says seriously.

I almost laugh and take another bite.

"Yeah?"

"You have a hawk nose."

I choke down the piece of hamburger and take a quick hit of Barq's. She leans forward and looks closely at my nose. I wipe my mouth with the napkin. "I'll have you know, young lady, I have a falcon nose."

She throws back her head and laughs. It's a deep laugh, one that goes on and on and she has to sit across from me now. It takes her a while to control herself. As she does, I turn my head to the side, and point to my falcon nose and let out a shrill bird cry. She laughs again until tears form in her eyes.

Just as she recovers again, two men come in and she has to work. As she takes their orders, two more men come in. And for the next twenty minutes, I watch her work, watch her step back and forth from the counter to the booths, watch that nice ass move away from me.

Each time she looks my way she smiles and I feel it, in that look, in the way she laughed. There's something passing between us. And I remember how my Daddy told me a Cajun secret, back when I was starting the long process of trying to figure out women. The Cajun secret was – get them to laugh.

"Dey laugh wit' you," he told me, "and dey feel good and dats not a bad ting, no."

I look out as a large brown pelican floats by on wings that have to be four feet across. The bird glides above the inlet canal, folds its wings and dives into the water. It rises a moment later, its bill gorged and I tell myself again, how much I like living in Bucktown.

•

"I hate this fuckin' place," Felice says as we walk into the homicide squad room.

"What?" I feign surprise. "It's so ... warm." I wave my hand at the cold, gray metal desks. "And smells so nice."

The air reeks of cigarette smoke and stale coffee. I lead Felice to my desk and point to the chair next to it. Tonight she wears a white cotton blouse, blue jeans and white tennis shoes. She could pass for a classmate of Angie.

Her face, void of make-up, looks younger than the hard nineteen years she's spent in the city that care forgot. Beneath the bright fluorescents, her brown eyes look lighter than usual and it occurs to me that her eyes are the same color as Sandie's. Deeper set, Felice has cautious eyes, leery eyes, street-wise eyes.

"So," she says as I plop in my gray metal chair. "You got some money for me, or what?"

I'd told her that to get her here. It's the truth at least. I open my briefcase and dig out a brown envelope. After she signs the receipt, I pass her two hundred in twenties. She makes a face and stuffs the money into the front right pocket of her jeans. Leaning back in the chair, she looks at the homicide vulture and shakes her head.

"Our day begins when their day ends," she reads the homicide slogan next to the vulture. "Some goddamn place you have here."

"So, how's it going on the street."

She turns back to me. "I thought you'd never ask." She folds her arms and says, "I have something for you."

I try not to look excited.

"Word on the street is that a fat-ass white boy who stays uptown is the killer. He hangs in the Ninth Ward."

I wait but there doesn't seem to be more. I almost ask her if the guy supposed to be a biker, but catch myself. I'm not here to give information, but get it.

"Where did you hear this, exactly?"

She goes about it in a roundabout way, but apparently it's almost common knowledge among the criminal element.

"Whoever he is, he's bad."

"How do you know that?"

"Every bad-ass brother I know don't want no part of him."

"Jesus, *nobody* knows his name?"

She gives me an impatient look. "I didn't say that. *I* just don't know it." A beat later she says, "Yet."

Chapter 8
ANY MORE QUESTIONS?

Just when I thought it couldn't get more complicated, the Task Force, after careful interviewing and re-interviewing witnesses, has come up with two different descriptions of our killer.

Three witnesses from the Cochran murder scene describe a tall, thin white man with salt-and-pepper hair. He fled the scene as the shots were still echoing. Four witnesses, two in a passing car, describe a heavy-set white male with black hair standing over the corpse of Patrolman J. P. Stevens. The fat man had a silver pistol in his right hand.

More than one killer? Our firearms experts are positive the same .357 Colt Python was used.

Sitting in the hall of the Criminal Courts Building, I examine Bob Kay's memo again, reading the descriptions from each witness. One gun, but two killers. What the hell is this? I know. I know. A good homicide detective doesn't speculate. We go with the facts. But *two* different descriptions? Two killers? Twice the chance for them to shoot off their mouths and yet we're hearing nothing.

The courtroom door next to me opens, and a black-clad Orleans Parish Deputy steps out and calls my name. I close my clipboard, rise and follow him into the nearly deserted courtroom. Some murder cases attract as much attention as a Saints game near the end of another losing season. As I pass the D.A.'s table, I lay my clipboard on it and move to the witness chair. Passing the jury, I look at each juror. They stare back at me with a jury's typical glazed look. Where do we get these people?

Still standing, I take the oath, sit and look over at the defendant. Seated between his two lawyers, the defendant looks like a middle-class business man in his nice dark blue suit. When I arrested him seven months ago, he was a severely fucked-up part-time roofer and part-time marijuana dealer. He killed his best friend with a hammer. Over a woman.

I don't remember him having gray hair along his temples. His drawn features are pale. Jailhouse pallor. Not much sunshine and fresh air in parish prison. His name is William Manesia, but everyone calls him Bubby.

Assistant District Attorney Peggy Stuart rises from the prosecution table. She's a big woman with short, light brown hair and large, dark brown eyes. She wears a dark green suit. As she picks up her legal pad, I notice Bubby taking off his suit coat.

Stuart starts my way and Bubby loosens his tie. Bubby places his tie next to his coat on the defense table. Stuart asks her first question. "Please state your name and rank."

Normally I look at the jury when I answer, but I'm too busy watching Bubby unbutton his shirt. No one else seems to notice.

"John Raven Beau, Detective, NOPD Homicide Division."

I glance at the judge, who's busy staring at the pen set on his desk. Judge Donald Lister has to be pushing eighty. Bubby's lawyers are too busy staring at me to notice Bubby removing his shirt. I look at the jury and twelve pair of eyes are looking right at me.

"Now, Detective Beau, on the afternoon of November seventeenth, did you have occasion to be called to the twelve hundred block of Upperline Street?"

"Yes."

Bubby drops his shirt on the defense table and his lawyers finally notice. Bubby stands and starts unfastening his pants. The lawyer on his left tries to grab his hand and Bubby slaps him sharply, which brings the judge out of his coma.

"Now wait just a minute," the judge says.

Bubby shoves his lawyers aside and takes a step back.

"You!" The judge points to the same deputy who escorted me in. "Stop that man."

Bubby has his pants down before the deputy can grab him. Thank God he's wearing drawers. Bubby howls like a wolf and tries to bite the deputy. Another deputy rushes over and grabs Bubby around the neck.

"Fuck you!" Bubby screams. "Fuck all of you! 'Specially that pork chop eatin' D.A.!'"

The deputy tries to put his hand over Bubby's mouth. Bubby bites the hand and the deputy howls. "Fuck the jury! I wanna ..." Bubby's voice fades momentarily.

"I wanna ... "

The deputies pull him to the floor.

"I wanna ... fuck that little blond in the jury!"

I glance at the petite blond woman seated at the far left end of the jury box. She bows her head as others look at her.

"Fuck all of you!"

The deputies lift Bubby and start carrying him out. He's handcuffed now.

"I want that blond to suck my dick!"

They slam into a railing and then into the wall before one of the deputies opens the a door and they fall through it.

"I wanna fuck that fat D.A. too!"

The door slams shut.

Peggy Stuart lets out a long sigh and starts back for the prosecution table.

"Um," my voice breaks the silence. "Any more questions for me?"

•

Seated at my desk, I go over the seventy-seven pages of print-outs of arrests and incidents at Bywater and Ninth Ward Bars. I use a yellow highlighter and after three hours, I wonder what the hell I'm highlighting. It's all so fuckin' random.

No name seems to dominate any of the incidents. Only a couple are repeated and most of the perpetrators are black. Rubbing my eyes, I go over what Sandie told me that evening at Café Du Monde. She said she was in a bar, probably in the Ninth Ward. Some bikers came in.

I reach into my briefcase and pull out my note pad. She described them as 'greasy-looking' men wearing leather vests and tattoos on their hairy arms. One of them said the murdered police officers were missing something. She let 'the big one' feel up her tits and he told her the cops were missing their badges.

Bikers. She was sure, back in that drunken stupor, that they were bikers. I pick up my phone and punch in the number to the Intelligence Division. The clock tells me it's after five so I don't expect an answer.

"Intelligence. Jones." A deep voice answers.

"This is Beau in Homicide. You got a minute?"

•

Detective Felicity Jones is seated behind his own gray metal desk. Pushing forty, Fel Jones is still in pretty good shape. Like me, he played a little college football at LSU. He has the darkest complexion, so black his skin seems almost blue. Smiling as I approach, he waves me to the chair in front of his desk. I try not to show how surprised I am that he's talking to me.

"So what's up?"

I tell him everything, about Sandie's statement, about my futile search for the correct bar, about us coming up with nothing, zippo, a big fuckin' blank.

"Y'all gather intelligence on gangs and bikers, don't you?" I ask.

"Yeah. But there isn't much here." He goes on to explain there's no biker gangs in New Orleans. No real gangs. There used to be a couple back in the eighties, but not any more.

"It's not like La Cosa Nostra, who've been open for business since before the turn of the century. You know we had the first Mafia family in the U.S. right here."

I think I heard that. Probably from Jodie.

Fel moves to a file cabinet, reaches in and pulls out two folders. He puts them in front of me and tells me to take a look. As I look at pasty mug shots of grubby-looking men, Fel explains how the biker mentality is one of rebellion, but not serious rebellion.

"No Marxists there. Most have driver's licenses, live in houses – albeit filthy houses sometimes. They just like to look different, dress different, ride bikes. You know, typical teen-ager mentality. Let's piss off the folks, tattoo our bodies, let our hair grow and don't wash."

Then he explains that it isn't all that simple really, but more like that than like a street gang. "We picked up word a week ago on the street that a biker might know something about Cochran's and Steven's murders."

Can't believe what I'm fuckin' hearing.

"In whispers. Nothing specific. No real intelligence. We have every informant trying to find out more." Fel leans back in his chair and lets out a weary sigh. "We put in long hours up here too, sometimes."

I go back to the mug shots, reading the descriptions next to some. They all sound the same.

"I sent a memo to Bob Kay this morning about it. But it's just a rumor at this point."

Some of the biker women look as rough as the men.

"People are so damn tight-lipped. There's so much heat from us on the street, it's frying them. We've got 'em scared. Got everyone scared. They're more scared of us than any cop killer."

It's my turn to let out a weary breath.

"I bet," Fel says, "I can count on one hand the number of cops who want to *catch* this killer. Everyone else is hell-bent on shooting him. This department is an armed camp of trigger-happy cops. It ain't healthy."

I have a hollow feeling in my stomach. He's right, of course. And I know, in the pit of my belly that *I'm* the one everyone thinks is the most trigger-happy.

Fel reaches over and taps the newspaper folded at the edge of his desk. "Glad to hear Costanza's was a good shooting, even though you'd never know by the press."

"I don't read the fuckin' paper."

"He'll fade some of the heat off *you*."

I look into Fel's brown eyes and see it there. Again, he's right on the mark. Why isn't this guy on the goddamn task force?

He taps the paper again. "They dug up some old Internal Affairs beefs against Costanza. They'll milk it for all it's worth. Make his life miserable for a couple weeks."

I close the folders. "Is there any way I can bring someone in here to look at these pictures?"

"Informant?"

I nod.

"Better if we bring the files to her."

Her? He's sharp all right.

"When?" I ask.

He looks at his watch and says he's got a dinner appointment at seven. Maybe we can do it on the way. I dial Sandie's number and get her machine. There's a knock on the door behind me.

"It's never fuckin' locked," Fel calls out.

Gonzales peeks in and tells me, "Kay's looking for you downstairs."

Before leaving Fel agrees to meet me with the file as soon as I get Sandie lined up. I thank him.

"Don't mention it."

I turn to leave.

"Seriously." Fel's voice deepens. "Don't mention it. We're not supposed to dispense this shit without an act of Congress."

He points a finger at Gonzales. "That goes for you too, Zorro."

As soon as we get into the elevator, Gonzales asks what the hell was all that. I figure the truth'll work here and explain that Fel's siphoning intelligence information to me and probably wouldn't like every swinging dick to know.

"Cool." Gonzales nods.

Bob Kay, all decked out in black, stands with three other black clad Task Force members. *Jesus.* Not another search warrant. Kay pulls a sheet of paper from his clipboard and hands it to me.

"It's from Intelligence. More rumors about bikers. I want you to get a hold of Jodie. She's tight with Felicity Jones. He's the only solid investigator in Intelligence. He might talk to you through her."

I keep my face from revealing anything.

Kay pulls me aside and lowers his voice. "Otherwise, we'll have to go through channels. You see, Fel and LaStanza used to be partners and LaStanza broke in Jodie and Jodie broke you in. They're still pretty tight."

It occurs to me that's probably why Fel spoke to me in the first place. Jodie.

•

Gonzales joins me for supper at Flamingo's the following evening. He's in another shark skin suit, dark blue with a black shirt and dark purple tie. I wear a gray tee-shirt with the emblem of London's Jekyll & Hyde Pub emblazoned in black across the front. A gift from an old girlfriend, she said it fit my personality. I don't agree, but the shirt goes well with the black dress shirt I wear like a jacket and my black jeans.

Angie is in her white uniform today, smiling as she seats us then goes to wait on the only other two customers near the front of the cafe, fishermen-looking men.

Gonzales gives her a good stare and says, "Who's the talent?"

"Angie and she's got too much brains for the likes of us."

Gonzales grins. "It wasn't her brains I was looking at."

I have to smile.

When Angie returns I order the usual and Gonzales orders the same without the onions. "Gotta keep my breath fresh," he tells her. "Never know who I'm going to kiss later."

She chuckles and walks away. Gonzales turns to watch her ass move away. I'm not so obvious, but I look too.

"You got something going with her?" Gonzales loosens his tie as the smoky scent of cooking burgers rises across the cafe. I shake my head.

Angie returns with our root beers. Her lipstick is more brown than red today and her hair thicker looking than usual. Don't know what she's done with it exactly, but it's fluffier and looks very nice.

"Since he's not about to introduce us," Gonzales says as he extends his right hand. "I'm Mike Gonzales and you're Angie, right?"

She takes his hand and nods.

"So. What you doin' when you get off tonight?"

Angie pulls her hand away and smiles at me.

"Moves fast doesn't he?"

I shrug.

"He who hesitates, is lost," Gonzales says.

Still looking at me, Angie says, "Tell your friend I don't date cops." She turns to him. "And if I were to, I prefer the slower moving, quieter type. Especially if they're part Sioux."

And she wheels and leaves and I don't hide the way I look at her moving away smoothly.

Gonzales grins broadly. "Well, you know where you stand now, don't you?"

I take a hit of Barq's.

Gonzales leans closer. "Seriously. A woman turns down a good looker like me, especially decked out in *this* suit, for the likes of you, you're in like Flynn."

"Flynn? Who's Flynn?"

"You know. I don't know. It's a saying."

I change the subject, going back to the reason for this meeting. Gonzales has been haranguing me to find out if Sandie recognized any of the mugs from Fel Jones's file.

"Thought maybe a face would jog her memory," I explain. "But another big zero."

"It doesn't make sense. Two different killers. Bikers are too disorganized to pull this off."

I hear myself repeating the homicide cliché, "Go with the facts, man. Go with the facts."

"Yeah? When the facts are slim, where does it leave us?"

I look out the window. "It's out there," I repeat another homicide cliché. "The solution's out there. We just have to hit the streets until we find it."

Angie arrives with our plates and ketchup. She backs up to the counter and sits on the stool next to our table, turning in the stool to face us. I take a bite of burger and look at her.

She tilts her head to the side and says, "Are you friends with any of your ex-girlfriends?"

I shake my head.

"I am," Gonzales injects. "One anyway. I go back and hit her a lick every once in a while."

I have to fight to keep from laughing at the silly bastard. *Hit her a lick?* What a loon, telling Angie something like that.

Angie's face is serious. "My ex-boyfriend wants to be friends. Go shopping on the weekend. Maybe take in a movie, if I'm not busy. Is that normal for a man?"

"No," Gonzales says as if she's asking him.

"What kind of shopping?" I ask.

"Window shopping. Shopping for clothes. Shoes. Make-up."

I can see the confusion in her eyes.

"Would you be modeling any lingerie for him?" Gonzales asks. "Or bathing suits?"

She shakes her head.

"Then he's an idiot," Gonzales declares.

Staring at the aquamarines, I ask, "When you say *friend*, do you confide in him? Tell him what you're feeling? Thinking?" She seems surprised at the question and tells me no, she doesn't confide in him.

"Then he's an acquaintance. Not a friend."

"The man's an idiot," Gonzales repeats, then fills his mouth, thankfully, with a large bite.

I take another bite and Angie looks over our heads, out the window.

"Can men and women really be friends without a sexual relationship?" Her voice is dead-pan serious.

"Nope," Gonzales answers.

"What about Jodie, you moron?" My voice is a little too high and the fishermen turn our way.

Gonzales leans closer and says, "Don't tell me you've never thought of going to bed with her. Ever?"

Jesus. I feel a sudden flush on my neck and hope to God it's not there on my face.

"Who's Jodie?"

I fill my mouth with another bite and thankfully Gonzales answers Angie's question.

When I finally look at Angie, she asks, "Do you confide in Jodie? Tell her things?"

I nod slowly and hear myself say, "She's a friend. I look up to her. Trust her. Tell her just about everything. We're friends. Padnas."

Gonzales raises a finger. "And if, one night, she looks you in the eye and starts unbuttoning her blouse, you'd tell her to stop, right?"

This isn't going well for me. I drink more Barq's and decide again, the truth is the best way.

"Of course I wouldn't. But that'll never happen. Ever."

"Touché." Happy with the response, Gonzales takes another bite.

I look at Angie and she's still staring out the window.

She speaks softly. "So there's always a sexual tension, isn't there? Between men and women. Unless they're related or one is completely gross."

"Some parts of Louisiana, being related is no deterrent." Gonzales adds that pearl of wisdom, which we ignore.

Angie turns her eyes to me and smiles shyly. "Thanks. Just curious." And she leaves for her other customers.

Gonzales waits until I look his way.

"Jesus. She always this intense?"

I nod and something clicks in my brain. Whoever this ex-boyfriend is, he's going to have to go shopping with someone else.

Chapter 9
A HUNDRED TIMES DOWN THE ROAD

The following three evenings are carbon copies of one another. Checking dailies at the office, chasing Sandie down and then Felice, linking up with Gonzales to see if he's come up with anything. End result is a big zero.

On my way home after the third carbon copy evening, I remember it's been exactly two months since Cochran was killed. Two weeks before, Stevens had been killed. The whole department is still on razor edge, wondering when the killer will strike again. I'm afraid, afraid all the heat's scared the killer away and we'll never catch him – or them.

Arriving in Bucktown with the dawn light, I look out at the canal at the early morning fog hovering above the still water. As I pull the Caprice against the curb, I spot a figure, sitting on the wooden bench next to the gate of *Sad Lisa*. It's a woman. She stands and puts a hand on her hip and a face from my past smiles at me. I climb out of the car and Buck yaps at me from the deck.

"Cute puppy," Sharon says.

"How long have you been here?" I spot her yellow Toyota parked down the lane.

"About an hour."

I walk slowly up to her. Sharon Merraid's brown hair is much longer now, well past her shoulders. Still straight, still parted down the middle, she has matching gold barrettes on either side. Her face is just as pretty and I feel my heart tug when she coyly bites her lower lip. Those familiar green eyes blink at me. Hard to believe she's standing here.

"You look very nice," I tell her.

"I was hoping you'd be happy to see me."

I've never seen the light blue blouse she wears but her faded jeans look familiar. We'd dated for over two years when I was a patrolman, when I worked those easy eight hour shifts, when I was so much younger. She's the one who gave me the Jekyll & Hyde shirt. Buck yaps louder now.

"How about some breakfast?" I step over to the gate and unlock it.

"It's not what I came for, but breakfast sounds nice."

Buck bounces in a circle, yapping even louder. As I step on deck, he rolls on his back and flails his paws at me.

"Watch out for the puddles," I warn Sharon, pointing at a yellow stain.

The houseboat's stuffy. Turning on the AC and ceiling fans, I open the windows and a semi-cool breeze quickly fills the room. I move to the small kitchen area and pull out two frying pans. Standing in the living room area, Sharon looks around and says, "It's like going back in time."

"What?"

"You haven't changed a thing."

"Buck's new."

Hearing his name, Buck yaps and then tries to howl, losing it in the back of his undeveloped throat. Sharon smiles, goes down on her haunches and pets Buck, whose tail is wagging so hard I don't know why it doesn't fly off.

"He's so cute. What is he, a springer or a setter?"

"Catahoula. It's the state dog."

Buck is eating this up, on his back now, flailing his paws as she pets his belly.

"Catahoula means *clear water* in Choctaw," I tell her. "See his blue eyes."

Sharon stands and moves to the sink and washes her hands. Buck must have peed on her too. I start up the eggs and two thick chunks of andouille, or what passes for andouille in the big city. Authentic Cajun andouille is more peppery, but Winn Dixie's version of this pork sausage isn't bad. It smells just as rich and makes my empty stomach rumble.

"Let me help." Sharon drops her purse on my easy chair and elbows me out of the way. I pull a can of puppy chow out for Buck and feed him while she cooks our breakfast. Watching her standing here I can't help notice the curve of her ass in those tight jeans. She looks at me and smiles.

"So, what *did* you come for?"

Her smile turns into a sad smile. She puts the spatula down and moves to me.

"This," she says as she wraps her arms around my neck, leans up and kisses me on the lips. A soft kiss, our lips barely touch but I know the familiar feel. Pressed against me for that brief moment jump-starts my body, like a charge of electricity. She pulls away and goes back to the stove.

Eggs, sunny side up, andouille and thick coffee-and-chicory, two slices of toast, properly buttered, is an excellent breakfast. A salty lake breeze flows through the window next to my small kitchen table, attached to the wall so it can be folded out of the way.

There's small talk. Sharon telling me about her new job at the bank. She's an officer now, promoted from teller. She still lives in the same apartment, half-a-house in old Metairie. She asks about Buck and about how *Sad Lisa* fared during the big flood.

"Fine. It's a boat."

She asks if I'm seeing anyone, but doesn't ask about the job.

We pick up the dishes and move to the sink where she kisses me again. Our tongues brush and a passion from long ago awakens in me. I pull her close and we kiss long and hard. Coming up for air, I take Sharon's hand and lead her to the stairs and up to the loft to my unmade bed. She drapes her blouse over the end table on the far side of my bed as I turn the window fan on high. I pull out my Glock and put it on the other table, along with my dress shirt and tee-shirt. Sharon ooches out of her jeans, leaving them on the floor next to her sandals. She stretches, standing in her white bra and bikini panties, her creamy skin glowing in the early morning light.

A thunder clap makes us both jump. I turn in time to see rain pelting the water outside. The sun beams through the rain water and I suddenly hear my Dad's voice telling me – if it rains while the sun is shining, the devil is beating his wife.

Sharon unsnaps her bra and drops it on her blouse. I stare at her round, perfectly symmetrical breasts, small pink areolas and tiny nipples, standing erect. I kick off my penny loafers and pull off my socks and jeans and black jockeys. I stand and stretch as a wave of windblown, rainy air flows through the window behind me. My dick is straight up like a flag pole.

Sharon leers at it as she works her panties down and for a moment we stand staring at each other's naked body. We climb on the bed, tossing the pillows on the floor. Sharon rolls on her back. I hover over her for a moment and kiss her throat lightly. I softly kiss my way down to her breasts, rolling my tongue over her nipples, sucking each for a moment. I kiss my way down to her belly, down to her silky pubic hair. I tongue her hair and part her legs with my hands. I circle her pussy with kisses, letting my breath fall on her pink slit. I kiss my way down her slender legs to the erogenous zones on the under side of her knees.

Sharon gasps, her hips gyrating slowly now, as I lick my way back up her inner thighs. She spreads her legs and I move my face between them. I hold back a moment and she pushes herself down to me. My tongue slides across the outside of her pussy. She cries out and I sink my tongue into her.

I reach up for her breasts and knead them as I work my tongue inside her. I pull back and start licking her in quick, smooth strokes. She humps against me and pulls at my hair. I continue licking, changing strokes to quick flicks, then back to long licks. I work her clit and she moans and pumps her hips to my licking.

Grinding her hips, Sharon rides my tongue. Her sweet, familiar taste in my mouth, I continue working my tongue until she pulls harder at my hair. I increase the pace and she cries out and yanks my hair. I push her hands away and continue working my tongue.

Her hips still gyrating, Sharon digs her heels into the mattress, trying to pull away from my tongue, but there's nowhere to go. Her head reaches the head board and she cries out to me to pull up. She wants my dick in her – now. But I keep licking and she gasps loudly and explodes against me. Her hips bouncing, Sharon climaxes against my tongue.

Her hips rise and I stay with her.

She bucks up and down and I stay with her.

She cries out and squeezes my head with her legs until my ears ache, and I stay with her.

Finally, her ass falls back to the bed and I pull away.

Gasping, she yanks me up to her mouth. We French kiss as Sharon reaches down to guide the tip of my dick to her pussy lips. I work my way in, through the hot wetness. She shudders at the penetration before we start a deep, grinding, hot fuck. Fast at first, I slow down and ride her in long, smooth strokes. Waves of cool air flow over us as we make love on my unmade bed. Sharon bites her lower lip, then opens her eyes to stare into mine as we fuck.

"Oh, Babe," she gasps.

I smile and kiss her again. She wraps her arms and legs around me and we continue. I slow down again but she won't have any of that, working her pussy against my dick. Her hands cup the top of my shoulders as I gasp and come in her in long, hot spurts. I feel my gushing and continue working my pelvis against her.

Sharon cries out even louder and comes again. She calls this one an inside climax and I work with it. She continues crying out until I'm spent, until I collapse on top of her. It's only then, when she quiets down, that I hear Buck down stairs, trying to howl again. I laugh and Sharon laughs and we lie there, with the cool breeze sliding over our hot bodies.

I roll off and lie on my back next to her. Sharon closes her eyes and I look up at the ceiling. Buck stops trying to howl. Another thunderclap echoes and the rain increases. The sky darkens somewhat. I blink and close my weary eyes and try not to feel the sudden emptiness in my heart.

•

Sharon lies napping next to me, still on her back. I'm up on my elbow, four hours after we'd made love, watching her.

My heart races again, but not from passion. It races from that sinking, deep, depressed feeling that we shouldn't be here.

What the hell is this? What were we thinking? Why have we rekindled this? Why have we just reached into the past for something lost long ago?

Jesus.

She sure took a long time coming back, after she walked away. The last words she said come back to me. "I can't take it anymore. I can't take that job of yours."

A patrolman then, I had started working twelve hour power-shifts in high-crime areas. She said all I ever talked about was the job. Criminals. Scum-bags. She said I told her the most horrendous stories. Jesus, I was only a patrolman then. You want horror stories? Try Homicide.

Try walking into a tenement, across a blood-splattered floor to the body of a woman sliced to death by a jealous boyfriend with a filet knife; try walking into a restaurant freezer where three bodies lie in frozen blood, employees executed by robbers; try interviewing a man whose sudden rage at his crying infant caused him to stop his car on I-10, pull the baby from its seat and smash its little head against the concrete; try interviewing that man without reaching over the interview table and smashing the life out of him.

Try missing Sharon Merraid so much my heart ached for months. Try turning around a hundred times down the road, hoping she'd be there. Sharon Merraid of the pretty green eyes and easy smile, she was another of my failures.

And today we went back in time, reached back for something ... that's gone.

The rain has stopped. The only sound is the water gently lapping against the side of *Sad Lisa*. I feel myself drifting again and hope I won't dream.

•

I feel her move on the bed before I feel her touch me, gently, her hand on my thigh. It reaches my dick and begins stroking it. A hard-on has no conscience. It rises nicely and Sharon kisses it, licks it, then starts sucking it. Her hair brushes my belly as her head moves up and down on my dick. My breathing increases and she caresses my balls as she sucks me.

When my hips start moving, she pulls up, climbs on me and guides my dick to her pussy. She sinks on me and rides my dick. I crane my neck forward and suck her breasts, nibbling her nipples. It always takes longer the second time around. We dig for the passion and grind and take our time fucking. I grab her ass when I feel I'm coming and bounce her up and down as I come again in her.

Sharon rolls off and says, "That was nice."

The fan cools our sweaty bodies. As soon as her breathing is back to normal, Sharon climbs out of bed for the shower. When she comes back, I'm still awake, but only barely. She dresses at the foot of the bed.

"Hey," she says softly.

I lean up.

"I know you're in the middle of something big." Her voice is deep and filled with emotion. "It's all over the news. Maybe, when it's over, you'll call me."

"You really want me to?"

She nods and bites that lower lip again. She dresses, leans over and kisses me softly on the lips and leaves. It's only then I realize I don't miss her anymore. I miss the way she was, the way we were together when her eyes were filled with love. There's nothing wrong with the passion, there never was anything wrong with the physical part. I miss that too.

Jesus, it's so damn confusing. I can't sleep. Not with the familiar smell of our sex on my bed. Who are we kidding? There's no way we can bring it back. It's gone. Couldn't she feel it?

Then again, maybe, just maybe we can start over, but we can't bring it back, not the way it was, not with that deep, complete love. No way. It's gone. Shattered like a porcelain vase dropped down a staircase.

I hear Buck moving around downstairs. The clock says it's three p.m. Time to walk him on the levee. Time to hose down the deck. Time to get started on a new fuckin' day. Time to wash my bed sheets.

•

As I walk into the squad room, late for another mandatory Task Force Meeting, I can't help thinking how hard it is to get Felice to open up. She's like a shadow, a one-dimensional person who won't let me know anything except on a need to know basis. I'd linked up with her an hour earlier. She's still working the case, but I had to pull every sentence out of her.

The squad room is full and I have to push my way to my desk where Tim Rothman sits, his feet up on *my* desk. He waves me to the chair next to my desk. I brush past a burly detective who glares at me.

"Hey, Two-L," Rothman calls out. "Lighten up and let him pass."

The burly detective growls back, "Mind you own business, fuzz-head. And my name ain't Two-L."

"Yes it is." Rothman grins as I sit.

The burly detective growls again and kicks a trash can out of his way as he rounds a desk to get away from us.

"Who the fuck is that?"

Rothman points to a skinny detective sitting ten feet away. "That's Bob Wilson, spelled with one 'L'. Nice guy. Works Burglary."

"So?" I feel I'm in the middle of a Fudd and Channard's not even around.

Rothman turns and points to the burly galoot. "That's Bob Willson, spelled with two 'Ls'. Also works Burglary."

"So?"

"So, he's Two-L and the skinny guy's One-L."

I shake my head. "You gotta have better things to do with your life."

"Not really."

Bob Kay comes in and most of us settle down. For the next twenty minutes, he lambastes us about how fucked up this operation is. And it occurs to me, isn't he in charge?

"The FBI's been trying to horn in on this operation from the start." Kay lets that chilling prospect linger in the air for a moment. A loud fart sound echoes, from the talented mouth of Tony Dunn, no doubt.

"They've been itching. Talking to the mayor. Sending us psychological profiles of our killer."

"What profiles?" Rothman asks.

"They sent three. One says it's a woman. Which one you want?" Kay is huffing now. "If we don't make some progress, they'll take over this Task Force. You know the drill. They have unlimited funds and the political know how to convince politicians to let them run the show."

Jesus. The FBI. All we need is them fuckin' this up. Hell, we can fuck it up by ourselves. Kay goes on to spell out new assignments. Thankfully, he doesn't mention me. When he assigns Bob Willson, the one with two "Ls" in his name, to parish prison, chuckles erupt. Seems some guards got information from some prisoners that might be useful. Two-L isn't amused. Poor bastard'll be spending his evenings in prison talking to junkies and stone-fuckin-nuts criminals who'll say anything to get out of their cells for a little while.

"Way to go Two-L. Couldn't happen to a nicer guy," Tim Rothman declares, then starts laughing. When Two-L glares at him, he laughs even louder, nearly falling out of my chair. Two-L seethes. As the meeting breaks up, I spot Two-L moving our way. He kicks a chair over and lumbers right up to us and leans over Rothman.

"Listen, you frizzy-headed Jew bastard. The name's Willson. W ... I ... L ... L ... S ... O ... N. That other name, ain't my name."

Rothman grins. "Yes it is."

Two-L is breathing pretty heavy now, his fists clenched.

"All right," Kay declares. "Y'all lighten up."

Two-L remains there for a few moments to make his point, then backs away.

Rothman puts his hands behind his head.

"Obviously, Two-L," Rothman adds, "someone in your family's dyslexic. Wilson is spelled with one 'L' as in Woodrow Wilson and Wilson tennis balls."

Two-L lunges and grabs Rothman's shoulder, raising his right fist. I grab his fist and he leers at me. "You want a piece of this, Cochise?"

Rothman pulls away and has to tell Two-L, "You're not only ugly, but stupid. He'll scalp you."

I let go of Two-L's fist and nod toward Rothman. "Go ahead and hit him."

Rothman's looks stunned.

I fold my arms. "Kay's watching. I can't hit you first. Go ahead and clip Rothman. Then I can break your ugly jaw, you fuckhead."

Two-L points his ugly jaw in my face and says, "Yeah?"

"Count on it. I haven't hit anyone in a while. I need the exercise."

Bob Kay steps between us, forcing us both back a step.

"What's this all about?"

Two-L waves me forward. "Come on, Geronimo. Any time."

"Wrong tribe, moron. Cochise and Geronimo were Apache."

Kay tries Rothman. "What's all this about?"

"Beau and I were just asking who the fuck was stupid enough to let dipshit Burglary detectives in this, anyway."

Tony Dunn belches loudly behind my ear and everyone starts yelling and pointing fists and it takes all of Kay's diplomatic skills to keep another cop from being killed. As Two-L and Dunn and the other burglary dicks, including One-L, back away, Kay growls, "Dammit! From now on, no one brings guns to a Task Force meeting. I *mean* it!"

Storming off, he adds, "Leave them in your goddamn cars. We don't need any more dead cops!"

I look at Rothman who crosses his eyes.

I point my finger at his nose. "Fuckin' trouble maker."

He nods, stands and stretches.

"You'da looked pretty goofy if that big bastard had hit you."

"Not as goofy as he'da looked with a broken jaw."

From the back of the room someone yells, "Beau. Line two!"

I pick up the phone. It's Sandie.

"Hey, Baby," she says. "His name's Mullet."

"Who?"

"Your damn killer."

Chapter 10
IN THE TWILIGHT ZONE

I found six men with the last name of Mullet in our files, as well as nine men also known as Mullet. Some fuckin' moniker. I also found one Mudfish and one Muddy and threw them into the mix.

It's taken me three hours to put together seventeen separate photo line-ups with seven different pictures in each, throwing one Mullet in each except the ones with Mudfish and Muddy. Amazingly, most of the men looked alike, fuckin' ugly or as well call them – *fugly*. Pretty boys aren't called Mullet.

Wearing a pink blouse and extra-tight, iridescent blue jeans, Sandie sits next to my desk. Her hair is curled and her face adorned with extra make-up. Bob Kay in a black suit and Gonzales, in a dark green shark-skin suit, stand on either side of my desk.

I pass the first line-up to Sandie, giving her the standard spiel. "If you see anyone you recognize, let me know."

"He in here?"

"If you see anyone you recognize, let me know."

She's disappointed with the first line-up. She shakes her head through the second one. Reaching the fourth picture of the third line-up, she lets out a screech. Kay and Gonzales jump forward.

Sandie holds up the picture and says, "I went to high school with him!"

I snatch the picture out of her hand. It's one of the fillers.

Kay and Gonzales back away.

"Jimmy Page," Sandie tells me. "I think I fucked him, but I'm not sure." She digs a stick of gum out of her purse and looks up at Kay. "He had the same name as the guy from Zed Leppelin. Very popular with the girls."

"Led Zeppelin," I interpret.

"Whatever."

We go back to the line-ups.

Just as we reach the second to last one and I'm figuring the Mullet she met doesn't have a police record, Sandie slaps one of the pictures down on the desk and yells, "It's him! This is the guy." She bounces up and down and claps her hands.

Kay and Gonzales hover over me as I pick up the picture.

A protruding brow over deep-set, beady eyes, a wide nose and a square, Neanderthal jaw, the man's dark hair is long and greasy looking in the picture. We can see the top half of his muscle shirt and tufts of kinky hair cover his shoulders. In police lingo, he's fugly as hell.

"You sure?" I ask Sandie who nods furiously.

I check the information on the back of the mug shot. "His name is Lloyd Singletary." I pull out my tape recorder and put in a fresh tape. Kay and Gonzales grab chairs and it takes a good forty five minutes to get Sandie's statement on tape.

"Actually, he remembered me," Sandie beams. "He was the big one who I let feel-up my tits that first night."

Jesus, if this ever goes in front of a jury, they'll fuckin' love it.

"I decided to hit some bars early and found him in The Honky Chateau Bar. Corner of Piety and Chartres at exactly four o'clock."

That's Bywater.

"I played it smart this time. I didn't get drunk and didn't talk about the killings. I just made sure he was the one and he was."

She pauses so I have to egg her on. "He was the one who did what?"

"Told me about the badges."

It takes a while but we get the whole story, including the fact that Mullet drives a maroon Harley-Davidson. Besides The Honky Chateau, he also hangs out at some uptown bars, but didn't tell Sandie their names. With the recorder still running I ask Sandie about the line-ups, how she went through fifteen before finding Mullet's picture. I have her sign and date the back of Singletary's picture, then put her initials on the back of every picture she viewed that evening.

When she finishes, she bounces in her chair and asks, "What now?"

"Tomorrow. We go back. Same time."

"Goody!" Sandie smiles broadly and I have to tell her she did well. Very well. Kay pays her another two hundred and Gonzales volunteers to take her home.

"I'll pick you up tomorrow at three p.m. sharp," I tell her.

"Make it three-thirty at UNO, I'm modeling."

As he leads her away, Gonzales asks, "You model?"

"Nude. At UNO. Beau didn't tell you?"

Gonzales looks back with raised eye-brows. "No. He didn't tell me."

"Why don't y'all come by UNO early. Y'all can watch."

Gonzales points a finger at me, his eyes like saucers. "Sure," he says. "It's a date."

Kay follows me to the computer where I pull up Lloyd Singletary's record. He's been arrested three times: DWI, aggravated assault, aggravated battery. Each arrest also included a charge of resisting arrest. Why am I not surprised? He's thirty. Exactly my age. At 6'5", he's a good three inches taller than me and outweighs me by a good fifty pounds. I point out his place of birth on the screen to Kay, who's now looking over my shoulder.

"Pea Ridge, Arkansas. A country boy."

"I'll get the Benton County Sheriff's Office on the phone." Kay picks up the nearest phone. "Somebody up there might remember him."

"You know Pea Ridge?"

Kay nods. "North of Beaver Lake. Just south of Mark Twain National Park. Beautiful country. Almost in Missouri."

Sure. It's gotta be the garden spot of fuckin' Arkansas. Sometimes, I feel I'm in a *Twilight Zone* episode. Just wish Rod Serling would step out and tell me *what the fuck is going on!*

•

The Honky Chateau occupies the first floor of a two story wooden building painted olive green. A red neon Jax Beer sign hangs in the only window, next to the only door, which opens to Chartres Street. Across Chartres is the concrete sea wall, the levee and beyond, the Louisa Street Wharf and the river.

Three motorcycles, a red pick-up and a yellow AMC Pacer are parked in the small shell parking lot on the Piety Street side of the building. Mullet's maroon Harley is parked nearest Chartres Street.

Sitting in my Caprice a block up Piety next to the rickety wooden fence of an abandoned house, I can't see the bar's door, but Mullet's hog is in plain view. Which ever way he goes on Chartres, we'll be able to follow easily. He shouldn't come back up Piety. It's a one-way. Of course, that doesn't mean much in New Orleans, where stop signs are only suggestions and red lights are run with impunity.

I have a partner now. Orders from Bob Kay, I'm no longer a lone wolf. I asked for Tim Rothman. He gave me Gonzales. Could be worse, a lot worse. Could have been sound-effect wizard Tony Dunn or bore-me-to-death-with-another-long-story Elvis Channard, or worse still – Two-L. At least Gonzales is Homicide. Like me, he was broken in by Jodie Kintyre.

Gonzales fidgets in his seat next to me.

"What's the matter, you got an itch or something?"

He glares at me. "Don't tell me you didn't get a fuckin' hard-on watching her model."

I did earlier, but I'm admitting nothing.

Gonzales fidgets again, trying to get comfortable.

So I tell him, "All right, no more suits."

"What?"

"You ride with me, you wear jeans and a dress shirt to cover your weapon."

Gonzales is in a double-breasted, navy blue suit with two-tone loafers.

"We wear ties in Homicide," he tells me. "Everyone except you, of course."

"Exactly."

We wait.

A skinny guy rounds the corner from the Honky Chateau and climbs into the Pacer, which actually runs.

"Looks like a refugee from a ZZ Top concert," Gonzales says and then yawns. "So, Kay showed line-ups to the witnesses from both murders but no one could pick out Mullet?"

I nod. Apparently the witnesses from Cochran's and Steven's murders didn't get a good enough look at the assailants to identify anyone. Mullet fit the general description of the heavy-set man standing over Steven's body, but barely.

"And we don't even know where this fuckin' Mullet lives," Gonzales says disgustedly. None of Mullet's addresses checked out. His driver's license is listed to an apartment he lived in three years ago. His hog is registered to another former address.

"No listing with the power company?" Gonzales asks.

I shake my head. "Or the gas company, phone company, cable TV company. And no one in Pea Ridge, Arkansas, heard of him."

"Jesus. He doesn't have cable?" Gonzales says in an exaggerated voice.

"Doesn't need it. He's got the Honky Chateau."

I don't bother telling him what Fel Jones said, how the Mullets of the world like living outside society. Fel angrily told me, over coffee this morning, that the Intelligence Division has nothing on Mullet. So far only Fel and Kay, Gonzales and I know about Mullet, besides Sandie who wore an extra short, extra tight minidress into the Honky Chateau a half hour ago.

We wait.

Gonzales is quiet for a good ten minutes, a record, before he says, "You gone out with that waitress yet?"

"Nope."

"Why not? Cops and waitresses go together like beans and rice."

I don't answer.

"You stupid or something?"

I don't answer, but I know that's no deterrent.

"She said she'd only go out with a cop if he was half-Sioux. That's more than a hint, Mister Native American."

Like a good plains warrior, I keep my face from revealing anything.

"If you were Latino, you'd be all over that little number. If you were Latino ... "

"Shut the fuck up!"

Gonzales actually shuts up.

"Keep your fuckin' advice, all right. I'm as much a Frenchman as I am Sioux. I don't need any help with women."

Gonzales settles back in his seat and mutters, "I think you do."

I let him have the last word, otherwise this'll go on all night.

Five minutes later, he asks, "If we follow this ass-hole, who's bringing Sandie home?"

"She's to call a cab. She's got money."

"I shoulda brought my car."

I squint at him. "You don't have a car." He's too new to Homicide to have a unit assigned to him.

"I mean my personal car."

Jesus.

I spend the next few minutes telling him how LaStanza used to drive around in his personal car. His rich wife bought him a Maserati. Jodie was self-conscious riding in it. One day, in broad daylight, they parked it on the street, walked around the corner and came back four minutes later to find the car gone.

Everyone ribbed LaStanza for months, even made up a song about inner-city thugs tooling around in his nice Italian sports car. Went to the tune from "Dead Man's Curve."

It went something like –

> I parked my car in the city one sunny day
> When some urbanites came and took it away
> Had to call a cab to get out of there
> Had to pretend to my wife that I didn't care
> So she bought me a new car with an alarm
> Made me promise to always leave it at home ...

I forget the rest, but it got funnier, something about driving to Dead Man's Curve via the Garden District and getting lost in the projects. For a moment, a vision of Sharon comes to my mind and our rainy afternoon in bed. I take in a deep breath.

"What is it?" Gonzales asks. "Angie, huh? You thinking about her, ain't ya?"

The hair suddenly stands on the back of my neck when I remember how Angie had asked about her ex-boyfriend and how I was wearing the Jekyll & Hyde shirt, the one Sharon gave me. Of course I'd heard her – 'I prefer the slower, quieter type. Especially if they're part Sioux.'

Why do I hesitate? I want to, but something in my gut tells me to hold back. Not now. Not while we're in the middle of all this. Then I remember Gonzales saying, "He who hesitates is lost."

I look at him and he's so bored he's glassy-eyed.

"He who hesitates is lost," I say. "Is that Shakespeare or the Bible?"

He shakes his head. "J. Robert Oppenheimer. The guy who built the atom bomb."

Cute. Real fuckin' cute.

Mullet comes around the corner and climbs on his bike. He cranks it up and drives off up Chartres. I follow, letting him have a good half block lead. A dump truck cuts in between us. I spot Mullet make a quick right. The dump truck stops at the stop sign and waits for oncoming traffic, like a good citizen. By the time I've made the corner, Mullet's bike's nowhere in sight. I head uptown, as if that'll do any good and spend the next hour cruising bars, but no maroon Harley. Just as I give up, Gonzales has to say it.

"I told you the only way to keep up with a bike is on a bike."

I say nothing until I pull back up at Headquarters. As Gonzales climbs out, I tell him I'll see him tomorrow.

"What's the matter with you?" he says, leaning back in. "Are you that spaced-out? Tomorrow's Saturday." He shakes his head. "I'll see you Monday."

I drive to Flamingo's and discover Angie's off. Probably out on a date. Thankfully Cecilia senses I'm in no mood to talk and leaves me alone. I order chili and sit quietly. I'll take Buck for a walk when I'm done, then pop an Abita beer and sit in front of the T.V.

Some Friday night I have planned.

•

Wearing my darkest sunglasses, I sit on the levee the following morning, the summer sun hot on my face. A surprising coolness is in the air. I look westward, in the general direction of Lake Maurepas and see thick cumulus clouds, like cotton, high in the sky. To the north, a line of cumulonimbus clouds with their flat gray bottoms, hover over the distant water. The rain's a good ten, fifteen miles away.

Buck's been sniffing around the rocks below for the last half hour. To my right, the lake is postcard pretty, its water shaded a blue-green tint from the bright sky. Sailboats and yachts cruise the unusually still water. The air smells fresh like Vermilion Bay after a rainstorm, salty but not stale and humid like the marsh.

The Choctaw called this lake – Okwata, which meant 'wide water'. The French re-named it for their Minister of Marine, Compte de Pontchartrain. When my Dad first told me about the lake bigger than Vermilion Bay, I thought Pontchartrain was a Choctaw or Cherokee name. After all, Pontiac was an Ottawa name. My father corrected me before I said something dumb in school, thankfully.

So how do I find out where Mullet lives? If he's our man or not, he knows about the badges. Maybe he lives with other bikers and they're involved. I have a bad feeling about this ass-hole. *He knows about the badges.* But how do I find out where he lives? Follow him, right?

Buck races up to me, licks my hand, then heads back down to the rocks and I remember how easily Mullet's Harley motored away from us.

So where does a Harley man hang out? And just as I ask myself that I remember the old Harley-Davidson Shop beneath the Claiborne overpass. I don't know how many times I've passed it and there's always hogs and bikers there.

It's a long shot, but what have I got to lose? I stand and whistle and Buck follows me back to *Sad Lisa*. Before leaving, I call Sandie to leave a message on her recorder and wind up talking to her.

"How'd it go last night?" I ask.

"Nothing. He's either smarter than I thought or just being cagey." She yawns. "Then again, I haven't been pumping him. And don't go there. I'm not a complete whore, you know."

"I never said you were."

I hear her breathing on the line.

"I'm taking a couple nights off," she finally says. "Going by my mother's. We have a family reunion across the lake. Fountainbleu State Park. Wanna come?"

I hesitate before saying, "Sure."

She laughs. "I'm kidding. I'm taking Scrumptious."

Still laughing, she hangs up and I know she's pulled my string. She got that hesitation out of me. We men think we're smart but women are smarter and much more wily. Especially when it comes to the human heart.

•

With my Caprice parked at the corner of South Claiborne and Clio, half hidden by an overflowed dumpster and an abandoned sofa, I have a good view of Hog Heaven across Claiborne, two short blocks away. Shaded by the overpass up to the interstate, Hog Heaven is a converted filling station. Looks like it was built in the forties with its rounded corners and stucco walls whose faded paint has peeled away in spots to show at least four different colors. I can still see a faded red Esso sign on the front wall. The words 'Hog Heaven' are painted in bright purple just above the door. Nine Harleys are parked there, three men working on one and four others sitting around drinking beer.

For the last three hours, six bikers have come and gone, but no Mullet. I couldn't be that lucky. If he does drop by, I'll have an easier time following him on wide Claiborne, at least I've convinced myself of that.

Wish I could just drive over and talk to them as they guzzle their brews and tinker with their bikes. Even if I went in disguise, they'd make me for the heat. Must be the way I talk. At the grocery last night, I'm in a tee-shirt and cut-offs, I ask a clerk where is the filé and he tells me, "Aisle three, officer."

Happens all the time. Jodie says its the way we ask direct questions, the way we look people in the eye with a more than subtle expectation of a quick answer that gives us away. I also think it's the way we're always looking around, always noting things around us.

I fight off a yawn and glance around again, making sure no one's sneaking up on me in this blighted area. Behind my car is a line of abandoned cars. Next to the dumpster is a one-story red brick building surrounded by a nine foot page fence with razored Contadina wire along its top. Across Clio, to my right, is a junkyard, also surrounded by a nine foot fence. The area smells of rotten bananas and burned tobacco.

This is the Sixth Police District. The *Bloody Sixth* has the most murders, robberies, rapes, the most abandoned houses, four housing projects, along with the manicured lawns of the Garden District. Opulence next to poverty makes life interesting. I settle back and watch Hog Heaven.

At five sharp, they close up and the six remaining bikers drive off up Claiborne. I wait a few minutes before leaving, knowing I've just wasted a day. Just as I access the interstate, it hits me and I slap the steering wheel. I didn't follow them because I didn't want to get spotted, especially with no Mullet in sight. But they left together in a pack, heading uptown. Sandie says Mullet frequents uptown bars. I knew I should have had more coffee today.

Maybe they'll be open Sunday.

I drop by Flamingo's and Angie isn't there.

"She's off," Cecilia says as she leads me to my booth. "Probably on a date."

Why do women always seem to know what I'm thinking?

It's unnerving.

Chapter 11
YOU GOTTA LOVE THE AMBIANCE

Just as I'm heading out the door Sunday morning, my phone rings. Buck barks at the phone and does a quick spin.

"Hello?"

"So what are you doing, today?" It's Jodie.

I tell her and she says, "Mind if I come along?"

Forty-five minutes later we're sitting next to the dumpster with fresh cups of coffee-and-chicory from P.J.'s. The strong smell of coffee momentarily overpowers the scents from the street, a mix of rotten bananas and motor oil.

Jodie glances around. "Jesus. Where do you find these places?"

"Nice, isn't it?"

Over night someone deposited a door-less refrigerator and a broken bathtub along the curb just outside the junk yard across the street. Jodie and I are both in jeans. She wears a tan blouse over a tank-top and I wear a dark brown dress shirt over a gold LSU tee-shirt. Although I'm sweating, Jodie's hair looks perfectly blow-dried, not a strand out of place. The woman doesn't perspire.

"So who told you about Mullet?" I ask, knowing the answer.

"Kay. He told Merten and me, swearing us to secrecy." She nods toward Hog Heaven, which has only two men working today. "You think he's going to drop by or something?"

I give her a Lakota saying. "The patient coyote will catch the rabbit when it comes out of its hole."

Jodie squints as she looks over at the filling station. "You didn't bring binoculars, did you?" She shakes her head. "I know. You don't need them. You and those Sioux eyes."

I've never told her my secret Lakota name but she's knows all about how well I can see. At eleven o'clock five bikers pull up and beers are distributed.

"Any of them Mullet?" Jodie asks.

I shake my head. She settles back in her seat and lets out a long sigh. "So, what district did you choose?"

A man pulls up on a reddish Harley and I look closely, but it's not Mullet.

"District?" I ask.

"If you'd bother to read the memos in your *In* box, you'd know the new chief is breaking up the Detective Bureau."

"What!?"

"We're going back to the districts. All plainclothes. Burglary. Robbery. Sex Crimes and even Homicide."

"That's stupid. How are we going to pick up trends? How're we going to know who's robbing people two districts away, who's raping uptown women, then getting in his car and driving downtown to rape a few? He expects us to *read* dailies and memos?"

Our new chief, a transplanted assistant chief from New York, is long on honesty but short on street smarts. Then again, he's new. He'll learn.

"The idea is to make us more visible on the streets, more accessible to the public."

I leave that idea floating in the heat. A few minutes later Jodie tells me she put in for the Second District. The uptown police.

"What about your old district?" she says as she looks around disgustedly at this typical Sixth District street. "You could work here again."

"That was LaStanza. I never worked the Sixth."

"Oh." It's not like her. She's embarrassed by the slip.

I keep watching Hog Heaven.

"Well, you better put in for something or they'll just stick you some place like the Fourth."

Jesus! The *Across The River Police*. Algiers. I've only been there a handful of times, always at night, always working a murder.

"You can put in for the Third. You live there."

Actually I live in Jefferson Parish, but that's close. A blue-gum dog races past us and I see it's chasing a rat.

"Now that you mention it, the Sixth might be the place. It's got the most murders, the most action." I wave at the abandoned appliances. "You gotta love the ambiance."

Jodie goes on about a Homicide Power Watch. Working out of headquarters, a small unit will handle big cases, heater cases. Maybe cold cases. She's pushing hard for it.

"Interested?" she asks me.

"Abso-fuckin-lutely."

At exactly noon, Hog Heaven closes up. We follow the four remaining bikers who dart off to Claiborne, cross three lanes to take a quick left on Martin Luther King Boulevard. The bikers spread out a little in the light traffic but come together at the corner of Simon Bolivar and park along the street outside a low-life bar with a hand painted sign out front that reads: Raton.

We drive by and make a u-turn and park facing them. About a dozen white-boy bikers are assembled outside, in this all-black neighborhood. They guzzle beer in the bright sunlight. Jodie and I draw curious looks from several women sitting out on the front stoops of their houses. They probably have us pegged as the police.

"Know what *raton* means in French?"

"Raton?"

"Yeah, the sign outside the bar. *Raton* is *rat* in French."

Jodie nods. "Fits."

The sun is brutal now and there's not even a hint of breeze. "Well," I say as I crank up the engine and turn the AC on high. "At least I have another biker bar for my informant to check out."

Just as I reach to shift the car into drive, a feeling comes over me. I hesitate and look back up M. L. King. A Harley slows and turns on Simon Bolivar, a maroon Harley. I watch as Mullet pulls his bike up next to the men outside the bar and stops to talk with them.

"What is it?" Jodie asks.

I point to the goose-bumps on my arm, then repeat another homicide cliché. "It's good to be good. But it's better to be lucky."

"It's him?"

I nod as Mullet starts to drive away. He stops again and continues talking. "You always bring me luck," I tell Jodie.

Still sitting on his bike, Mullet takes a beer from a compadre and drains it. He tosses the can in the gutter and stretches. Looking up momentarily at the sun, he yawns. The men in the street back away as Mullet turns his bike around in the street and heads away from us, back up M. L. King.

I try not to follow too closely, but as we near Claiborne I close the gap so he doesn't get through the light without us.

He makes a leisurely illegal left turn on Claiborne and we follow. Staying in the center lane, he's not going very fast and I hope he's going home after an all-niter, instead of just starting out for the day.

Mullet slips into the right lane as we pass Jackson Avenue. He increases speed slightly, then slows and takes a right on Third Street. I take the corner slowly, just in time to see him hang a left on the next street. When we get to the corner of Third and South Derbigny, I look to my left and see Mullet climb off his hog and cross a tiny front yard to the front porch of the third house from the corner. A playground is in front of us. So I cross Derbigny and drive next to the playground while Jodie looks back.

"He went inside the third house."

I pull up against the curb and look through the six foot page fence, what we call a hurricane fence, surrounding the playground. Mullet's Harley is parked next to two others in front of an unpainted shotgun camelback. Several junked motorcycles rest on either side of the small front porch. The house is sandwiched in a line of other shotgun houses, many of them boarded up. The neighborhood is semi-blighted with about a third of the houses abandoned. Some are downright shanties.

Four black women and two older black men are out on the front stoops of the houses across the street from where we sit to check out Jodie and me. A group of boys shooting baskets at the covered basketball court in the playground, a few feet up from where we sit, stop playing to look at us.

"We stay, we're going to get burned," Jodie says.

I nod and pull away to circle the block and get a layout of the area. The playground is Taylor Playground, running along So. Derbigny from Third Street all the way to Washington Avenue. Behind the playground is an elementary school. As we drive around to Washington Avenue, I hang a left on South Roman, which runs a half-block through the playground. I stop momentarily next to a huge oak tree.

"We can watch him from here," I tell Jodie, nodding across the playground to Mullet's house. He'll have to be really sharp to spot us through two page fences, across a wide, block-long playground and through an oak tree.

"We'll gonna stay today?" Jodie asks.

"Naw. I think he's just come home from an all-nighter. No need to push our luck. How about some lunch?" I ask Jodie as I pull away.

"Sure."

"You name it. The Camellia Grill? The Columns? How about some Chinese?"

Jodie pulls her hair back with both hands and says, "Wendy's."

I give her a screwed-up face look.

"I think I'm addicted to their double-stacks with cheese," she says and smiles for the first time today.

Who am I to argue?

•

I look out the porthole at the moon as I lay in bed. It's large and yellow in the distant sky. I hear Buck moving around downstairs. He can't sleep either.

Jodie called it a Homicide Power Watch. I'd like that, to work with her again regularly and not as her junior partner either. Guess that's why she called this morning, that and to get out together on something. I miss working with her. Guess she feels the same way.

Curiously she didn't mention her latest boyfriend, the podiatrist. She's been seeing the guy for about a year, told me his name more than once, but for the life of me I can't remember it. He's older. Pushing fifty, I think. Met him once. He's prematurely gray, hair more white actually. Quiet and nice, the perfect man for someone like Jodie. Dependable. Solid. There when you need him. Not many foot emergencies, at least that's what Jodie tells me.

I roll over and face the dark side of the room and close my eyes. I take in deep, measured breaths, steady breaths and slowly feel myself slipping away. *Sad Lisa* seems to drift beneath me ...

And I dream again.

Of my Dad.

Of one particular, lazy Saturday afternoon.

In the swamp, autumn lasts one day, two at the most. The stifling heat gives way to one perfect day, a bright day with cool air. It is the day before the first cold front reaches down from Canada and turns south Louisiana into a damp, cold, miserable land of winter rains and chilly winds blowing across the flat land all the way to the Gulf of Mexico.

I dream of the autumn day of my twelfth year, sitting on thick grass next to a coulee off Vermilion River. My father knows this permanent coulee well, this deep gully fishing hole next to a huge weeping willow, whose branches reached over the coulee. I sit on one side of the tree, my father on the other side. Holding my slaughter pole, that extra long bamboo fishing pole my father cut and shaped for me, I watch my cork rest in the smooth, brown water. A worm impaled on the new stainless-steel fishing hook my father bought in Abbeville, I held the nylon string taught, just as my daddy instructs. His face beams at me when my cork bounced slightly.

Slowly, I move the tip of the pole to my right, keeping the string tight and fell the fish strike, the cork going straight down, the tip of the pole bending. I pull up firmly and the fish is hooked. It yanks back and nearly pulls the pole from my hand.

"Stand up," my father calls out, putting his pole down.

I stand and pull up as hard as I can. The fish darts away and my foot slips and I go down on one knee. My father heads my way, but I stand quickly and start backing away, still holding the pole high. My father told me, more than once, to just walk backwards. "No fish 'round here gon' pull a eighty-pound boy in de water."

The fish feels like a gator in its struggling. The pole dips and looks like it'll break, but doesn't. I continue backing until the cork comes out of the water. The fish yanks again and I hold firm until it comes out of the water, sailing and flapping to land on the bank. I jerk the pole again and pull it higher up the bank and see it's a yellow cat, the best eating catfish, thick and round. We weigh it later at Burke's Fish Hut and it's over thirteen pounds.

That night we cook it, along with the six channel cats my father caught and the two sac-a-lait I managed to catch. My mother made cornbread. My father's face beams at me as we eat our fish. My mother, so quiet, sits and smiles at me, telling me that was the biggest catfish she's ever seen. For years, my father bragged about that yellow cat. I see his face clearly, the slight stubble of beard on his chin, the dark creases along his cheeks, his bright eyes.

I wake suddenly to the smell of my father's tobacco-laced breath. A deep pain in my chest, I sit up and try to catch my breath and discover I'm crying. I settle back down and wipe my eyes. Buck yips once downstairs and I take in a deep breath. Even after all these years, it's hard to believe my father's really gone. Still hard to fathom a world without him.

I close my eyes and envision a woman, a silken-legged beauty with full breasts and nice round hips. The face I give her is from a woman I saw once, as she crossed St. Charles Avenue by Audubon Park. She wore all-gray, a smart business suit with a skirt short enough to show the smooth lines of her sleek legs. Dark haired, she had a round face and full lips colored a deep red.

I was stopped in heavy traffic as she crossed in from of my police car. She turned and looked at me for a long moment. I don't think a week has passed when I didn't think of that dark haired, alluring, New Orleans beauty.

•

Parking my Caprice against the curb next to the large oak on South Roman, I point across Taylor Playground to the unpainted wooden shotgun house. "That, my friend, is where Mullet lives."

Gonzales pulls off his sunglasses and squints.

"No shit?"

"No shit."

"How'd you find it?" Gonzales puts his sunglasses back on. He's wearing black jeans today, a gray dress shirt unbuttoned over a black Saints tee-shirt. He gleeks me, peeking over the top of his sunglasses.

"It's called good police work."

He shoves his glasses back up and settles in the seat. I tell him the plan. We'll follow Mullet to see what uptown bars he frequents, maybe see who he hangs with. Maybe, if we're lucky, we'll see who else lives with him. The place has three bikes parked out front.

Gonzales pulls out his binoculars. "Can't see any plates, except Mullet's." The bikes are pointed the wrong way.

"So, how'd you find it?" Gonzales asks again. So I tell him and he laughs and agrees, it's good to be good but better to be lucky. Six kids move into the playground and start tossing a football.

"Think we can get a warrant?"

I'm not sure if he's serious or pulling my chain, so I say, "For what?"

"To search Mullet's. Maybe sneak in when he's not there, come up with the gun or badges."

I tell him we don't have enough to convince even the friendliest judge to give us a search warrant. Besides, once the neighbors see us go in, and they will, Mullet will know we know. If he's our man.

"Maybe we can convince Sandie to wear a wire. Get Mullet to incriminate himself."

I've run this by Sandie and she's against it, big time.

"I might have to let someone feel me up," she said. "And my clothes are too skimpy. I'll get caught."

The football bangs against the fence near us and one of the boys fetches it. He gives us a good stare. Without invisibility cloaks, Gonzales and I can do nothing but act as if it's natural for two white boys to be parked in a plain-as-hell, four-door Chevrolet on So. Roman in the middle of the afternoon. Might as well be in a marked unit.

"Good catch," Gonzales says as one of the boys makes a one handed, running catch.

"I was a running back. Didn't catch many passes at Rummel." Gonzales gleeks me again, peeking over the top of his sunglasses. "Believe it or not, I was all-district twice."

"I was all-state twice."

"No shit?" Gonzales sits up. "What position?"

"Quarterback."

Gonzales removes his glasses. "You were an all-state quarterback. Which state?"

"Here. Holy Ghost High School, Cannes Brulcé, Louisiana."

"Holy Ghost?" Gonzales' voice is loud enough to get the boy's attention. "Cannes what?"

"Cannes Bruleé. It's a village off Vermilion Bay." I point to the boys who've stopped playing to watch us.

Gonzales nods. "Village? You making this shit up, or what?"

I crank up the engine.

"Where we going?"

The kids are moving our way slowly as I pull away. "We don't wanna be the talk of the neighborhood."

Gonzales puts his sunglasses back on and gleeks the kids as we leave, then turns back to me. "All-state *quarterback*?

"Holy Ghost is a 2A school. We won the state championship my junior and senior years."

Gonzales gives me a know-it-all look. "2A? OK."

That's why he's never heard of us. Archbishop Rummel and the other big Catholic schools in New Orleans are all 5A schools. Championship games on TV and all. I wheel the Caprice toward headquarters, taking our time.

Gonzales still gives me this unbelieving look, as if he expects me to say I'm kidding any second. So I ask, "Did you play any college ball?"

"Nope. You?"

"LSU. Two years. Tore up my knee in spring practice my sophomore year."

Gonzales shakes his head. "You were a quarterback. At LSU?"

"I wasn't first string."

Gonzales folds his arms and tells me he's going to check out this shit. I laugh. Hope I'm there to see his face when he calls the athletic department and finds it's all true. An RTA bus pulls away from the curb and almost crashes into us. I brake hard and tap the siren as we breeze past. Fuckin'asshole.

"That school. Holy Ghost." Gonzales pauses a moment. "Is that a *senior* high school?"

Fuckin'clown.

We're on Claiborne when Matt Sinclair calls me on the radio.

"Go ahead."

"Just want to let you know Andrew Porter just made bail."

"Who?" I answer although the name's vaguely familiar.

"Your CI," Sinclair reminds me and as soon as he says it I realize Andrew Porter is Felice's old man.

Jesus. Nearly fifty counts of burglary and he's rolling out of Parish Prison.

"What the fuck happened?" I ask Sinclair as I punch the accelerator.

"What else? A judge reduced his bond. And you can't say fuck on the radio."

"10-4." I wheel the Caprice up the overpass to I-10. "And thanks," I tell Sinclair before slamming my radio down on the seat. Gonzales gives me a minute before asking what the fuck was that. So I tell him the old, familiar story. How, in New Orleans, no bond is high enough because there's always another judge who'll come along and reduce the bond. Fuckin' judges. I swerve around a minivan doing twenty in the fast lane and Gonzales holds on.

"Where we going?"

"Gotta find Felice before Porter does."

"Felice who?"

I glance at Gonzales who has both hands on the dash board.

"Oh, yeah. I forgot to tell you about her."

As I weave my way through the usual mob of dumb-ass drivers, I tell Gonzales the Felice story.

"So," he says when he can get a word in. "What're we gonna do with her when we find her? You got room on your boat for a boarder?"

Chapter 12
THEY'RE DINGBATS

Felice walks into the apartment, stops next to a plush, beige sofa and turns back to me.

"You know I can't afford this." Her face is drawn, void of make-up, which makes her look even younger than usual. She wears a cut-off tee-shirt and faded jeans, white tennis shoes with frayed laces.

Jodie moves around me and says, "I told you, it's free."

"Nothin's free, white girl." Felice puts a fist on her hip and looks around the apartment.

Jodie moves through the living room and opens the bedroom door. I see a king-sized brass bed inside. Prim in a light yellow suit, Jodie's perfect page-boy hangs around her pale face. The living room looks like a display in an upscale furniture store. Porcelain lamps with white smoky-glass shades, a cream colored love seat, a coffee table and matching end tables of reddish-brown cherry wood. A huge entertainment center, also made of cherry wood, covers and entire wall. There's a state-of-the-art stereo system and a Zenith TV with a screen that has to be thirty inches. Gonzales lets out a high pitched whistle. He's still wearing his sunglasses.

Felice drops her bag and moves into the bedroom.

Jodie shrugs. "Told you. LaStanza's wife owns the building. No problem."

"She that rich?" Gonzales asks.

"Yep." Jodie goes on to explain how LaStanza married into old world money, how his wife's family owns banks in

Switzerland and Luxembourg. Not to mention the biggest bank in Louisiana.

Then Jodie smiles and says, "Next time I'll wear a black tee-shirt too." She taps a finger on the fleur-de-lis emblem on Gonzales' tee-shirt. My tee-shirt is solid black and the dress shirt I wear over it is navy blue. I hear the toilet flush beyond the bedroom. Felice comes out shaking her head.

"How long am I supposed to stay here?"

"Until we can think of something," I tell her.

"What you gonna do. Kill Andy?"

No, I tell her. We're going to have a talk with him. Make sure he knows that if anything happens to her, I'll scalp him. See how he likes going around with a scar covering his entire head.

"Yeah." Felice gives me a I-don't-fuckin-believe-anything-you-say look and plops on the sofa.

I reach under my dress shirt to the scabbard next to where my Glock is tucked in the waistband of my jeans. I pull out my nine-inch, black, obsidian Sioux hunting knife, step over and show Felice the sharp side of the blade.

"Sioux knives are sharpened on one side only. See?" I twist the knife back and forth.

Gonzales lets out another high-pitched whistle.

Felice folds her arms and says, "We have another problem."

"What?"

She looks away. "Your killer," she says dryly.

Turning back she doesn't blink those large chocolate eyes as she stares into mine. Then she says, "Your killer's name is Clyde."

•

Sitting at my desk chair, I look at the clock on the far wall. It's seven-thirty in the morning and I'm so tired my eyes burn. The vulture wavers in its perch above the star-and-crescent badge.

"What day is this?" I ask my partner.

Gonzales is dozing in the desk chair next to my desk.

"It's Thursday, you dummy." Tim Rothman steps up and leans on the corner of my desk. "Guess it's no sense asking you why the fuck we been called here. You don't even know what day it is." He moves away and asks, "Coffee?"

I nod and close my weary eyes. My mind won't let me doze. Flashbacks of the last few days blink behind my closed eye-lids, like a videotape on fast-forward. Felice told us she came up with the name Clyde at a bar on Chef Menteur Highway. Seems Clyde, a scrawny white male with black and gray hair, has been shooting his mouth off that he used a Colt Python .357 magnum to murder two cops. Not many people know a Python was the murder weapon. Clyde drives a Harley. Another fuckin' biker.

An exhaustive check of police records surfaced too many Clydes with criminal records to narrow our search. Not one Harley-Davidson is registered to a Clyde anywhere in Louisiana. Un-be-fuckin-lievable. Beside, Felice has never seen him. The men who told her Clyde was shooting off his mouth were typical bar flies, ugly men with red, drinkers noses.

Clyde could be the 'tall, thin white man with salt-and-pepper hair' the witnesses described from the Cochran murder. Mullet could be the 'heavy-set white male with black hair' seen standing over the body of P.J. Stevens. Maybe, just maybe, we have two important pieces of this puzzle.

Felice's old man, Andrew Porter, is just as hard to find. Everyone, and I mean everyone, we talked with claimed he skipped town as soon as he made bail. We put some fear into his relatives, but they didn't seem to want to have anything to do with the wonderful Mr. Porter either.

Four o'clock this morning, I had coffee with a drunken Sandie back at Cafe Du Mondé. No, she hadn't been to bars searching for Mullet. She'd been out with Scrumptious and partied 'hard into the night'. That quote was followed by a loud, "Woo. Woo. Party time!" Which caused an elderly man at the next table to spill his coffee.

I took her home and left a note for her, telling her we had to talk when she was sober. I didn't dare give her Mullet's address. No telling what she'd do. I'd feel a lot better if I had more control over my informants.

Bob Kay's voice brings me out of my trance. I blink open my eyes and see the office is full now. Two-L Willson glares at me from the coffee pot area. I'm too tired to think of anything to say to fuck with him. Three men in nice suits stand next to Bob Kay at the front of the office. Kay is trying to get everyone's attention. Rothman taps my shoulder and points to the Styrofoam cup of coffee on my desk.

"Gotta be Feds," I nod toward the suits as I turn myself around and dig my sunglasses out of my briefcase. At least the light from the federal radiance won't hurt my eyes.

Kay introduces the nice suits as FBI special agents. "They have something important to announce," Kay says as he steps aside.

The tallest of the agents, a balding man who looks a lot like Patrick Stewart of the *U.S.S. Enterprise, Next Generation*, steps forward and announces the FBI has prepared a psychological profile of the killer in the recent shootings of police officers. I take a sip of coffee. It's tar black and tastes like bottom-of-the-pot grunge. I take another hit.

The tall agent holds up a sheet of paper. "This psychological profile of our killer is being passed out to one and all." The other two agents start passing around sheets of paper.

Rothman leans close to me. "Did he say *our* killer? Who invited these chumps, anyway?"

I fight back a yawn and take another hit of coffee. I wish it were stronger. I want to taste grounds. "Hey," I tell Rothman, "I thought psychological profiles were just for sex killers."

"Yeah, but this is the FBI. They can do *anything*." His eyes bulge in mock surprise.

The agent arrives with the sheets of paper and I wave him off.

"I'm drinking," I explain, raising the coffee cup. He puts a sheet on my desk and hands one to Rothman. The tall agent tells us, in simplistic sentences, as if we're school kids, that the FBI has marshaled its mighty resources, resulting in the profile, which he reads to us, point by point.

"Number One. Subject is a white male between the ages of twenty-five and thirty-two."

"Number Two. Subject lives in the greater metropolitan area."

Somebody in the back coughs and it's contagious as several more officers cough louder. Fuck, we thought he lived in Detroit. Rising slowly, I dig my mug out of my desk drawer, move to the coffee machine to start up another pot.

"Number Three. The subject is left handed."

Jesus. They *are* good.

"Number Four. The subject is not religious."

Somebody laughs aloud.

"Damn," Tony Dunn shouts. "There goes my church surveillances."

I empty two of the pre-packaged packs of coffee and chicory into the filter.

"Number Five. The subject is single, however, if married, there is a great deal lot of stress in his married life."

"Yeah. He's a fuckin' killer!" Two-L finally says something intelligent.

The Captain Picard look-a-like is unruffled. He waits for the chuckles to die down.

"Number Six. The subject has a high school education, possibly some college."

College educated bikers. Why the fuck not? Could have gone to Auburn.

"Number Seven. The subject is intelligent with an IQ between 120 and 130."

This is sounding more like science-fiction. I look back at the pot and it's nearly full. I wipe out my mug. It was a gift from Jodie. It's black with a neat red print that reads. If we're not supposed to eat animals, why are they made of meat?

"Number Eight. The subject has a white collar job."

So much for my biker theory. I fill my mug and take a sip. It's stronger and a little thicker than the grunge. All right. Weaving my way back to my desk, I see the FBI guys are winding down now. Sitting again, I lean back with my coffee and wait.

Bob Kay takes over and assigns several men to work with the FBI and their profile. He looks my way but, thankfully, my sunglasses are enough to keep me out of that trick bag. I take another hit of coffee.

The tall FBI guy steps forward again and asks if there are any questions about the profile. He seems perplexed that we have none. I look around and no one's gonna do it. I can't resist, so I pick up the sheet from my desk and raise my hand. He points a finger at me.

"Excuse me, Captain Picard. Did you just beam down with this shit, or what?"

Kay blanches. My comrades let out a long-held-in laugh, which reverberates. Gonzales finally wakes up and looks around as if he's in a bad dream. Tony Dunn waits for everyone to catch their breath before he makes a gong sound, followed by a good imitation of a toilet flushing.

"Hey, Beau?" Rothman shouts over the laughter. He has the coffee pot in hand. "What the fuck is this? Swamp piss?"

•

Before I go to work that evening, I find Angie at work, finally. Maybe it's because I haven't seen her in a while, but she looks extra pretty. I don't remember her uniform skirt being that short. Her legs look nice and sleek as she leads me to my seat. She's done something to her hair. It looks fluffier. The sculptured lips, painted in dark brown lipstick, smile nicely at me as I sit.

"Haven't seen you in a while."

She nods and tells me she's been working mornings. At four p.m., I'm the only diner. I order the usual. She returns with my Barq's, gives me a Marisa Tomei smile and says,

"Are you still *friends* with Sharon Merraid like Mike Gonzales is *friends* with his old girlfriend?"

"What?"

"Like your partner. Do you just 'hit her a lick every once in a while'?"

The acid in my empty stomach churns. Her eyes stare intently at me. I let out a long sigh. "How do you know Sharon?" Instinctively, I've answered a question with a question. Lawyers have taught me that.

"She's been coming in here. We started talking about *Sad Lisa*. She's very friendly."

Angie looks out the window, giving me a long look at her pretty face in profile. And it hits me again. She's too young and too pretty and I've got too much shit going on in my life. Maybe I should just tell her yeah, I fucked Sharon. I'll tell her Sharon is my occasional *warm receptacle*. I'll say something really stupid like that and run her off. But I don't. Why? Because the way she asked. She's interested in me. God knows why. My looks aren't good enough to end my bad luck with women.

Angie turns to me again and says, "Sharon thinks she's still in love with you."

Jesus. What can I say? Do I give her the line Rhett Dutler gave Scarlett when she told him she was in love with him? Do I say, "That's her misfortune."

No. I'm no Rhett Butler. So I tell her how it ended between Sharon and me.

"She didn't want me to be a cop. She wanted me to open a business, like a barber shop and we could live in back and I'd be there all the time."

Angie nods and puts her knee up on the bench across the table. Her skirt rises nicely.

"It's called nest building," she tells me. "Women are nest builders. Men are hunter-gatherers. That's why men hate to go to shopping malls with their girlfriends."

"Except your old boyfriend."

She almost smiles. Joe slides my plate on the counter and gives me a friendly wave. Angie retrieves my plate. As she returns, I tell her. "Hey. Maybe we could introduce Sharon to your old boyfriend."

It's a stupid suggestion but Angie smiles again and slips into the booth across from me. Those eyes stare right into me. As usual, Joe's burger is delicious.

"Actually," she says. "Sharon came back to you on the rebound."

She's caught me with a mouthful. All I can manage is a, "Huh?"

"She broke up with her bank teller boyfriend."

Why does this girl always seem to know more than I do about my life? Maybe I should ask her who's killing the cops.

"At first I felt sorry for her," Angie says. "But that's life, isn't it? Love's hard."

"Harder than solving murders."

Jesus, sometimes I can't believe the things that come out of my mouth. I take another bite of burger.

"Just ask Romeo and Juliet," she says. "And Rhett and Scarlett and Scott and Zelda."

The door opens and four men come in. Angie gives me a look of resignation and climbs out of the seat. Adding, "And

162

Cleopatra and Antony and Zhivago and Lara and Prince Rudolf and Baroness Mary."

She heads for the four men who have slipped into the first booth. As she's handing them menus, an elderly couple comes in. As I eat, I watch Angie move from the booths to the counter and back again as she serves her customers. Just as I finish my burger, Angie brings me another Barq's.

"Rudolf and who?" I ask.

Backing away, she answers, "Rudolf and Mary." Then adds the word, "Mayerling." Whatever that means.

I drink my second root beer slowly. Outside several shrimp boaters are drying their nets, reminding me it's time for me to get to work. I climb out of my booth and Angie comes over with the check. I can see in her eyes, she wants to talk more.

"Why do you leave me such big tips?"

Again, she's changed direction. My Daddy told me that's why hurricanes used to be named for women. "De hurricane. De heavenly storm dat change direction on a dime, yeah."

The aquamarines are waiting for my answer.

"I like the service, here. You're a good waitress." For a moment I regret describing a full-time student by her part-time job. But her eyes tell me she's not offended.

"You don't have to leave big tips."

"You earn them."

She turns away and I leave a five dollar bill on the table and pay Cecilia the nine dollar check at the register.

•

Detective Elvis 'Elmer Fudd' Channard stands talking with a bored-looking Anthony Dunn in the center of Henry Clay Avenue. Channard has his little arms folded. He wears a tan sport coat with dark blue pants. Dunn, who wears a dark blue sport coat and tan pants, turns to Gonzales and me as we step up.

"Hell. Look at you two. No more ties, huh Gonzales?"

Channard stops his soliloquy a moment, but quickly continues, " ... and the woman cuts her own grass, with one of those push lawn mowers, the kind without a motor ..."

I spot Bob Kay standing between two marked units along the downtown side of the street. He'd called us on the radio, forty minutes after I left Flamingo's and ten minutes after picking up Gonzales. Kay nods our way and starts walking over.

" ... and she has one of those upright vacuum cleaners with the big bag. She takes it outside and vacuums her sidewalk ..." Channard hasn't lost a breath.

I move around him as Bob Kay steps up and points to a small apartment complex to my right. "Someone spray painted a message on a dumpster in back," Kay tell us. "About the cop killer." He's left his coat in his car and wears another white shirt over his dark blue bullet-proof vest.

"And?" I ask.

"And we found two dead cats in the dumpster."

Gonzales moves around Channard whose voice rises, " ... and she has at least five different wigs. A red one. Brunette. Blond. Blue and Pink ..."

"How'd the cats die?" I ask Kay.

He takes in a deep breath. "Decapitated."

That'll kill 'em, all right.

" ... and she never goes out. Except to cut her grass or vacuum her sidewalk ..."

Gonzales turns to Channard. "What the fuck you talking about?"

Blinking, as if he's just noticed us, Channard says, "The woman who lives across the street from me. She's peculiar. She has this big bird in some sort of cage ..." The Fudd continues.

"So what do you want us to do?" Gonzales asks Kay.

"We need to interview everyone in the apartments."

" ... and she feeds it mice, I think. Or maybe hamsters. Or maybe gerbils. I can't be sure ..."

I lean around Channard and pretend to be looking for something on his back. Gonzales and Kay start moving away, only my partner stops and asks what I'm looking for.

"The fuckin' *off* switch."

Dunn makes a loud fart sound. "Give up. There ain't none."

" ... and she wears the strangest clothes ... and ..."

We leave with Channard's voice echoing behind us.

"Hey," Dunn calls out angrily. "Don't fuckin' leave me with him." He hurries after us.

I catch a whiff of cigarette smoke as we move between the small apartment buildings, each suspended over a blacktop parking area jammed with pickup trucks mostly. The green dumpster is behind the left building next to a white Chevy Suburban up on cinder blocks. Spray painted in bright red on the dumpster are the words: COP KILLER HATES CATS.

A bespectacled crime lab technician is dusting the outside of the dumpster.

"One dead cat was on the far side of the dumpster." Kay points around the side. "The other was inside."

Dunn makes a helicopter noise. Around the back of the dumpster I find a pentagram painted in black.

"Pentagram?" Kay moves around to where I am. "Jesus," he says. "Don't tell me this thing's got Satanic implications."

"Better call your FBI buddies," I tell him. "Only *they* have the power to take on Satan." I pull out my note pad and head to the nearest building, knock on a hollow-core wooden door with a brass number 1A on it. A woman with dirty blond hair answers. She wears a white undershirt and baggy red gym shorts, a cigarette dangles from her lips. She nods at me, turns and yells to a teen-aged boy sitting on an orange sofa. "See. I told you they'd figure out who did it."

I hold up my credentials and she backs away, waving me in.

"OK, officer. He's all yours."

The boy won't look at me as I enter and stand next to the beat-up coffee table. He's about fourteen with short-cropped red hair. He wears a black, oversized Saint's *Who Dat?* tee-shirt and extra baggy denim shorts that go past his knees. He's barefoot.

"Well, Nottoway," the woman says. "You gonna tell him or do I have to?"

Nottoway? Jesus, the kid's probably named for the famous plantation house up by Bayou Goula.

The boy folds his arms. "You fuckin' tell him!" He looks at me for the first time and his dark brown eyes squint fiercely. And it occurs to me that his mother is smarter than she looks. Nottoway is an Algonquain word which means *rattlesnake*.

Sometimes it's that easy. Just knock on the right door.

A half-hour later, I'm leading the way back to Henry Clay Avenue, Gonzales, Kay, the crime lab technician and Dunn in tow. We leave this heinous crime scene in the capable hands of the two Juvenile Detectives Kay summoned twenty minutes ago. The crime amounts to two counts of violating Louisiana Revised Statute 14:102, Cruelty to Animals. A fuckin' misdemeanor in Louisiana.

Nottoway and two of his buddies, out of boredom, decided to liven up the apartment complex by decapitating two cats and painting the pentagram and message on the dumpster. It was a lark, a youthful indiscretion, a cool-as-fuckin-hell bitching rush. The girls would notice them now. Fuckin' A! They got the fuckin' Task Force out enmasse. Too bad Kay hadn't called Captain Picard and the FBI boys. I'da loved to see how they handled this. I could use the training.

Channard is standing in the same place in the street. Guess he's been guarding the cars. He steps in my path and says, "Is Jodie coming?"

"I doubt it."

"So, what happened?"

I stop so I don't run him over and take in a deep breath. "If you promise not to ask any questions, I'll tell you."

He nods furiously and I tell him. Gonzales waits politely for me. As soon as I finish, my partner adds, "Dumb shits."

Channard turns and looks at the apartments. "Dingbats," he says.

"Fuckin' dingbats is right," I agree and start heading for my car.

"No." Channard points to the buildings. "The apartments are dingbats. That's an architectural term. Built in the fifties and sixties. Apartments with parking beneath. Brick and wood, painted in pastel colors."

I keep walking, but my partner has to ask Channard, "What the fuck are you yakking about now?"

"The apartments. They're dingbats. Probably built in the fifties and sixties. Apartments with parking beneath. Brick and wood, painted in pastel colors."

Unlocking my car door, I call back to Gonzales that if he wants a ride, he'd better get the fuck over here. Channard remains talking in the middle of Henry Clay Avenue. Pointing to the apartments and waving his arms around as police cars pull away, some peeling out.

God, I love police work.

Chapter 13
THIS OUGHT TO WORK

My casework has degenerated into maddening surveillances of Sandie in barrooms, Felice in more barrooms and Mullet in even more barrooms.

Three nights after visiting the dingbats, Gonzales and I are parked against another curb, down the street from another barroom, this one called Pluto's on Camp Street. Mullet's Harley is parked with a dozen other bikes a block away. Gonzales dozes next to me while I sit as far down in the seat as possible in the dark car. A couple neighbors have already peeked out at us, probably figuring we're the heat, especially in my stripped-down Caprice.

My mind wanders back to Flamingo's. Angie looked so good this afternoon. In a pair of faded jeans and a white buttoned blouse, she had two gold barrettes in the hair, pulling it up on the sides. It made her look a little older, more sophisticated. Three shrimpers sure thought so, repeatedly calling her back to their booth, flirting with her big time. Two were middle-aged, but one was young, closer to Angie's age than me. She seemed to like the flirting. Like a true plains warrior, I kept my face expressionless as I ate. It bothered me, seeing her laughing and cutting up with the men. But I didn't show it.

A black dog races past the Caprice, as if something's chasing it. I sit up higher and see nothing. I settle back and my eye-lids feel so heavy, I have to fight off sleep. It's hard. I feel myself drifting ...

The sound of a hog starting up brings me out of my dozing and wakes Gonzales with a start. A green Harley pulls away from Pluto's as my partner and I both sit up and stretch.

"Wish we had more coffee," I say.

"Jesus." Gonzales yawns. "OK, so we have another one of Mullet's hangout for Sandie to check out. Why are we still here?"

"Got anything better to do?"

My partner sulks against the door, stretches his legs again and folds his arms across his chest. He's in black jeans tonight. I'm in faded jeans.

"Tell me something to keep me awake," Gonzales says. "Seen any naked women lately?"

Not answering him won't shut him up, but it's worth a try.

"Why don't you tell me about the four guys you shot?"

He's serious. "Come on. How'd they happen? It'll keep me awake."

My memory re-winds to my rookie year. I had parked my car across Magazine Street from the Second District Station and was heading in for four p.m. roll call ...

"Come on. Tell me a story. Tell me. Tell me. Tell me. Tell me."

Jesus. I raise a hand and just give up.

"The first man I shot was outside the Second District. He was in a cowboy outfit. Ten gallon hat, leather vest, boots and spurs, two nickel-plated revolvers in a double holster rig. He even wore chaps."

"What?" Gonzales sits up.

"Leather trouser things cowboys wore over their denim pants. Protected the legs from thorn bushes."

Gonzales nods. He's awake now and listening intently.

"He walked up to some cops standing outside, including my partner, Tim Rothman. The cowboy stopped about twenty feet away, spread his feet and told the cops to *draw*. He had his hands over his guns, like a gunfighter.

"Ever the clown, Rothman took out his notepad and drew a stick figure of the cowboy and showed it to him. Everyone laughed, except the cowboy. That's what caught my attention as I crossed Magazine from where I'd parked my car – the laughter.

"The cowboy drew both guns and fired. He blew out the windows of the police car Rothman was standing next to, and sent everyone diving to the sidewalk. I pulled out my .357 and dropped him with two shots."

Gonzales smiles widely. "I remember that. I was in the academy. He was a mental wasn't he?"

I nod. "In and out of Mandeville. Bought the guns by mail-order. I had no trouble in front of the Grand Jury, but caught hell on the department. Injun kills cowboy." The streetlight at the corner blinks then goes out. I look around, but it's quiet. Guess the neighbors will have to call the power company when they get around to noticing.

"What about number two?"

Six months later. Armed robber from the K&B at Carrollton and Claiborne got into a running gun battle with police. Buncha shots fired by the police that evening. Three hit the robber. All from my gun.

"I caught him crossing Carrollton. Another good shooting."

Gonzales starts drumming his hands on the dashboard. "This is better than T.V." He's doing *Wipeout*. "Continue."

I point to his hands and he stops.

"Number three was a month after I came to Homicide. Jodie and I jumped a rape-in-progress call. We arrived with two patrolmen. Jodie had me cover the side of the house while they went in the front door.

"The rapist jumped out of a window and charged at me with a butcher knife. I fired four times. He took two in the chest and two in the head."

"I remember that one too. Didn't you have a little trouble with the Grand Jury with that one?"

"Yep." I tell him how a woman in the house next door swore I didn't yell "police" and that I executed the man after he was on his knees. Hell, I didn't have time to yell anything and the trajectory of my bullets proved he wasn't on his knees when shot.

"My fourth shooting was Exchange Alley."

Gonzales starts drumming *Wipeout* again as my mind flashes back to the alley. It seems so long ago. My partner quiets down for a while and I'm thankful for that. Mullet comes out at midnight, climbs on his hog and we follow him home.

"Wasted fuckin' night," Gonzales complains as we drive away from South Derbigny.

"Not really. He didn't go out and kill a cop, did he?"

I feel Gonzales staring at me, but won't look over at him until he says, "Seems to me you're plagued."

"Plagued?"

"Shooting people. You're plagued by being a good shot while everyone else misses."

He might have a point. So I have to ask, "By the way, how good a shot are *you*?"

"Fuckin' horrible. That's why I don't mind hanging around with you, Cochise."

"Wrong fuckin' tribe, Zorro."

•

Five minutes after five the next evening we follow Mullet to Pluto's. Ten minutes later, Sandie, in an iridescent yellow body suit, climbs out of the back seat of our car and goes in. Gonzales and I, both in all black, wait outside.

Predictably, the FBI has taken over our Task Force. Not officially, of course, it's a joint venture. Kay is still in charge. The Bureau just tells everyone what to do. As an act of defiance, more than believing I'm really on to something, Kay has shielded me and Gonzales from the assignments handed out daily by the men in the nice suits.

"They mean well," Kay explained earlier that afternoon.

"They're too cerebral," Gonzales complained. "This is a street thing."

Both are right of course.

"Well," Kay added, "they have one thing we've been needing."

"And that is?"

"A printing press. They can print up as much money as we need." With that Kay handed me ten one hundred dollar bills to split between Sandie and Felice.

Now, as we sit as inconspicuously as we can down Camp from Pluto's, we wait. A boring hour passes. Half way through the second, I look over at a sign next to the willow tree we're trying to use as cover. The sign is white with red lettering that reads: This Is A Drug Free Zone. There's a drawing of a hypodermic needle with a slash through it, like a no smoking emblem.

"Those signs really work," I tell my partner.

"What?"

I point to the sign. "A few weeks ago I saw two guys standing next to one of these over by the Melpomene Projects. They were about to make a deal, when one of them noticed the sign, slapped himself on the forehead and said, 'Wait. We can't deal here.' They walked two blocks over to make their deal."

Gonzales taps down his sunglasses and gleeks me. I bend my chin down and return the gleek, looking at him over the top of my glasses.

"Don't get too fuckin' weird on me, Crazy Horse."

At least he got the tribe right. No way I'm telling him how close he is to my ancestry. According to my grandfather, that is.

•

At first, the number of people milling around the street doesn't seem out of the ordinary. Mostly kids, several breeze by on roller blades. Ignoring us, they laugh and cut up as they pass. It isn't until four men carry a large folding table out of a house and set it up on the sidewalk, do things seem strange. Another man wheels a barbecue pit over to the folding table and starts up the flames. The crowd, a nearly even mix of black and white faces, grows quickly and I look around to see if a parade is coming. People are standing in the street now and sitting on nearly every front stoop. Everyone seems actually friendly. I have that *Twilight Zone* feeling again.

Pulling off my sunglasses, I ask my partner. "What the fuck's going on?"

"Huh?" He's dozing again.

"What the fuck are all these people doing?"

Gonzales takes off his sunglasses, seems to notice the crowd for the first time and chuckles. He puts his glasses back on and settles back in his seat.

"Don't you ever listen to the news?" he asks.

God, I love a good quiz.

"It's National Night Out Against Crime."

"Oh, yeah. This ought to work. I guess the police can take the night off." My sarcasm is barely past my lips when the loud report of a gunshot echoes behind us. I jump out of the car, my Glock in both hands as I crouch. A horde of people run past us. At the end of the block I see several adults jumping and shouting. A half dozen roller-bladers round the corner and head our way at full speed.

Moving around the car to the sidewalk, I jog toward the corner. Gonzales is right behind me as we approach a screaming white woman. Two screaming black women see our guns and point to us, as they screech louder. Turning the corner, I spot two men holding down a large black man who has a blue steel revolver in his hand.

"Police!" Gonzales shouts behind me. "Freeze!"

I ease over and step on the hand holding the revolver. The man yelps when I reach down and twist the pistol from his hand. It takes a few minutes to discover our perpetrator, the man with the pistol, has taken a pot shot at the roller-bladers who had the audacity to steal some of the popcorn from the perpetrator's large bowl on the table in front of his house.

"I'm tired of them damn hooligans!"

We pass the gunman to a uniformed officer who also heard the gunshot as he passed in his marked unit.

"Hey," the patrolman calls out. "Y'all ain't handling this?"

I point to my star-and-crescent badge, clipped to my belt above the left front pocket of my jeans.

"Homicide," I tell him. "See any dead people here?"

With a disgusted look on his face, the patrolman walks to his car with the perpetrator.

Gonzales chuckles. "Hope they don't find a body."

"Some fuckin' National Night Out Against Crime, huh?"

"What you complaining about? You almost got to kill number five."

One of the roller-bladers is standing next to my open door.

"I made sure no one stole anything from y'all car, officer," he tells me, a smirk on his young, dark brown face. I look inside and our portable radios are still there. At least the car keys are in the front pocket of my jeans.

"Thanks," I tell the boy. "How was the popcorn?"

"Very good," he says as he wheels away. "I'm going for the rest."

We drive, carefully, past Pluto's to set up on the other side of the bar. We have to watch for Sandie in our rear view mirrors now. I glance at my watch and it's barely seven. The sun won't be going down for another hour and a half, at least.

"Some fuckin' Night Out Against Crime," I grumble again.

Gonzales lets out a long breath. "Now, that's something you don't see every day." He points straight ahead and I look out the windshield at a very large, naked man running toward us. I'm speechless. Behind the man is an equally large woman, also naked, also running toward us.

Stumbling up to our car, the man leans his hands on the hood and gasps for breath. I climb out just as the woman arrives, puts her hands on the man's back and struggles to catch her breath.

The man looks at me and tries to speak. His face is contorted in pain and I hope to God he's not having a fuckin' heart attack, not on the hood of my car.

"Call ..." The man struggles to speak.

"Call ... police."

I point to my badge.

He nods, bends his head as he takes in another deep breath, and raises a hand for me to wait. I look back and Gonzales is still in the car, gleeking us with his mouth open like an imbecile. It takes a minute but the man gets it out. They were robbed. Pointing up the street, he tells me there are others, victims at a private party.

"They took our clothes," the man adds as I hustle them into the back of my car. The man recovers enough to lead us to what looks like a walled garden at the corner of Camp and Pleasant Street. As we park, I notice the strong scent of body odor coming from the back seat.

The man starts to get out and I ask him not to. "Just roll the windows down, OK?" My car's gonna smell like a Ninth Ward dumpster.

"They're inside that gate." The man points to a six foot wooden gate. "It's a private park."

"Are the robbers still around?" I ask as I climb out.

"No."

"What did they look like?"

"Black," the man says. "Young. Three of them. We heard a car leave after they took our money and clothes."

Gonzales follows me to the gate. I pull it open and peek in. There's a well-tended garden to my left, a pool to my right with a large, latticework wooden shelter beyond where about twenty naked people stand huddled together.

"Some fuckin' night out against crime," I tell my partner as we step into the small private park that smells of freshly cut grass.

They are mostly couples, women hiding behind men who have their hands in front of their genitalia, thankfully. All stare as us as if *we're* naked. A tall blond woman steps out from behind her skinny male companion, puts her hands on her hips and says, "What took you so long to get here?"

It's hard not to look at her oversized breasts. She has a neatly trimmed, blond bush and long, shapely legs.

"We were on stakeout," Gonzales says, sunglasses in hand now as he gives her a closer look.

"That's no excuse. Can't you see we need help?"

A gray-haired man inches forward, his pretty brunette companion keeping as close as she can to his back. She stares at me with large brown eyes, her pretty lips quivering in fear. I take off my dress shirt and pass it to the gray-haired man for her. As he hands it to her and she dons it quickly, I get a momentary peek at her slim, naked body.

The skinny man snaps at the blond, telling her to get back and cover up. I notice the blond's blue eyes for the first time as she tells him, "If they haven't seen a naked woman before, it's their problem!"

The sound of screeching brakes turns me around. Just as I make it to the gate, I see two uniformed officers walking toward the front of my car. The naked large people are standing outside my car, arms folded.

The nearest officer, a middle-aged black man with a thick moustache, sees me and hold his arms out, palms up. "What the fuck is this?" His name tag reads: Kolberg. Nice German name.

"It gets better," I tell him. I wave the large couple forward and invite the uniformed officers into the garden. The stunned look on their faces almost starts me laughing. As they take in the sights, I tell them how some enterprising street thugs had the audacity to take advantage of the National Night Out Against Crime. Both officers look at me as if I'm speaking Russian. I shrug and tell them they're gonna needs some jackets and blankets. Waving to my partner, I start back toward the gate.

"Wait," Kolberg calls out, "you leaving?"

"You can call for a Robbery team." I keep moving. "Get my shirt from the pretty lady with the brown eyes, OK?"

"Y'all ain't Robbery?"

"Homicide," Gonzales growls as he passes. "See any dead people here?"

"Just the two that were outside a minute ago."

Real fuckin' funny. Glancing back as I reach the gate, I see the blond woman standing in front of Kolberg, hands back on her hips as she chews him out.

"Jesus, what a fuckin' evening." I have to readjust myself as I try to sit in behind the steering wheel. "All I fuckin' need."

Gonzales jumps in and asks what's wrong as I crank up the engine and drive us away.

"What do you think? I got a fuckin' diamond cutter in my jeans."

Gonzales laughs.

"And you didn't get a hard-on looking at the blond or the pretty brunette?"

He puts his sunglasses back on. "Yeah. But I already came in my jeans. I'm all limp now."

I almost run into two parked cars. Laughing so hard, I stop the Caprice in the center of the street.

My partner gleeks me again and says, "What?"

"All fuckin' limp?"

He grins, which causes me to laugh even harder. I finally get going again. Wiping tears from my eyes as we approach Pluto's, I see Sandie standing in the middle of the street, her hands on her hips. She looks like a big canary in that yellow jumpsuit. I jam the brakes and struggle to put the car in park as my partner and I laugh so hard, we have trouble catching our breaths.

Sandie walks up. Gonzales is slapping the dashboard and my side is killing me.

She moves to my window. "What the hell's so funny?"

I try to tell her but can't get past the word limp, which causes my partner to bounce in his seat as he roars, pointing a finger at me as if *I'm* the lunatic.

Sandie climbs in the back seat and says, "What's this smell?"

It takes several minutes before my partner and I can communicate intelligently.

Sandie shakes her head. "When you two jack-asses are ready, I'll tell you what Mullet told me before he drove off ten minutes ago."

It still takes me half a minute before I can ask, "OK What'd he say?"

"He said he thought it was about time another cop got his brains blown out."

The laughter disappears instantly.

Chapter 14
BECAUSE HE WORE BLUE

Mullet doesn't come home that evening.

The next morning, the ruthless summer sun bakes the interior of the Caprice as my partner and I sit beneath the large oak on So. Roman Street. I stare through the metal fences at Mullet's house, but my eyes are so weary I can barely make out the place.

"Where the fuck arc they?" Gonzales stretches and looks behind the car for our relief. They should have bccn here and hour ago.

As I look into the rear-view mirror, Jodie's white LTD pulls up behind us. Climbing out, I stretch and move wearily to Jodie who rolls down her window and tells me she's relieving us while the task force serves warrants.

"Channard and Dunn will relieve me in a couple hours."

I thank her and start back to my car but turn back.

"Warrants?"

"The FBI guys have come up with information out of Desire."

Jesus. They're searching the projects again. What did Gonzales call them? Cerebral? Stupid is more like it. Searching the city's largest housing project when everyone knows white boys are doing this.

It seems to take hours to drop off my partner and drive home. Buck bounces on deck and yips and runs in circles as I bring him inside and give him fresh food. As if in a daze, I go out and hose off the deck and put more dry dog food in Buck's outside food dish and fresh water in his bowl.

Racing back out on deck, Buck scampers to the gate and barks, his tail wagging. God I'm so tired, but I go in and get his leash, and my spare sunglasses and take him across Orpheum to the levee and let him run. I sit on the hot grass.

Buck is already down by the rocks. I lean back and close my eyes. The sun is warm on my face and I roll on my side. When I was twenty, I could stay up all night and not feel a thing. Damn am I getting old or what?

•

It takes a few seconds to realize the wetness on my face is Buck licking me. I wake and look at my watch. It's been two hours.

"Come on, boy." We move back to *Sad Lisa* and I plop down on the couch. No way I'm climbing to the loft. Just as I'm getting nice and comfortable, the phone rings. I catch it before the answering machine clicks in.

"Hey, Babe. Did I wake you?" It's Sharon.

"Yes, actually. Worked all night." I bring the phone back to the couch.

"I thought I'd come over."

"Not now," I tell her. "I'm dead. I mean really dead."

She asks if I've been avoiding her. I haven't returned her calls. Peeking at the answering machine I see the light blinking and can't remember the last time I even checked the damn thing. Sharon goes on about our relationship, about commitments and other serious matters, only her words fade in a jumbled heap. She keeps talking and her voice lulls me, draws me into a nice dozing state.

"Hey!" She wakes me. "Did you fall asleep on me?"

"I told you. I'm dead."

She hangs up on me.

Before I can put the phone on the floor it rings again.

"Yes," I snap. "What is it?"

"You awake?" It's Jodie and the catch in her voice causes me to sit up. I have to hold my head.

"What is it?"

"A Sixth District officer is missing."

A cold shower revives me enough to clear my eyes. As I brew extra strong coffee and chicory, I check my answering machine to see if Sandie or Felice have called. Sharon left three messages to go along with four hang-ups.

I take the coffee with me. Racing past Flamingo's I glance inside, but only Cecilia's there. I slap my blue light up on my dash, hit the siren as I roll through the red light at Old Hammond Highway and hang a left, punching the Caprice as I fly into Orleans Parish. Before I reach headquarters, I hear it on the radio. Another Sixth District unit has found the missing officer's car off Tchoupitoulas near the Washington Avenue Wharf. By the time I get there, it looks like a cop convention.

I spot Jodie's blond hair from a half block away as I park on Tchoupitoulas. Gonzales is with her. He wears another black Saints tee-shirt and jeans. She's in a white blouse and black skirt, her nine-millimeter in a black canvas holster rig. Dennis Merten, wearing an ill-fitting brown suit, moves to cut me off. The perpetual scowl on his dark face seems furrowed into a permanence.

I slow down and ask him, "Anything yet?"

He shakes his head and rubs his chin and it's the first time I've ever seen him unshaven. Jodie sees me and waves me forward. I step away from my lieutenant who growls. "You enjoying the vacation, or what?"

I must be exhausted because it takes me a few steps to realize. He's been up to his ass in regular murders while I've been sitting on my ass on useless stakeouts. I look back at him and shrug.

"We're spreading out," Jodie says as she moves past me. She waves her hand around. "Search every fuckin' building."

I go back and ask Merten if he'll go with me. Without a word, he leads the way to the nearest abandoned warehouse. We find a boarded-up side door with several wooden planks missing. Merten kicks in more planks and we go inside. Thankfully, he has a flashlight. So I follow him across the empty first floor. All we find, all the way to the third floor, is trash, empty soft drinks cans and fast food bags.

We can't even break into the next warehouse, which has steel plates covering its windows and doors. Merten wipes his sweaty brow with his coat sleeve as he leads me to yet another abandoned warehouse. My light blue PANO tee-shirt is soaked and my faded jeans already streaked with grease and dirt.

When Jodie calls me on the radio, just as Merten and I have found a window to climb into the third warehouse, I feel a sickness in my stomach. She asks me to 10-19 her position, then tells me she's a block up Tchoupitoulas from my car. I hurry over and see a crowd of blue outside a two story brown brick building. Along the side of the building, in faded white paint, is a sign that reads: Studebaker of New Orleans Parts and Service.

Kay towers over the crowd as he stands next to an iron gate. He sees me and calls me forward. I press my way through the crowd of cops. Kay points to the gate and tells me to go in. He stops Merten behind me and starts talking about a thorough canvass.

Moving through the partially open gate, I see the FBI's Captain Picard step into a doorway at the far end of a wide alcove. He's followed by three more men in prim suits, each carrying a silver metal case. I follow them to a stairwell and up to the second floor. With most of the high windows broken out, the wide second floor is bathed in bright sunlight. I stop in the doorway and take in the surreal scene.

Carefully watching where they step, the four feds take a roundabout route to where Jodie stands a good thirty yards away, her back to me. Two uniformed officers stand off to her left. One looks like he's crying. My gaze moves to Jodie's right to a crumpled figure slumped on the filthy floor. His powder-blue NOPD shirt is streaked red and black with coagulated blood. Dusty sunlight, streaking from above, illuminates the body in a macabre heavenly light.

I remain in the doorway and study the area. It doesn't take long for me to see footprints in the dirt. I go down on my haunches. Looks like three sets entered the room and two sets returned to the doorway.

The men with the silver cases lay them on the floor in the far corner. One pulls out a camera while another pulls out a tape measure. Jodie leads the two patrol officer my way, walking along the walls back to me. We step back out of the doorway as the camera flashes. I don't have to watch to know the cameraman is taking long distance pictures from each corner. Carefully he will move forward for close-ups of the body.

Jodie instructs the officers to go downstairs and each write a follow-up report as to what they saw when they discovered the body. Her face is flushed, her hair unruly. Unlike me, there's not a hint of perspiration on her as she quietly tells me the officer's name was Peter James, two years out of the academy. His nine-millimeter is still in its holster. They used his own handcuffs to manacle his hands behind his back. Looks like he was shot twice in the head by a large caliber weapon. The top if his head is blown off.

The hum of a hand-held vacuum cleaner sounds behind us and we step back into the room. The cameraman is bent over the footprints and takes a close-up photo. A sound behind us turns me around as three additional men in nice suits reach the doorway. Each carries another silver case.

Jodie slowly leads me downstairs where Kay and Gonzales wait with Tony Dunn and Elmer Fudd Channard.

"Who's watching Mullet's house?" I ask immediately.

"We have two units there," Kay answers, placing a weary hand on my shoulder. I have to fight to keep from brushing it off. Although we're in a wide alcove, I feel confined, smothered. But I don't brush off the friendly hand. The torment in Kay's eyes won't let me.

Jodie explains that Dunn will be the case officer on this case. He nods wearily. He's now responsible for the report and ultimately, for catching the killer, although I'm sure the Task Force is about to be expanded and we'll all be lost in a sea of police. Kay's scratchy voice tells us nearly a hundred officers are canvassing the area, searching the ground outside, covering every angle. As his voice fades and we're engulfed in a sickening silence, we move apart.

Gonzales sits in the doorway leading upstairs where the FBI lab is meticulously processing the crime scene. Kay moves to the opening of the alcove and leans against the wall. Dunn sits several feet away, his head in his hands. No sound effects now. Jodie finds the cleanest spot on the near wall to lean against, Elmer Fudd a few feet away, sneaks peeks at her, as if none of us can see. He's dying to say something, but even he knows better.

I find the farthest corner and sit crossed-legged and close my eyes. But there is no way I can rest. I keep seeing the crumpled body, keep wondering what Peter James thought before the bullet tore through his mind. Why was he riding alone? I know the answer to that. Manpower shortage. But how did they get the jump on him?

I see Cassandra's face again, ashen and gray in death, her shirt saturated in blood. Shaking away the image I try to imagine Angie's face smiling at me as she sits across the booth. But the image I see is sad, troubled as the aquamarine eyes stare intently at me.

Faintly, I hear chanting. As it become clearer, I realize it's in my mind. I hear the deep voice of my grandfather and uncles as they sing the sad death chant of our ancestors. It resonates in my mind and brings me to another plain, where a great calming waits. I drift, as if on a cloud. My eyes snap open and I'm content to stare at the dirty floor. The acid in my stomach eats at me because it's my fault. If we had just called for a unit when the fat naked people ran up to us, if we would have stayed on assignment, if all those useless surveillances hadn't dulled our senses, if ...

There are so many ifs.

And Peter James is dead.

•

It's like coming out of a trance when Captain Picard comes down the stairs to confer with Bob Kay. Jodie steps over and I rise slowly and join them just at the agent confirms the officer's badge is missing.

"We've recovered a projectile in the room. We think another is still in the brain." The agent talks lowly, his voice deep and sad. "We've also found two partial latents on the handcuffs and one very good print."

I cut in. "I have a copy of Mullet's fingerprints in my briefcase."

The agent turns to me and asks, "Whose prints?"

Kay explains and the agent nods. Apparently he's been told of the thin lead I've been following.

"We'll need an original set," he tells me and I'm on my way to Criminal Records for Lloyd 'Mullet' Singletary's fingerprints.

An hour and a half later, when the FBI fingerprint expert looks up from my desk and tells me it's a match, I feel my neck redden, my pulse rise, my eyes narrowing. I don't have to ask him to repeat it because Captain Picard does and the expert looks down through his magnifying loop and says, "Positively."

Dunn lets out an excited whistle.

"Son-of-a-bitch!" Kay looks stunned. Picard is amazed, as if I'd pulled a rabbit out of a hat. Gonzales blinks at me as if *he's* suddenly in *The Twilight Zone*. I look at Jodie and there's a knowing look in her hazel, cat eyes. I know. *It's solved*, but far from over.

Elmer Fudd pats me on the back as I reach into my desk drawer for a warrant form. And I wheel and grab his arm. My partner steps forward and pulls my hand away.

"Don't congratulate us," Gonzales says. He lets go of Fudd's hand. My partner's voice rises, "Don't anyone fuckin' say it was a good job, because it wasn't."

The faces around us don't understand, except Jodie who softly reminds everyone how we were supposed to be following Mullet. I know it's my fault. It'll always be my fault. At least, when I finally look in my partner's eyes I don't see as much anguish there. At least he isn't blaming himself as much as I. Then again, it was my surveillance.

Jodie softly says, "In a few hours, we'll be witnessing the autopsy of a twenty-two year old boy who's dead solely because he wore blue."

•

Strong coffee and chicory keeps me going, for now.

It's nearing midnight as I sit in my Caprice beneath the So. Roman oak. Jodie brushes her hair out of her face as she peers through the binoculars across the playground to the unpainted wooden house. My keen, sharp Sioux eyes, are too tired to do us any good.

At least Gonzales is home, hopefully getting some sleep. I swallow the last of my coffee and its heat momentarily soothes my scratchy throat. I know I'm pushing exhaustion, but I can't go home, not yet.

The autopsy of Peter James surfaced the second bullet, lodged at the base of his skull. It isn't in as good shape at the other bullet, but firearms examiners are sure it came from the gun that killed Cochran and Stevens. They're also sure they can make a match if we come up with the Colt Python.

Jodie forced me to eat a Wendy's double-stack with cheese a little while ago, but it did little to ease my bellyache.

I can't find Sandie and can't find Felice and no one, not even the entire department and the FBI can locate Mullet.

Dunn put out an All-Points-Bulletin and we have people set up outside The Honky Chateau, Pluto's, Hog Heaven and the Raton bar. Fel Jones has units checking every known biker hang-out in the city as well as Jefferson and St. Bernard Parishes.

Felice hasn't been at the apartment where we stashed her. And her auntie hasn't seen her for days. We'd cruised the bars along Chef Menteur until four a.m. Sandie hasn't answered the messages I've left on her machine, nor the two notes I slipped under her door. *Jesus to hell*, why am I always a step behind? God, don't let me get an informant killed too.

"I hope we catch this bastard alive." It's the third time tonight Jodie has reminded me we need to know who was with Mullet on Tchoupitoulas Street.

"I know. I know."

Jodie looks at her watch and tells me Wilson and Willson will be relieving us at midnight. Then she surprises me with, "Think I'll write a book about this case."

Why not? The public loves true crime stories.

"It'll prove my devolution theory."

I almost smile.

"No doubt the human race is devolving, moving backward, crawling back into the fuckin' primordial soup." Still peering through the binoculars, she adds, "Take Mullet. He's closer to a Neanderthal than even a Cro-Magnon, much less a Homo Sapien."

A car turns off Washington behind us, but it isn't our relief.

"Hell," I tell Jodie. "The Sioux still wonder why the inferior white men were able to take the sacred lands from the people God chose to care for that land."

She bats her eyes twice at me before going back to her watch.

"To the Sioux, the Black Hills of Dakota are the center of the universe. It was ours from the earliest times, until the white devils came and took it. Man for man the Sioux were superior. Yet the white devils prevailed. Maybe the Neanderthals were meant to rule."

"Center of the universe? That why your mother went back?"

"Yep." After my father died, my mother returned to the Black Hills, to her family, to the center of her universe. I didn't, of course. I guess the center of my universe is my father's center – the flatlands of Louisiana. Although I feel the fierceness of the Lakota in my blood, I am also a Frenchman, like my Daddy.

Another Caprice turns off Washington and pulls up behind us. I see Two-L's oversized head behind the steering wheel. Without even a wave, I start up the engine and drive away.

•

The alarm clock wakes me at five p.m. to the echo of the Lakota death chant. Rising, as if from another trance, I feel groggy. A quick shower later, I don another black tee-shirt, black jeans and black Reeboks. Between petting and feeding Buck, I slip my Glock into its canvas holster at the small of my back, and slip my obsidian knife in its sheath, tying it around my calf on the inside of my left leg. I pull on another navy blue dress as I leave.

Starting up the Caprice, I realize I'm still hearing the chant, in the back of my mind. My hands shake as I hold the steering wheel.

"I'd better eat something."

I pull away quickly. Passing Flamingo's, I see Angie leaning against the counter and talking to Cecilia. I hit the brakes and slide into the parking lot. Cecilia scolds me as I enter, telling me I shouldn't spray shells all over the place. Angie smiles, grabs a menu and starts for my booth.

"No, I need something to go." I'll wolf it down as I drive.

"Oh."

I order the usual, skipping the drink. Angie passes the order slip to Joe who has already started my burger.

"Why the big hurry?" Angie's voice is low and serious.

"Did you know him?" Cecilia asks from behind me.

I shake my head and Angie's eyes seem to grow darker.

"Know who?"

I tell her another police officer's been killed. Her mouth draws tight. A whiff of Joe's burger passes over us, smelling so damn good.

"So you're going to play shoot 'em up again," Cecilia asks.

Angie leans forward. "What does that mean?"

I turn and give Cecilia a stern look. And she rolls her shoulders. That's what I get for sliding on her shells.

"What does she mean, shoot 'em up?" Angie's voice wavers.

I stare back into her eyes and tell her Cecilia's joking. We're searching for a killer, but the last thing we need to do is shoot anyone. She doesn't seem convinced. Angie leans an elbow against the counter. "Guess you won't be watching TV tonight. *Mayerling* is coming on." There's that word again.

Joe flips my burger and drops onions on top.

"What's *Mayerling*?"

In a distant, hollow voice, Angie tells me it's about a tragic love affair between an Austrian Crown-Prince and his mistress. Watching her explain the sad story, I force myself to not look at my watch. *Jesus*, I've got so much to do.

Joe slaps cheese on my burger. He seems to sense I'm in a hurry.

"I think you'd like it," Angie says.

I nod as she stares intently into my eyes, again. For several long seconds we remain motionless. Joe quickly packs the burger and fries into a paper bag, stuffing extra napkins inside and clears his throat to get Angie's attention. As Angie passes me the food, I see something in her eyes that makes me want to stay. She doesn't even try to hide it. And I have no response.

"Be careful," she says as I back up and pay Cecilia.

I nod and try to give her a tip. She wants no part of it.

"See ya' later," I say and turn to leave.

"What's with the big knife?" Angie asks behind me.

Backpedaling, I answer quickly, trying to be funny. "I'm not supposed to shoot anyone, but no one said I couldn't scalp 'em."

The disappointment in Angie's eyes makes me feel like shit.

Chapter 15
IS HE DEAD?

I slip another note under Sandie's door, figuring I'm heading for the Chef to search for Felice, when headquarters calls me on the radio.

"A Reverend Holliday is calling you from Charity's Emergency Room. Want the number?"

"Negative. I'll head there."

Whatever the reverend wants can't be good. Nine minutes later, I park the Caprice behind Charity Hospital and jog up the ER ramp. Holliday, also in all black, stands just inside the door. The look on his face confirms, it isn't good. He raises his left hand and shows me one of my business cards.

"You know a girl name Felice Marquee?"

Jesus, no.

Holliday nods over his shoulder. "She's been beat up." He lowers his voice, "And raped."

I wince and my stomach feels as if it's twisting in a giant knot. I follow the reverend through the waiting room of bent-up folding chairs and coughing people to the trauma rooms which reek of alcohol swipes and other sickly-smelling antiseptic odors. Holliday stops outside the fourth cubicle and opens the curtain for me, but stays out. A nurse stands over Felice who lies on her back beneath a green sheet. Her bare feet are exposed.

I open my shirt to show my badge and the nurse goes back to dressing a long wound on the left side of Felice's jaw. I see black stitches there. Easing around the bed, I move up to Felice's face and her eyes are open, staring at the ceiling. Her lips are swollen twice their size and bruises mark both sides of her face.

I call her name but she doesn't react. I call out again and the nurse moves her head over Felice's and nods almost imperceptibly.

"She's ignoring you, officer." The nurse's voice is as antiseptic as the smell here.

"What's her condition?"

"The doctor's outside." Again the chilly voice. "Dr. Adams."

I find Dr. Adams when he steps out of the next trauma room to write something on a clipboard. I identify myself and ask about Felice's condition.

"She's stable. Lacerations on her chest and face. Probably a broken rib or two. We'll have to set her jaw, which is fractured and she's been raped, multiple times." His voice is staccato and without feeling. He moves past me through another curtain into another trauma room.

Reverend Holliday sits in the waiting room. I tell him Felice's condition and ask how he knows her.

"I don't. One of the nurses called me when she found your card." He rubs his unshaven chin. "Told you I'd put word out everywhere about this case. Including your name."

I thank him and ask if he'll call Felice's auntie while I call headquarters. A half hour later, while the good reverend comforts Felice's auntie, I escort two detectives from the Sex Crimes Unit to Felice's cubicle. Dr. Adams joins us as they hand him a rape kit.

I wait in the hall beyond the waiting room. I can't let this get to me. I have to remain calm, keep my mind clear. I have to fight the rage growing inside. The death chant starts up again, echoing from deep within. I want to shout. I want to yell. I want to run, somewhere, anywhere. I want to chase down the men who did this and scalp them. Maybe slice a throat or two. I want to feel their warm blood on my hands.

Jesus, help me.

Although my radio's turned down, I hear Kay's voice call me. I pull the radio out of my back pocket, turn it up and tell Kay to go ahead.

"I'm working with you tonight," he says. "Pick me up at the office at eleven-thirty."

"You there now?"

"10-4."

I walk to the nearest pay phone. He answers as if he's in a hurry and before I can tell him about Felice, he says, "Sandie just left a message for you."

"Where is she?"

He pauses at my shouting. "Don't know. She left the message with the desk. Here, I'll read it to you. 'Been getting your notes. Will call soon. I'm getting close'."

"Dammit!"

"What's going on?"

Calming myself as best I can, I tell him about Felice. When I pause for a breath, he tells me he's coming right over and hangs up on me. Out in the waiting room, the auntie looks at me with loathing. Holliday moves toward me. He has a question. "What's going on with these search warrants in Desire? You know white boys are doing this."

"Everybody knows now. We have a suspect. The FBI ran those warrants, but won't be running any more there."

"Your suspect's a white boy, correct?"

I nod and thank him again for calling me about Felice. He puts two heavy hands on my shoulders and tells me I don't look so good.

"I'll look worse before this is over."

Ten minutes later Kay rushes in. His vest is outside his shirt tonight and he carries a shotgun to go along with the nine-millimeter on his waist. He's accompanied by two uniformed officers who both look like rookies. Before he reaches me, the two Sex Crimes detectives step out of the trauma room.

Both are black, the woman is Sergeant Darlene Wilson. Short and stocky, her skin is only a shade darker than mine. Her eyes, however, are much darker brown. They flash fiercely as she tells us a elderly white couple found Felice lying along Almonaster Avenue, almost ran her over. They brought her directly to Charity but left before anyone got their names. Almonaster, that's only a mile or so from Chef Menteur Highway.

"Felice say anything?" I ask.

"She grunted a few sentences. Said she was working for you. They're setting her jaw now." Darlene glares at me. "She was raped multiple times. Why wasn't anyone backing her up?"

I could say she didn't want any backup. I could explain how she wouldn't even let me know where she was going. But what's the use? It's my fault. I sent her out in the night and this is what she got.

Darlene turns to Kay. "We've got units hitting the Chef bars." She and the other detective step away from me as if I'm the source of the stink in the room. I look at Kay and he's all owl-eyes as he stares back.

"I've got to find Sandie."

He nods. "I'll stay here and talk to Felice when she's ready."

As I head for the door, Kay tells me not to worry about So. Roman. He'll get someone to take my watch there.

At midnight, I'm pulling away from the Honky Chateau. I've already talked with the two task forcers, who are set up outside waiting for Mullet. I'd described Sandie to them, went in the bar myself to make sure she wasn't there.

I head for the next bar. I'm hitting every Bywater bar Sandie and I checked out that night she told me she first heard about the badges. I'm checking *every one*. A night watch juvenile team has been checking Sandie's place periodically, but our elusive red-head is no where to be found. I have a bad feeling.

She's not at The Getted Bar nor Wayne's Funky-Butt Pub nor a real slimy dive called Grapp's off Franklin Avenue. At two-thirty, as I climb back into the Caprice, my partner calls me on the radio. His voice is low and serious.

"10-19 So. Roman. Our perpetrator just arrived with two other subjects."

•

Jodie and I set up in my Caprice a block up So. Derbigny at the corner of Fourth Street. Tony Dunn, with the arrest warrant and search warrant, sits down Derbigny just past Third Street with an unhappy Elmer Fudd who wanted to sit with Jodie so badly he called 'dibs' out loud. Jodie looked at him as if he was retarded. It took Jodie a good twenty minutes to calm down. "Like I'm up for 'dibs'. I think I'll swat that fat fuck across the back of his head."

We have ten units, a total of twenty officers, armed and ready. We plan to wait until four a.m. to hit the house. Give 'em time to get good and drunk or good and sleepy. The FBI waits up Washington Avenue. No way they're dirtying their hands on the apprehension. Bob Kay, with Gonzales in what is now the command car, is parked beneath our tree on So. Roman. He hasn't called for SWAT. This is a Task Force Operation. Kay left Darlene Wilson with Felice. I think that's the best move we've made all night.

Mullet had gone inside with a tall blond biker and a Latino-looking biker. Their three bikes are still parked out front, two on the sidewalk. At two a.m., the main lights go out. The light from a TV in the front room goes off shortly before three. Forty-five minutes later, we climb out of our units to don our gear.

I put on a black Kevlar helmet and wrap an armor-plated bullet-proof vest around my torso. So does Jodie. I help Jodie adjust her helmet. We follow Tony Dunn and Elmer Fudd to the front door, which has only a door lock, no dead bolt.

Mercier and Costanza are right behind with two uniformed officers who will cover the door, and our backs, once we go in. Other officers climb into the back yard and surround the house on both sides.

I move next to Dunn as he lifts his right foot and slams it against the door just above the lock. The door crashes in and Dunn goes in low. I go in high with my nine-millimeter in my right hand and my flashlight in my left.

No one's in the front room.

Dunn reaches the hallway as I crouch at the other door. Mercier and Costanza step in.

Jodie shouts, "Police!"

Mercier tosses a flash grenade down the hall as Costanza tosses one in the room ahead of me. We duck and close our eyes as the grenades go off.

I rush into the kitchen with Costanza right behind and it takes a moment to see we're alone. Someone shouts behind us and a shotgun erupts. Several quick shots follow and I lead the way back into the front room.

"He's down," Mercier yells.

Voices shout outside and a hail of gunfire erupts from the backyard. Twenty seconds after we entered, we turn on the lights to find the blond haired biker dead in the hall. The other two never made it off the back porch. All were armed with sawed-off shotguns.

Jodie checks Dunn and Mercier then turns to me and Costanza to see if we've been hit.

The back porch is covered with blood and smells of gunpowder. Five shadows move toward us, like black-clad ghosts. They'd made sure no one got off the porch. Constanza eases forward and check the Latino. Dead.

As he moves to check Mullet, pulling the long hair away from the man's face, it hits me. It's not him. He's too small.

"Dammit!"

I back into the house, pushing my way past Elmer Fudd. Dunn makes a loud burp sound followed by a 'Zowie' and two pings, like sonar from some submarine.

Where the fuck is Mullet? I press my back against the wall, close my eyes and think. The chanting returns, as if I push an invisible 'play' button. I feel a sudden calming as I shut out the voices, the footsteps, the smell of death.

Blood! I see blood.

Sandie.

"Where you going?" Jodie shouts behind me as I run to the front porch and leap off. Kay and Gonzales pull up behind me as I drive away. Punching the accelerator, I head the wrong way down Third Street to Claiborne. I make it to Jackson Avenue in five heart-wrenching minutes, running every light, nearly causing three wrecks.

I take the stairs three at a time, withdrawing the Glock on the way up. Sandie's door is cracked open. The door frame's been shattered, the floor littered with splinters from the frame. I lean close and listen. All I hear is my heartbeat. I peek in.

The only light filters through the open window at the far end of the living room. I think there's a fire escape there. The curtain floats in on the summer breeze. I step inside and ease through the living room toward the first bedroom. Empty. So is the second bedroom. I move back through the living room and stop at a creaking noise at the far end of the room near the open window. I go down on my haunches and wait long seconds.

I creep silently into the kitchen and wait. The hair on my arms tingle and I feel goose-bumps. Someone's there. I feel it. I strain to hear. Breathing. I hear breathing. Ahead and off to my left. I raise the Glock and a flash is instantly followed by the explosion of a large caliber weapon. The refrigerator door flies open and another round strikes it.

As the echo dies down, I hear screaming. A woman's voice screams behind me as I wheel around and rush back into the living room. A large figure jumps out the window. A chrome revolver reaches back in and sprays the apartment with four more shots. I duck back into the kitchen as the cabinet below the sink opens and Sandie crawls out.

"Beau!" She reaches for me. "Beau!" I pull her to me and take a second to make sure she's not hit.

"Stay!" I push her away and race back into the living room, firing three quick shots at the window as I rush it. There's no return fire. I wait two seconds and carefully peek out at the black iron fire escape. There's a noise below. Two more shots ring out, echoing with the sound of thunder. Magnum rounds. He's reloaded.

I hear hurried footsteps. He's running away. I crawl out on the landing and see the big fuck, greasy hair flapping behind as he heads down the well-lit alley behind the apartment house. There's a high brick wall in front of him. He's going the wrong way.

I hurry down the ladder and tumble to the pavement as another round strikes the ladder above me. Jumping into a doorway, I hear him slap the wall a good thirty yards away. He's trapped. I let it sink in a couple seconds and then call out, "Mullet!"

He lets out a yell of frustration, more like a growl.

"You're trapped. You stupid fuck!"

A bullet strikes the wall near me. I hear feet running. *He's rushing me.* Another shot ricochets above me and I have to do the unexpected. I dive out, flat on my belly, arms straight out and aim at him. He fires again and I squeeze off a round, which strikes him, sending him head first to the pavement. Mullet screams and rises, holding his left leg. He points his gun at me again and I hear it click and click again. He's out of bullets.

I get up. He wavers as he stands, points his revolver at me and pulls the trigger again. It's a Colt. I recognize the classic ramp sights.

"Click it again and I'll blow your brains out!" I step toward him and he throws his gun at me, missing me by inches. Even hunched over, he's a bear of a man. Mullet sucks in a deep breath and lunges at me and I drop my aim and blow out his right knee.

He collapses five feet in front of me. Stepping around him as he writhes, I press the muzzle of my Glock against his temple.

"Quit moving!" I search him carefully, then step back and holster my weapon.

Mullet's face, slick with sweat, glares at me. His teeth gritted, he's in real pain. Good. I slowly back away and find his gun up the alley. It's a .357 magnum Colt Python with a four inch barrel, standard issue walnut checkered grips. I look around for my radio, which has fallen out of my back pocket. I find it beneath the fire escape ladder. Making sure my voice is calm, I call headquarters.

"Go ahead, 3124."

"I need a Homicide Supervisor and an EMT unit. I have the suspect down." I give them Sandie's address and tell them we're in back, in the alley.

Jodie cuts in, "Suspect? Did you say *suspect*?"

"I've got Mullet."

The fool is trying to crawl away. I step back over and nudge him in the left leg where I shot him and he doubles up.

"Stay still, fuck-head!" Unsheathing my knife I slice off a strip of Mullet's shirt and wrap it around his knee cap, which causes the big man to flatten out. He breathes heavily, eyes closed tightly now. I pat him down, make sure he doesn't have another weapon.

My legs feel suddenly weak so I sit cross-legged in the yellow glow of the alley lights and wait for everyone to show up. Wiping perspiration from my brow, I see my hand is shaking. I look up to check where I'd fired through the open window and see there's a three story brick wall across the alley. Looks like the rear of some business. I shake my head. I'm in another alley, aren't I?

Watching Mullet sucking in breaths, I try not to envision Peter James' head, try not to remind myself what Mullet has done. But I can't. My hands begin to shake and I want to blow this fucker's brains all over the pavement so badly, I can taste his blood in my mouth.

I close my eyes and try to envision the Dakota sun setting on the Black Hills. And the death chant echoes again in my mind. Long moments later, my heart aches and yet I feel a great calming inside. My hands stop shaking. Turning around, I cup my hands around my mouth and call up to Sandie.

She peeks out the window.

"I got him!"

"Good! Is he dead?"

"No."

She pauses a second. "What the fuck you waitin' for?"

To get the whole story, Jodie would say. This slimy bastard is our only chance at getting the story. A siren echoes in the distance. Another seems to answer. Tires screech to a halt up the alley and a car door slams. I stand, spot the unmistakable form of Lieutenant Dennis Merten move out of the darkness into the alley. Flashing red lights and a high-pitched siren confirms the EMTees have also arrived.

Merten's coat flaps as he steps quickly. "He dead?"

"Not yet."

Merten turns and tells the EMTees to fuckin' hurry. He rushes past me and goes down on his knees next to Mullet. I step back as two white-clad EMTees race up, each carrying a medical bag. Merten moves out of their way, watches them a minute then slowly walks back to me.

I point to Mullet's gun and Merten glances at it before his dark face moves in front of mine. He looks at me incredulously.

"I don't fuckin' believe this shit!" He shakes his head. "I do not fuckin' believe this."

I give him the inexpressive, plains warrior stare. Then I turn and head back for the fire escape.

"Where you going?"

I point upward, jump, and grab ladder and pull myself up.

Chapter 16
KNOW WHAT KIND OF KNIFE THIS IS?

Six hours later, after giving two statements, after enduring another superintendent's hearing to justify why I shot yet another person, I sit in an uncomfortable metal chair outside Felice's room at Charity. No, in my statements I didn't say it was my fault, although *all* of it is my fault. I'll go down that road alone. What they got out of me was 'just the facts' as Jack Webb would say.

My Daddy loved *Dragnet* and we watched it late at night on our black and white TV. I'm not about to tell anyone that on the fuckin' department. I blink away the image and close my eyes as I hear Sandie's voice again, asking me why I didn't kill Mullet. Sitting on her couch, every light on in her apartment, she'd wrapped herself in a pink blanket. Her make-up smudged, her face was streaked with tears as she looked up at me. I sat next to her and tried to take her hand, but she pulled it away.

"I heard him scratching at my door," she said in a hollow voice. "All I could think was ... hide under the sink."

A tear rolled down her cheek.

"I heard him searching for me." She started rocking back and forth. "How'd he find out where I live?"

"He's not as stupid as he looks."

Sandie suddenly slapped my shoulder hard.

"And you're not so smart either."

She stopped rocking, leaned back and closed her eyes.

"I found out *why*," she said in a whisper. "It's like a gang with no name. In order to become a member ... they have to kill a cop with a special gun."

"Mullet tell you that?"

She shook her head. "Word on the street. Everyone's been talking about it, especially since the last cop got killed."

Lt. Merten had stepped into the living room, followed by a crime lab tech with a camera. I get up to show them the bullet holes and my shell casings. Pulling me aside, Merten told me Mullet was going to make it and Jodie was in route to Charity and Kay wanted me immediately, at headquarters.

The sound of footsteps brings me back to the present. Darlene Wilson turns the corner down the hall and heads my way. She wears a dark suit this morning. Seeing me, she avoids my gaze as she turns briskly into Felice's room.

I readjust my Glock and lean back and wait. Fifteen quiet minutes later, other footsteps approach. Jodie rounds the corner. In black slacks and a black jacket, she carries a carton with three Styrofoam cups. As she gets closer, I see the coffee's from Café Du Monde.

She sits next to me and I catch a whiff of her mild perfume when she leans close to pass me a cup. "Extra strong," she says as she takes a cup herself.

We each take a sip.

"Mullet's not talking." Jodie's shoulders slump. "He's down the hall in a nice comfy bed and I can't get a damn thing out of him." She shakes her head at this personal defeat. Hell, if anyone could get the big bastard to talk, it would be Jodie.

"We found Cochran's and Steven's badges in a chest-of-drawers in Mullet's bedroom."

"The Python from the alley?"

She nods and takes another sip. "A match. And he almost killed you with it too." She looks down, sadly, as if she's given up on telling me I almost got killed ... again.

"Dunn and the FBI are dismembering the place," she add. "Haven't found Peter James's badge yet."

The effect of the coffee is immediate. I sit up. Too bad it's going to be temporary. I'm so damn tired my eye-lashes ache when I blink.

"Any word on Peter James's funeral?"

"His parents are burying him back home in Oregon."

I stare at the closed door of Felice's room as I tell Jodie about the scrawny man named Clyde who'd been shooting his mouth off that he used a Colt Python .357 magnum to murder cops.

"That was the lead Felice was following."

"None of the three bodies on So. Derbigny were named Clyde."

I nod. "He has salt and pepper hair."

The door opens and Darlene Wilson steps out, sees us and stops. Jodie holds out the third cup of coffee. Darlene gives me a long stare then takes the cup, tucking her clipboard under her left arm. Surprisingly, she moves around me and sits on the chair to my left. After sipping her coffee, she crosses her leg and opens her clipboard.

Looking at her notes, she says, "Felice doesn't want any part of you. So there's no sense waiting out here." Her voice is scratchy but the edge is gone. "She doesn't remember the name of the bar she was in, but it was on the Chef. The man she was looking for, Clyde, came in with four other men. They locked the door and confronted her, demanding to know why she was asking about Clyde. They tore off her clothes, beat and raped her."

Darlene looks up at me. "She doesn't remember being dumped on Almonaster, but remembers someone pointing a gun at her and pulling the trigger but the gun didn't go off. Probably a misfire." Closing the clipboard, Darlene stands. "We've hit every bar along the Chef and will hit 'em again, so there's no need for you to go pursuing this. Understand?"

I look her in the eye and say nothing.

"This is a rape case." She turns to Jodie. "Not a murder."

I stand and stretch.

Darlene asks Jodie. "Do you have any control over him?"

I cut in. "Which way is Mullet's room?"

Jodie points down the hall and says it's to the right. "You can't miss it. Cops all over the place."

Darlene leaves without even saying good-bye. Jodie closes her eyes and leans her head back against the wall. With her lips pursed and her hair fluffed around her lean cheeks, with the sun streaming in from the window at the end of the hall, she looks ten years younger.

She's right, there's no missing Mullet's room. Two black-uniformed Orleans Parish Sheriff's Deputies guard the door. Tim Rothman and a patrol officer lean against the wall across the narrow hall. When Rothman notices me, I ask him, "Where the fuck have you been?"

"Desire. Goddamn Picard had me boldly go where no man has gone before – without transporters or phasers. Heard you've been up to your usual no good."

I pull out my Glock and hand it to him and step across the hall into Mullet's private room. The lone window has bars on it. Mullet lies propped up in bed, his right arm handcuffed to the bed rail, both legs in bandages and suspended by ropes from the bars running down each side of the bed. His deep-set eyes glare at me. He lowers his head so his protruding brow can make his eyes more menacing. Probably practiced that look in jailhouse mirrors made of stainless steel.

"What the fuck you want?"

I move to the right side of the bed.

Mullet's greasy hair has already made a stain on the white pillowcase and the room smells bad, like a garbage left out in the rain.

"I said what the *fuck* you want?"

I pull my note pad out of my back pocket and the pen from my dress shirt pocket. "Names," I tell him. "I want to know who was with you on Tchoupitoulas Street."

"Fuck you!" He defiantly sticks out his Neanderthal jaw. "I want my fuckin' lawyer."

"Names," I tell him. "I'm not going to ask you again."

I stare into his eyes, giving him the cold, warrior stare. He tries staring back, but blinks eventually, huffs and looks away. I keep staring. He won't look back now, content to readjust his sheet, then lean back.

I keep staring. He tucks his free hand behind his head and closes his eyes. "You know," he says. "I can't wait to get back in jail. I'm a hero. I'll be king of Parish Prison. King of the cop killers."

"You're going to die."

He laughs at me.

"You're going to get the death penalty."

When he looks back he sees my face hasn't changed expression. He sees my eyes still boring into his eyes.

"Death penalty!" Mullet laughs again. "Yeah, in ten, fifteen years maybe. Hell, I wouldn't have lasted ten years on the street."

I move so fast he doesn't even see me pull out my ten-inch knife, doesn't even have time to yell. Grabbing a chuck of greasy hair, I yank it hard and press the edge of my knife against his forehead. The beady-eyes leer at my blade.

"Know what kind of knife this is? It's obsidian. A Sioux knife, the same kind that scalped Custer and his men at Little Bighorn."

I twist the blade and draw a line of blood.

"See how it's sharp on one side only." Raising the blade swiftly, I slice off a chunk of Mullet's hair. "Makes scalping easier."

Mullet lets out a scream so loud the deputies rush in with Rothman and two doctors. I let go of Mullet's hair and calmly slip my knife back in its scabbard. On my way out I tell Rothman I should have really scalped him.

He hands me my Glock and says let's shoot him.

I storm away. Behind me my old partner tells the doctors, "He's part Sioux, you know. A stone, cold killer."

•

Captain Picard does a double-take as I approach the front porch of Mullet's house at six p.m. sharp. He's never seen me in a suit.

"So, how's it going?"

He tells me it's going fine. I can see three agents inside the house, one with a hand-held vacuum, the other taking measurements.

"By the way, what is your name?"

"Special Agent Thomas Kirk."

I grit my teeth and force myself not to howl in the man's face. It takes several, teeth-grinding seconds before I can ask, "Come up with anything with the name Clyde on it?"

Kirk shakes his head.

I rub my hand across my freshly-shaved chin, pull out my note pad and walk around to the side of the house. The first bike still has blue paint on its rusty gas tank. I jot the serial number in my note pad and move to the next piece of biker junk. By the time I've circumnavigated the house, I've secured thirteen serial numbers and four license plate numbers.

"Seriously," I tell Kirk as I pass him a business card. "If y'all come up with anything with the name Clyde, please let me know."

Kirk nods slowly. Stepping away, I spot my partner approaching with Elmer Fudd Channard.

"I thought you were at the hospital?" Gonzales spreads his arms. In a bright blue shirt over a tee-shirt and jeans, he points to my navy blue suit. "What's with the get-up?"

"We wear suits in Homicide, partner."

As I turn to leave, Channard calls out, "Have you seen Jodie?"

•

A previous owner of the turquoise Harley-Davidson without any wheels, parked behind Mullet's house, was one Clyde Pailet, Box 11206, Highway 11, New Orleans. I stare at the name on the computer screen. The hair on my arms stands straight up.

I run Clyde's name through criminal records. Also known as *Swamp Rat*, he has arrests for simple battery, aggravated assault, aggravated battery and burglary. He spent six years in Parchman for Auto Theft. He got out six months ago. *Jesus*, he was arrested three weeks ago for aggravated assault. So much for parole violations, he was released on bail the next day.

Swamp Rat? I check his place of birth. Pearl River, Louisiana. Right next to the Honey Island Swamp. I run the address in the computer and a vehicle currently registered at the Highway 11 address is a gold Harley Davidson listed to C. L. Pailet.

I print out Pailet's record. Five minutes later, a clerk at Criminal Records passes me a color image of forty year old Clyde Pailet who stands six feet tall and weighs one-eighty. His craggy face has sunken cheeks and a jailhouse tattoo of 'CP' on his forehead, backwards as done with a mirror. Clyde has medium length salt-and-pepper hair, just like the man seen fleeing from the Cochran murder. I put together a photo line-up and call Darlene Wilson on the radio.

A half hour later, I'm standing in the hall outside Felice's room with a reluctant Darlene Wilson. "We'll see if this works," she says skeptically as she takes the line-up into Felice's room. When she doesn't come out right away, I sit. When she doesn't come out a half hour later, I know we've found our Clyde. She has to take a statement.

An hour after entering, Darlene comes out.

"I hate to have to ask," she says, "but how'd you come up with him?"

I tell her about the motorcycle and add, "I'll call you in the Bureau with a script of his house." She'll need a detailed description of the house for her search warrant.

"I told you. This is a rape case. I don't want you involved. And that's an order."

I want to tell her she can stick those fuckin' sergeant's stripes up her ass, but I opt for the more diplomatic route. "In case you haven't figured it, we need each other."

There's a subtle change in her eyes. Maybe she agrees. Maybe.

Sure, she's the one who can get an arrest warrant and search warrant for Clyde Pailet, and her rape case is all we have right now. But Cochran and Stevens and James are dead and there's no way I'm not going to Clyde's.

•

Clyde's house is a camp actually, suspended on creosote pilings off Highway 11 along the Irish Bayou Canal not fifty yards from eastern Lake Pontchartrain. Set up in my Caprice in a cut back off the two-lane, black-topped highway, I watch the place carefully. There's a screen porch surrounding the unpainted, wooden house which has a corrugated tin roof. The small shell parking area in front of the house is empty. A long wooden walkway connects the house to the shell lot.

This semi-wild part of town almost reminds me of home. The camps, the clapboard houses, the occasional brick house lining the highway have absolutely nothing in common with the wrought-iron balconies of the French Quarter, except being within the same city limits. Behind the camps, the wide expanse of the lake, dotted with small cypress islands, could almost pass for Vermilion Bay.

The smell is different, of course. Highway 11 smells of kerosene and car exhaust and only faintly of marshland. New Orleans East is a vast swampland dotted with the occasional subdivision, dissected by elevated roadways, like Chef Menteur Highway two miles to the south of where I sit. Highway 11 rings the eastern boundary of the city as the

Seventeenth Street Canal, where Angie is probably waiting on tables, rings the western edge of town.

Darlene Wilson's dark blue Ford Taurus leads the long line of units flying up Highway 11 from the Chef. Blue and red lights flashing, the high-pitched whine of their engines decelerate quickly, followed by the screeching of brakes. Behind Darlene's Ford is the armored car SWAT unit. I climb out of my car, stretch and casually cross the street.

Nine black-clad and helmeted SWAT officers bolt from the back of the armored car. They race across the shell lot. The men in front carry large bullet-proof shields. The next two carry a black battering ram.

Stepping next to Darlene, I fold my arms and watch the spectacle of someone shouting 'Police!' and the door crashing beneath the weight of the battering ram, of the SWAT team climbing in and out of doors and windows, buzzing around the porch like killer insects.

Bob Kay, wearing a SWAT vest outside his suit coat, leads a line of Task Forcers from the cars to Darlene and me. Gonzales, in a dark green suit, gleeks me. Rothman and Channard and One-L and even Two-L are there, along with two crime lab technicians. Dunn gives us his impersonation of Al Pacino's "Whoo ah!" from *Scent of a Woman*.

The SWAT teamer with a silver stripe around his helmet gives us the all-clear with a wave and Darlene leads us, single file along the walkway that creaks and moans with our weight. The SWAT team passes us, their heads bowed in disappointment.

Kay passes out rubber gloves to each of us as we enter. Our search is disciplined and meticulous. Seven minutes after entering, Elmer Fudd Channard calls excitedly from the first bedroom. "I found it!"

We wait, but all he does is repeat himself. "I *found* it!"

"Found what?" Kay replies.

"The badge."

It's lying in the top drawer of an end table next to a double bed with yellowed sheets and a headboard featuring several bullet holes. We take turns peeking at it, see it has James's badge number, before a crime lab tech moves forward to take pictures and secure it.

After seeing the badge with dried blood still on it, we continue our search in complete silence. We find two Colt .38 revolvers, a Taurus .22 revolver, a sawed-off Winchester 12 gauge shotgun and two pounds of marijuana wrapped in aluminum foil. We also find nine Polaroids of Clyde and his compadres. Mullet is in two of the pictures, which were taken on the porch of this house.

As the technicians start dusting for fingerprints, we move to the porch. The sky is purple and green, the clouds above the tree-line across the highway are blood red. Behind us the lake is already in darkness.

Bob Kay taps me on the shoulder and asks me to follow him down the walkway. I spot Merten leaning against Darlene Wilson's car. When we arrive, he unfolds his arms and tries to smile at me. His face doesn't crack, but if that's a smile, I'm a fuckin' astronaut.

"We want you to take a week off." Kay says this looking up at the sky.

Merten nods and the smile fades back into the familiar scowl. "And when you come back, you come back to our platoon." He blinks at me, as if he's just realized I'm in a suit.

"Am I suspended?"

The both say no in unison. Emphatically. Kay leans against the car and tells me I've done a helluva job on this case. Hell, I solved it, he says. I'll get a commendation. I'm the one who put it all together, he says, his voice rising. Without you, he says, he doesn't know when we'd have solved this damn thing.

He pauses for a breath and Merten cuts in. "We don't want you shooting this last ass-hole." He folds his arms. "You haven't taken a vacation in nine months. Take a week."

Merten's eyes reveal there's no way I'm talking my way out of this. Even if I remind him it's my fault, it'll do no good. Probably do a lot of harm.

"We have the whole department looking for this guy," Kay says. He won't look me in the eye.

Merten does as he says, "Take a goddamn week off. That's an order."

Chapter 17
GUESS YOU GOT A LOT OF GIRLS

Nine o'clock the next morning I'm out on the deck of *Sad Lisa* with Buck who's giving me a curious, blue-eyed stare.

"A week," I tell him. "What the hell do I do with a week?"

Buck leans forward, his butt up in the air, and barks twice.

"Am I pathetic, or what?"

I move to the gate and look over at the green tarpaulin covering my old car as it sits parked next to the dock at the bow of my houseboat. Turning, I almost trip over Buck on my way to the engine room where I pull out one of the spare car batteries.

"Come on," I tell Buck as I lead the way out to the car.

I pull the tarp off of my '79 dark green Thunderbird, open the hood and replace the battery. It grinds a little when I start it, sputters, then cranks up smoothly. I let it idle.

"It's about time you see a swamp," I tell Buck as I climb out.

He's too busy sniffing tires to answer. I wash up quickly and pull down a bowl, filling it with ice to put on the floorboard for Buck. Slipping the Glock into the waistband of my black jeans at the small of my back, I grab a shirt to cover my weapon and my knife on my way out with the bowl.

"You're going to love this," I tell Buck who goes down on his back, flailing his paws at me as I pass. "You're a swamp dog."

"John?" A feminine voice calls out behind me.

I turn and Angie is there, arms behind her back. She has her hair in barrettes again and wears a pink sleeveless top and jeans.

"Are you all right?" She twists her head to the side.

"Sure." Then I realize. "You've been reading the paper again."

Her face reddens slightly and she steps forward, focusing those aquamarines at me.

"You weren't at work last night."

"I took a couple days off. Exams."

Buck bounces over to her, yips, then sniffs her white tennis shoes. She bends over to pet him and he rolls on his back.

"Watch it. He'll pee on you."

She yanks her hand back and laughs in that deep, Bacall voice. "He's sure cute." She looks past me at the car. "Going somewhere?"

"Cannes Bruleé."

"Where?"

"Little village where I grew up. By Vermilion Bay. South of Abbeville."

Angie shakes her head.

"South of Lafayette."

"Oh." She takes in a deep breath and says, "Can I come?"

It's not often I'm at a lost for words, but I recover quickly with, "Sure. If you're brave enough to travel in this." I nod to the T-Bird.

"Can I help you load up anything?"

I put the bowl on the floorboard on the passenger side, explaining Buck might overheat in the car and the ice will melt and he'll have something cool to lap.

"AC doesn't work in the old car."

"May I use your phone?"

"Sure." I lead her on to *Sad Lisa* and watch her curious stares as she looks around. She leaves a message for her father, telling him where's she's off to. She's careful. I like that.

"You always carry that?" she asks as I pick up my knife.

"My Daddy told me to never go in the swamp without a knife." I pat the Glock. "And we have to eat, don't we?"

She laughs again. Good, she gets my bad jokes. As soon as we get in the T-Bird, Buck scrambles on my lap, puts his paws up on the steering wheel and busies himself looking out the windshield. I crack the windows and the warm breeze flows over us as we drive away from Bucktown for the interstate.

Angie pets Buck head. "Is he really a swamp dog?"

"Catahoula. It's the state dog. An Indian dog."

I tell her how the word *catahoula* means clear water or beloved lake in Choctaw. "Because they have blue eyes."

Accessing the interstate, I give the T-Bird's eight cylinders the gas and she slips smoothly into traffic. One of the big, later Thunderbirds, my car is heavy with a nice comfortable ride. With the windows cracked, a fresh breeze floats around us.

"How far is it?"

I start laughing at that, which makes Angie laugh back at me.

"About three hours, if we're lucky."

"Good," she says, crossing her legs. "We'll have plenty of time to talk."

It occurs to me this is our first time alone, except for Buck. We glide through Metairie and Kenner and slip into St. Charles Parish. Buck finally settles between us as we cross the Bonnet Carré Spillway, riding the concrete bridge over a vast swampland along the southern edge of Lake Pontchartrain, which lies nearly motionless to our right.

"Beautiful, isn't it?" Angie nods to the moss-covered cypress trees.

"Wait 'till you see Vermilion Bay."

I ask about her classes and learn some of the differences between UNO, The University of New Orleans and LSU, Louisiana State University, where we had an active campus life. A commuter university, UNO sounds more impersonal. When I mention the differences, Angie is very curious about my time and LSU.

"I hear about the drinking and wild parties."

"I only went there two years. On a football scholarship." I explain how I tore up my knee. Dropped out and meandered down to New Orleans.

"To most of us Cajuns, New Orleans is Paris."

She tells me her father went to LSU for a couple years. Her parents divorced ten years ago. Her mother re-married and lives in Tennessee. She doesn't volunteer and I don't ask why she lives with her father. We transverse Ascension Parish in silence and I'm amazed how natural it feels just having her there. We don't have to make small talk. I feel my heart beating and recognize that tell-tale sign.

We cross the Mississippi at Baton Rouge and she starts talking about LaSalle and DeSoto and vast American forest-swampland that once covered as far as we could see. I tell her about the fierce war dogs DeSoto brought with him, dogs used to ward off Indian attacks. Apparently some of the dogs escaped captivity, some captured by the Choctaw.

"Ever see a red wolf?"

"At the Audubon Zoo," she says. "Small for a wolf, aren't they?"

"Apparently DeSoto's war dogs mated with the red wolf, which produced the mottled spots, muscular shoulders, and blue eyes of the Catahoula."

Buck raises his head as if he knows we're talking about him, licks my hand then nuzzles his face against Angie's leg. She strokes his fur softly. "Hard to imagine this little guy being fierce."

I finish the thought, "Or able to move silently through the swamp with the cunning of a wolf."

"He doesn't look very cunning."

"If you look at his face closely, you'll see a close resemblance to Disney's Goofy."

She laughs again.

We pass cotton fields and corn fields as we cross the long flat land. Turning off the interstate at Lafayette we eventually ride past rice paddies and wide fields of sugar cane.

"My Daddy worked the cane."

"Tell me about him."

I tell her he was a sugar boiler by profession. Worked from one sugar mill to another each season. Godchaux's. Domino's. He was also a pipe-fitter for the mills.

"What does a boiler do?"

"Boils the cane into molasses. Ever use cane syrup on pancakes?"

Angie nods. "My favorite."

Eventually, past Abbeville, the road narrows into a two-lane blacktop as we move through the marshland Cajuns call the floating prairie. The cypress forest closes around us. We cross three wooden bridges over bayous to a road with no white stripes. I slow down as we cross Crooked Bayou.

Looking around, Angie lets out a sigh. "Gorgeous," she whispers, as if something out there can hear us. Buck climbs back in my lap, paws up on steering wheel as we ease through the vast swamp. Spanish moss drips from the cypress tree like beards of long dead Spaniards. I roll the windows down completely to let in the rich scents of the swamp. There's no smell like it. The air is thicker, heavy with oxygen, carried on the sweet smell of chlorophyll from the flora, along with the sourness of decay.

I turn down a shell road and circumnavigate a log in the road, through more cypress until the road rises slightly. We move next to the brown water of Bayou Brunet. The cypress gives way to a stand of oaks and suddenly we're there. I turn off the road and pull up against a wooden fence, once painted white. Angie lets out a high-pitched sigh as Vermilion Bay opens in front of us, vast and olive green. The sun shimmers off it and a nice warm breeze floats from it.

I let Buck out and he races to the fence, sniffs it, cocks a leg up and pees on it. Angie stares at the bay, a hand over her eyes. I turn my eyes to an unpainted wooden house to our right, half-hidden at the edge of the bayou, the swamp its backyard. A typical Cajun house with porches in front and back, it has a high-pitched roof. A red pick-up is parked next to the house. At its rear is the dock my father built, a pirogue tied to it.

My throat tightens.

"It's lovely here," Angie says. "And so peaceful."

I wave my hand at the wide bay. "When the rain comes in, you can smell it first, rich and damp." Shielding my eyes, I look at the bay. "The clouds build. Tall, gray clouds. Suck the humidity right off the bay and it becomes almost cool, even in the dead of summer."

I turn back to the house. "It comes down in sheets, in waves, peppering the swamp, bending the branches of the big oaks and fluttering the cypress moss and it's like the sky's falling. Fat raindrops hammer the tin roof like thousands of nails falling from heaven."

Angie moves to me and stares at the house. "That was eloquent."

Me, eloquent?

I point to the house. "After my father died, my mother sold it and moved back to South Dakota to be with her people."

"The Sioux."

Nodding, I tell her, "This land doesn't belong to my family any more." There's a catch in my voice. I clear my throat as if something's caught there.

The screen door opens and two dark haired boys rush out, the door slamming behind them. The boys run around to the far side of the house, out of sight. For a moment, I wonder if their father teaches them the wonders of the swampland as my father taught me.

Looking at Angie, I can see it in her eyes. She won't say it, but the house is little more than a shack.

"My great-granddaddy built it."

I don't tell her it's a *daubed* house, its walls filled with swamp mud and moss to keep the house almost cool in summer and warm in winter. I don't tell her that the stairs on the front porch lead to the attic where I slept.

She puts a hand on my shoulder for a moment as she looks around again. "I'm serious. This place is *so* beautiful."

"That's what the mosquitoes think and the gators and cottonmouths."

Buck sniffs along the edge of the swamp, but doesn't go in, thankfully.

I can't stop staring at the house. "I guess a part of me will always belong here." Can't believe I said that aloud. But I continue the thought. "My mother's father, up in Dakota, used to tell me how the white man believes the land belongs to him. The Sioux believe we belong to the land. I guess I feel both ways."

Taking in a deep breath, the familiar scents fill me with a deep heartache. I close my eyes. This is where I belong. This is the only place I've ever belonged, with my daddy here on the swamp. A pain stabs me deep in my chest as I see my father's craggy face. And I remember, with unforgiving clarity, the long, beautiful summer of my youth.

Every school I went to – I didn't belong. I didn't belong at LSU. I don't belong in Bucktown and hardly in New Orleans. And it hits me hard, as I stand here, that I'll never belong again. Because it's gone. That time is gone.

Blinking my eyes, I feel tears and look away from Angie, lest she notice. Buck scampers over and rubs his nose against my leg. He senses something is wrong.

"Are you all right?" Angie touches my hand.

I nod but can't stop the damn tears. Pulling away, I cover my face and fight the tears.

Angie's voice comes faintly. "You don't have to hold it in."

I grit my teeth and struggle though the sadness. I can't let it out. Not here. Not now. Eventually, the tears subside and I wipe my face quickly and take in a strong breath and look away. "If my Sioux grandfather could see me now, he'd call me a bad name."

"What name?"

I take in another deep breath, still struggling to calm myself. Looking into the aquamarines, I explain. "In the code of the plains warrior, the Sioux and Cheyenne, a warrior never shows emotion. Unlike the white man, who is known to show his anger and even cry in front of everyone, if a Sioux warrior did the same, he would be called *Woman Face*.

Angie laughs and immediately covers her mouth with a hand. I laugh too.

"No way," she says. "No one could call you woman face with that square jaw and falcon nose. Anyway, you're only half Sioux."

"When my daddy died, I was a *Woman Face* for a long time. Guess I still am."

I take her hand and lead her back to the car.

"How about lunch?"

"Good. I'm famished."

I call out to Buck, but he's too busy sniffing a frog. I have to go get him and he actually growls as I pick him up. I put him next to the bowl and he laps the cool water. As we pull away, Angie tells me she's a half-breed too, half-French and half-Italian. I can't help but laugh. *Half-breed*, huh?

Aunt Lillian's lies on the edge of the swamp, just outside Cannes Bruleé. Suspended on pilings, the white wooden building has a tin roof and seating out back, little gazebos where Buck can ramble around. On our way up the stairs, I tell Angie this place has the best nutria gumbo and fried armadillo. She pokes me in the side.

"Real cute." She takes my hand as we step inside to the strong smells of filé gumbo and boiling crawfish.

We carry our plates out to the gazebo closest to the swamp. I go back and let Buck out of the car and he races right for the swamp, but doesn't go in. Good city dog. As Angie takes her first mouthful of crawfish etouffee, scooping a spoonful of the thickly seasoned crawfish tails and white rice, I take a sip of icy Barq's. She makes a yummy sound and I start in on my crawfish bisque.

"So that's how it's done," she tells me as I use the butt on my spoon to dig out the crawfish stuffing from the shells. Mixing it with the rice and gravy I taste it. Wonderful. Buck's yipping turns us around. A huge box turtle has emerged from the swamp and lumbers across the grass, Buck circling it and yipping.

"Lucky that's not a snapper."

So Angie and I share our first meal together in the shelter of the small gazebo, beneath the strong Cajun sun next to the vast swamp where I hunted and fished away my young days and nights. Later, we drive through Cannes Bruleé and I point out my old high school. A large sign in front of Holy Ghost reads: *Go Riders!*

"Holy *Ghost Riders*?" Angie asks incredulously.

"State champs my junior and senior years."

"What position did you play?"

I tell her I was an all-state quarterback, believe it or not.

"Quarterback, huh? Guess you got a lot of girls."

Shaking my head, I tell her, "I was ... um ... sort of ... well not part of the crowd."

"What does that mean?"

"My daddy worked part-time. My family. Um, we were on relief."

I can see in her eyes, it's not registering.

"I went to catholic school without paying tuition."

"What? On a football scholarship?"

"No. I never knew we were poor until I got to high school. I remember overhearing a girl I had a crush on telling her friends I was cute and all, but poor as a church-mouse."

Angie's eyes are suddenly red.

"We always had enough to eat. I just, uh, didn't have nice clothes, stuff like that." I take one last look at the school as we move away. "Stuff that doesn't matter ... now."

"But it mattered then, didn't it?"

Turning off Landrieu Avenue, I take her along Breaux Lane where fine southern homes of wide verandahs and manicured lawns line the street.

"We actually have rich people here too."

"So many trees," Angie says.

"If you look closely, you'll see the houses were built around the trees or between them." As they carved our village from the Cajun floating prairie, the founders of Cannes Bruleé didn't believe in cutting down trees.

Before leaving the village, I pull over at a small grocery store "I want to get some authentic boudin and andouille to take back home."

Angie climbs out, making sure Buck doesn't get out. He barks at us and I tell him we'll only be a minute. I ask the woman behind the counter for ten pounds of andouille and ten of boudin. She wipes her hands on her white apron and gives me a strange look. Her graying hair in a bun, she's about my mother's age. She goes about cutting and wrapping the spicy pork sausage we call andouille and the boudin, white sausage made with rice, ground pork, chicken and vegetables.

The woman brings the packages to the register. She gives me that same strange look and says, "You gotta be Calixte Beau's boy."

I nod.

"An weren't you de quarterback dat went to L.S. and U.?"

"Yes, ma'am."

"What happen to you? It was zif you fell of de eart."

I pull ID folder out of my back pocket and show it to her. "I'm a cop." I dig my cash from my front pocket.

"Get on wif' youself!" The woman laughs loudly, which causes Angie to laugh too.

I interrupt the laughter, asking for another slice of andouille, which she also wraps in white paper. On our way out, she calls out, "You came back soon, child. I can believe Calixte Beau's little boy a cop. I knew you turn out to no good, yeah."

I give Buck the slice of andouille and he attacks it, then laps more water before settling on the seat between us. Driving through Acadiana, I take Angie to St. Martinville and show her the little statue of Evangeline.

"That's Delores Del Rio," I tell Angie. "The stature was cast in her image. She played Evangeline in the movie back in the 1920s."

Buck sleeps most of the way home. As we close in on the city, I feel sullen, feel it all closing in on me again. Angie asks what's wrong. I tell her about Felice and about Sandie and Mullet. I tell her about So. Derbigny Street and the alley behind Sandie's. I tell her about the blood we found on Peter James' badge. I ramble on until I'm describing Cassandra's lifeless face.

Angie says nothing when I finally stop talking. The sunlight still has a good hour or two to go by the time we pull back into Bucktown.

"If you'll have dinner with me," I say as I park the T-Bird. "I'll make you the most succulent boudin you've ever tasted."

Angie seems relieved that I've come out of my funk and we unpack. Fixing Buck a can of gourmet dog food, I flip on my police radio out of habit. The traffic seems normal.

"This is so cozy," Angie says as she steps around the houseboat. Noticing the loft, she says, "So that's your bedroom."

An excited voice rises on my radio, the whoop of a siren echoing in the transmission. I turn it up.

"706, headquarters."

"Go ahead, 706."

"I'm in pursuit of that gold motorcycle, northbound on Highway 11!"

Jesus Christ – *Clyde*.

Chapter 18
THE SAVAGE BAYOU

I step over to my closet, pull off my shirt and put on a black tee-shirt and put the Glock and place it on the end table next to my sofa as I unfasten my belt. I slip on my canvas holster, along with two ammo pouches.

"What's happening?" Angie stares at me with wide, suddenly frightened eyes.

Nodding to the radio I tell her that's the last killer they're chasing. I sit on my sofa, pull off my white leather Nikes for my black canvas Reeboks, then fill the two ammo pouches with magazines of 147-grain, semi-jacketed hollow-point ammunition. Slipping the Glock into its holster behind my back, I reach down and tie my knife to my leg.

Angie steps in front of me. "You're leaving?"

"I have to."

"But ... I thought ... you were off duty." Her lower lip quivers.

I stare into her eyes for a long moment, step around her and grab a dark blue shirt from my closet. Slipping my handcuffs into the waistband of my jeans, I snatch up my radio. Angie hasn't moved. I step back in front of her.

"You can stay. Is your car here or did your Dad drop you off?"

She's breathing heavy now.

"Maybe you should go home."

"My car's at Flamingo's but I'll stay with Buck."

The voice on the radio screams that the bike has made a U-turn and is heading toward Chef Menteur Highway. Angie reaches for my face, but stops.

"I *have* to go."

"I know." Her eyes glisten.

As I turn to leave, she grabs my arm, pulls me back and kisses me softly on the lips. She lets go of my arm and whispers, "Be careful."

I reach behind her neck and pull her to me and kiss her lips as softly as I can. In a deep, steady voice I tell her, "You may not believe this, but I'm always careful."

Taking her hand I lead her to the door and ask her to lock me out. I wait for the click of the dead bolt before running to my car.

•

The T-Bird's engine whines as I dash to the interstate, dodging slower cars, blowing lights when I have a shot, gunning it when I'm clear of traffic. Clyde's bike turns on the Chef. To my surprise, he's heading back into town instead of east toward the Honey Island Swamp and the great state of Mississippi.

As soon as I hit I-10, I floor it. It takes me eleven minutes to transverse half the city, cross the Industrial Canal and blaze through most of New Orleans East. The T-bird's big V8 is flat-out flying. The gold motorcycle pulls another U-turn and heads back toward Highway 11. I take the Paris Road exit, wheels screeching, barely catch hearing the pursuing officer tell headquarters the bike has turned up a gravel road off the Chef. Headquarters asks where.

"I'm not sure," the officer replies. "There's a sign." Three seconds later the officer shouts, "It's Bayou Sauvage ... National Wildlife Refuge ... Trail. Runs off the Chef toward the lake."

Other units respond, their sirens whooping over excited voices. Six minutes later, I barely see the sign as I blow by it at eighty miles and hour. I pump my brakes and bring the T-Bird to a tire-screaming stop, wheel it around and turn up the gravel road. Riding along a small levee next to Bayou Sauvage, I have to stop quickly again as I almost pass three parked police cars and a gold motorcycle lying on its side in a shell parking lot to my right.

I scramble to the bike and recognize the license number. It's Clyde's, all right. I pull out my Glock and walk quickly to the brown building at the end of the small parking area. A white sign on the building reads: Take a Hike. To the building's right is another sign on the railing of an elevated wooden walkway that runs into the vast swamp beyond. That sign reads: Ridge Trail Through Swamp.

A sound turns me around as a door opens and a uniformed officer comes out of a bathroom. Zipping up, the officer freezes when he sees me pointing my gun at him. I pull the Glock down and tell him I'm Homicide.

"All of you in the bathroom, or what?"

His name is Billiot and it takes him several seconds to explain the biker ran off down the ridge trail. "We all went after him, but he jumped the rail and went into the swamp. Who the fuck ever heard of a swamp in the city limits?"

Footsteps on the walkway turn me around again. Two officer come walking back along the ridge trail. One is a sergeant who raises his hand and says, "He must be a fuckin' swamp rat or something. He just vanished."

The second officer brushes his shoulders briskly. "You should see the fuckin' spiders in there!"

"Which one of you jumped him first?"

The spider-scared officer says he was prowling around Highway 11, looking for that damn gold bike and jumped the bastard.

"Good work." I step around them to the walkway. "Is he armed?"

"I didn't see anything."

"What's he wearing?

"Dark green shirt and black pants. It's that guy Pailet, all right. Salt and pepper hair."

"Come on," I tell them as I move forward. "Show me where he jumped the rail."

"Why?" the sergeant answers. "We got SWAT coming. And Chief Kay's in route."

"SWAT?" I try not to keep my voice down. "It'll take them a good hour." I point to the west where the sun hovers at tree top level. "We don't have enough light."

The sergeant shakes his head. "Kay's getting bloodhounds."

"From where? Kentucky?!" My voice echoes.

"No, Angola."

"From the penitentiary? That's a two hour drive. Maybe three."

I point to the spider-scared cop whose name plate reads: Anderson. "Show me where he went in." I'm backing quickly down the walkway. Anderson lowers his head and follows.

The canopy closes over us, tall bottom-land hardwoods – oak and cypress and sweetgum trees, all dripping Spanish moss. We follow the zig-zag wooden walkway suspended over soggy, black mud. I scan the trees for movement.

Sugarberry trees stand next to huge magnolias and the occasional elderberry tree.

"He went in here." Anderson points to our left.

I see deep footprints in the bog. Re-holstering my Glock, I carefully climb over the rail and drop lightly next to the footprints, which lead off straight into the deep marsh.

Anderson curses as he jumps away from a large spider web. "Fuckin' spiders are bigger than my hand."

I shush him and tell him in a harsh whisper, "Those are golden silk spiders. They won't bother you." A black, fierce-looking silk spider, nearly three inches in diameter, moves slowly along its web, it's long yellow legs flexing, showing off the black tuffs of hair at its leg joints. "Just don't let it bite you."

Anderson goes down on a knee.

Clyde's wearing cowboy boots. I stand and follow the footprints.

"Whoa," Anderson calls out in a muffled voice. "You're going in after him?"

I turn and tell him to wait back by the bike in case Clyde doubles back. Hearing a tractor-trailer rig ramble along the Chef behind Anderson, I point over his head. "And set up a perimeter along the Chef, I-10 and Highway 11."

It's about three miles to Highway 11 to the east and about the same distance to I-10 to the north. If we surround the area, we'll have Clyde trapped. Over my shoulder I add, "And watch Bayou Sauvage in case he swims it and heads for Bourbon Street."

"Hey!" Anderson calls out, stopping me again. "Want my flashlight?"

"Did Clyde have one?"

Anderson shrugs.

"Just tell the ass-holes with the bloodhounds I'm in here."
I don't have to worry about SWAT. No way they'll soil their
pretty black uniforms in a swamp.

Stepping around an oak as wide as any in City Park, I
follow Clyde's footprints across the boggy marshland. The
sound of cars fades quickly, replaced by the incessant buzz of
insects. Two mosquito hawks dance past my face as I wipe
away a mosquito biting my neck. As the evening draws close,
I'm going to curse myself for not wearing a long-sleeved
shirt.

Clyde's tracks are easy to follow in the daylight and I
pick up the pace, keeping a wary watch where I'm headed, in
case of ambush. Moving around a ten-foot, prickly palmetto
bush, I hear my Daddy's voice telling me how its fruit is a
favorite of robins, crows and raccoons. I stop and listen and
ahead, very faintly, I hear something moving through the
brush. I follow the sound and the footprints. In the dappled,
early evening sunlight, long shadows cover the foliage.
Moving as silently as I can, I press on past brambles and wild
camellia bushes, ducking beneath large spider webs
suspended between trees.

As I ease around another oak, a crow caws loudly off to
my right . I stop and peer through the long trumpet vines
dangling from the oaks thick branches. A brown lizard
scampers up the creeper vines, wrapped tightly around the
oak's thick trunk. A sound behind me turns me around in
time to see a squirrel scramble to a sweetgum tree. Wiping
sweat from my eyes, I continue through the steam, following
the footprints. Another mosquito bites my neck and I wipe it
away, as well as two on my left arm.

Concentrate. I have to concentrate on the prints and what's ahead. The fetid, almost sweet scent of the swamp gives way to air so thick, it's a struggle to breath without gasping. The footprints open up. He's moving faster. I increase my pace through a stand of sugarberry trees. The footprints lead to a cluster of dwarf palmetto bushes. Clyde's pushed his way through the prickly spires. Several are broken and more bent.

I move around the bushes and pick the prints up on the other side. Clyde seems to be making a bee-line straight north. He's heading for the interstate. I step up my pace through a thick grouping of bald cypress and immediately I'm in ankle-deep water. Clearing the trees I see a wide expanse of water ahead. In the distance are more trees and an elevated roadway – I-10.

Dotted with cypress knees and tall cypress trees, the wide pond glimmers in the fading sunlight. I take a few hesitant steps and I'm up to my knees. No way Clyde's out ahead, I'd be able to spot him. I slide back to the nearest cypress and lean against it.

Three feet away, a black cottonmouth glides past. At least five feet long, its vicious triangular head sticks out of the water, tongue darting as it sniffs the steamy air. The chilling cry of a bobcat off to my right startles me and I almost jump. *Jesus*. I close my eyes and listen hard for anything but only hear my Daddy's voice again, telling me how the bobcat cries at the setting sun, announcing its meal time.

A horde of mosquitoes settles on my arms and I wipe them off and move around the tree back to the marsh. I have to find Clyde's trail again before the light is gone. I'm a swamp man. My Daddy raised me that way. Except for the fuckin' moccasin and the smart-assed bobcat, I feel at home here. Reaching the boggy marsh, I spot a gator mound and give it a wide berth. Female gators protect their nests ferociously. An adult gator can easily run down a man in mud.

Finally, I'm on firmer ground. Pausing, I examine the area for footprints. None. Concentrating my senses, I feel I must veer more to my left, skirting the pond. Clyde had to have gone that way. Ten feet later, I spot a fresh scrape against a cypress tree and see Clyde's footprints along the edge of the pond. He's going in and out of the water, moving more easterly now.

Deep in the swamp the high-low call of cicadas echoes through the summer evening, rising and falling like an out of tune accordion. Rounding another cypress, I stop and study the black mud around me. A particularly mean mosquito bites my left wrist. I squash it and scoop up some mud, rubbing it on my arms and neck to keep some of the blood suckers away.

The beating of wings turns me to my left as a Louisiana blue heron rises from the swamp. Silhouetted against the orange sunset, it does my heart good. It's a good omen, I tell myself as I press on. I get a momentary view of the eastern sky, which is already dark. There's a full moon hovering there. Another good sign. Even with some clouds, the night may be bright enough for me to track.

Clyde's footprints lead out of the water back into the marsh and in a straight line toward Highway 11. God, I hope they've cordoned off the area. I follow the tracks in the fading light. Under the heavy canopy again, it's much darker.

I follow the tracks for a good half hour, but don't spot Clyde. Walking bent over, in order to see the footsteps, I move through the twilight until I can see the tracks no longer. Finding a tree, I stand against it and wait for the dusk to die away, wait for my eyes to adjust.

Slowly, moonlight begins to filter through the canopy. If Clyde's still moving, he's getting further away, but a *patient* tracker will grow old and die an old man in his bed. Here in the swamp, a tracker who hurries may find his prey too quickly. I force myself to wait for the moonlight.

A snorting to my right brings me to pull out my Glock and lean around the tree. Moments later, I spot a shadow ahead, low to the ground. It snorts again and I recognize the sound. The shadow moves slowly away. I can barely make it out, but it's a feral hog, digging its nose in the mud, ferreting out truffles. My Daddy and I killed a razorback once. He slew it with one shot of his twenty-two rifle, right through the hog's eye. It didn't drop right away, but we had no trouble tracking it.

Suddenly I hear a slap off to my left. A human voice curses and slaps again.

Thank God for mosquitoes.

Ducking away from my tree I creep toward the sound. Carefully, silently, I move through the marsh, using whatever moonlight I can. Trees are darker and so are the bushes I must navigate around as I walk on the balls of my feet. A sound from behind stops me. The deep howl of bloodhounds echoes through the swamp. Jesus, they got here quickly. And I realize it could be some local hunter's dogs. Wait a minute. I remember a Levee Board police officer who raises bloodhounds.

A movement off to my right catches my attention and I see Clyde for a second, too far away to shoot at, as he steps around a tree, heading south now, straight for the Chef. I pursue him directly, Glock in hand. I hear him snapping through bushes, moving quickly. I pick up my pace. He can't hear me if he's making so much noise. Increasing my pace, I try to close on him. Clyde grunts and I stop, going down on my haunches. It takes a few seconds, but I hear him moving again, away from me, this time more easterly. My God, is he heading for Highway 11 again?

Thankfully Clyde continues his breakneck movements. I don't have to be as careful. He doesn't know I'm here. Pausing every few steps, I listen to make sure he's still moving. I just need to keep him within earshot. No way I can catch him without running.

I move through a spider web and quickly remove it before its creator crawls on me. Thankfully there's no painful bite. I keep checking my arms and hair as I continue. Have to be more careful. Pausing again, I can't hear Clyde.

I strain to listen and hear a faint sounds of passing cars. We're close to Chef Menteur Highway and I can't wait. I have to reach it before Clyde. A vision of him flagging down a ride or racing across to whatever's on the other side propels me quickly toward the road. Can't count on the area being cordoned off.

It's lighter ahead and I increase my pace around bushes I can now see. Stepping through a line of live oaks, I almost fall into the wide ditch alongside the highway. Large streetlights, more like floodlights, suspended on high poles across the highway, cast a dim glow over the entire area.

I back up to the nearest tree and scan the wide, four lane blacktop. The other side looks like an extension of the same wooded, marshy swampland. Of course, there are no cops lining the road. I should have known. The only cops I've ever seen cordon off an area was on T.V.

A noise to my left turns me back to the woods. Something moves a good fifty, sixty yards from me along the far side of the line of live oaks. I ease over to the next tree and watch but there's nothing. Seconds slip into minutes. He's there. I feel it. He's just beyond the tree line. He's waiting.

To cross the road? Or is he waiting for me?

Breathing as quietly as I can, I move my hand in slow motion to scrape the mosquitoes off my arms. I fold my arms to help keep the blood suckers away. Patience. I run it through my mind again. I must have patience. I know he's there.

He may be a swamp rat, may even know this swamp better than I, but I am also of the swamp. I grew up here. Blinking sweat from my eyes, I examine everything straight-on. Then turning my head, I study the area from the corner of my eye, looking for anything that angle could reveal. I watch for motion, not shape, but see nothing but the trees and bushes.

I sense something else, something from within. It's a foreboding. This will be an important night in my life, of this I have no doubt. Maybe a little fear has crept into my heart. Before battle, a Sioux warrior prepares himself, painting himself, chanting the ancient songs, hardening all the soft places within, thus denying his enemy a spot to wound him.

As I wait, I steel myself, hardening even my heart for this task.

Chapter 19
YOU KILLED OF MY TRIBE

Headlights from each passing car flashes through the swamp, especially the westbound cars making the long curve a hundred yards down the Chef from where I stand pressed against trumpet vines wrapped around a tall live oak. I watch for any movement in the swamp, but there is nothing.

If I'd thought to slip my radio into the back pocket of my jeans, I could have called the cavalry a half hour ago. No, I can't think of what might have been. I have to concentrate on the terrain, on movement, on sounds, anything that will tell me where Clyde lurks.

It's taken a while to realize the ditch alongside the road narrows dramatically several feet away from where I am. If Clyde is where I feel he is, he won't have to jump the ditch to bolt across the highway. He can just step over it.

A sinking feeling begins to gnaw at me. What if I'm wrong? What if Clyde has slipped back into the swamp and is heading for Highway 11? He could be there soon, hitching a ride. A breath of warm air flows over me from the swamp. My shirt, drenched in sweat, feels almost cool for a moment. The loud blast of a horn blares as tractor-trailer rig rounds the long curve and barrels my way. I squint at its high-beam headlights.

I feel a shiver, as if an invisible finger has caressed my spine. I automatically go down on my haunches. Four thundering heartbeats later, the truck blows by. Closing one eye to the high-beams, I count to three and switch eyes. I hear boots on the blacktop and spot him, running flat out. Clyde's crossing in the wake of the truck. Sixty yards away, he's almost across the highway. I step away from the tree and raise my Glock, fixing the reflective white front sight through the rear sights at the running figure. My foot slides forward and I slip into the ditch.

Climbing out, I see Clyde bolt into the woods just beyond the far streetlight.

Dammit to hell.

Can't let him double back and set up for me across the road. I suck in a deep breath, rise quickly and race across the wide highway. Pumping hard, I bear down until I finally dash into the trees. I swing around a tree to stop myself. My feet sink in the bog. I listen closely as I watch the highway to make sure he doesn't double back across.

Nothing.

Moonlight, filtering through the canopy of live oaks, gives me a good view for at least twenty yards in the swamp. Off to my right, it seems lighter. Slowly, I realize the tree line ends about thirty yards away.

I step around the tree and move forward in the direction where Clyde went in. Moving carefully, I navigate through the trees past the streetlight to where Clyde entered the woods. The unmistakable imprint of a boot heel marks the spot. Crouching, I follow Clyde's footprints through the trees. Several yards later I lose them in the darkness. I creep forward and find another footprint beneath a opening in the canopy. He's headed straight through the trees for the lighted area beyond.

Inching along, I spot the outline of a wide marsh beyond the tree line. As I arrive at the end of the trees, I see ribbons of water, glimmering with moonlight, cutting through thick marsh grass. In the moonlight, the earth is lighter than the sky, which is black as pitch along the horizon.

I look for movement, scanning from side to side, strain my eyes, hoping to catch him move. As the long minutes pass, I look for anything that is different in the landscape and spot something in the distance, straight in front of me. An indistinct blot is there. I stare at it and finally, it moves. He's crawling away from me, crawling instead of walking. He knows someone's following.

Slipping the Glock into its holster at the small of my back, I go down on my knees and follow the blot. I pick up his trail twenty yards later and slip into it, hoping I'm not producing my own blot as I move toward him. Looking back, the tree line is darker behind me. I should produce no silhouette as I move steadily after him.

Coming to the first ribbon of water, I see it's about fifteen feet across. Probing with my hands, I sink into it but it's not deep enough to wet my belly. I cross it as smoothly as I can, trying not to cause a ripple.

Climbing back on to the marsh grass, I look for the blot, but it's gone. Has he stopped? Is he lying in wait for me? Is he just resting? I flatten myself and wait. Something crawls over my arm and I resist swatting it away. A mosquito stings my neck.

I wait.

My Daddy's voice echoes the reminder he'd told me time and again as we moved through the deep swamps along Vermilion Bay. "Be one wit' de' swamp, ma boy, and de' swamp be one wit you."

When I was ten, I used to run that through my head again and again, a favorite childhood ditty. I wonder if he's watching me now, as I lay in this marsh, trying to be one with the swamp in a game far deadlier than any imagined when I was young and the world was one adventure after another.

Like the time we hooked a young gator in our trout line ...

The blot rises directly in front of me and moves away, like a turtle. I know I must ignore the inner eye of my memory and focus on the world around me. Be one with the swamp – I follow, keeping to the trail Clyde has left in the rough marsh grass, crawling slowly and steadily. The blot moves in and out of sight as Clyde continues through the grass.

It is slow progress and the night deepens as we continue across the wide marshland. Moving through a swarm of mosquitoes, I push them away from my face and wipe the sweat from my eyes.

I pause a moment to listen and remember my grandfather's gravelly voice reciting the old rallying cry of Sitting Bull and Crazy Horse. "Today is a good day to fight. A good day to die." I know what my Daddy would say to that. "A good day to die? Zif. I ain't never seen one a dem, no."

Pushing the voices away, I continue. The second band of water is wider, and deeper. I have to stand and walk across hunched over in order to keep the Glock and ammo magazines dry. Reaching the other side, I go down on all fours on the grass and something splashes behind me. I freeze. A turtle, I tell myself, or probably or a fish. Could be a gator, but I don't look back. I watch out front.

If a warrior drowns, his spirit can never go to the land of ghosts. His spirit will remain trapped in the water forever, cold and lonely, moaning in eternal grief. Nothing in that old saying about being eaten by an alligator.

An icy finger traces itself across my spine again and I realize, the swamp rat's trail is too easy to follow. I roll to my right quickly and pull out the Glock. Fiery muzzle flashes and the explosion of magnum rounds in front of me drive my face into the grass. Two more shots explode.

My heart thunders in my throat as I force myself to look up and aim the Glock. I blink my eyes, trying to get them to adjust to the blackness again, but I keep seeing yellow dots from the muzzle flashes.

"If you ain't a fuckin' cop, quit following me ass-hole!" Clyde's voice echoes in the open marsh. "If you are. You're about to die!"

Perspiration stings my eyes as I squeeze the damp, rubber grips of my Glock. Aiming it, I wait for the blot to reappear. I hear something. A sloshing sound, followed by footsteps.

I suck in a deep breath, let half of it out and wait.

Only the sound fades and I realize. He's running away from me. And I can't see him. It's so dark ahead. Glancing up, I see a wispy cloud moving in front of the moon.

I rise to my knees and see a mound ahead. There's a rise, probably a levee. Instinctively, I move to my right, angling for the rise in front of me. Moving quickly, with knees bent, I hurry forward, watching and listening.

Footsteps echo off to my left, sounding as if Clyde's made it to solid ground. I pick up my pace and nearly fall over a dwarf palmetto, its spires pricking my legs through my jeans. Suddenly I'm on solid earth. Stepping cautiously, I continue up a levee until I feel something sharp underfoot. I reach down and it's rocks. My hand touches something cool. A rail.

I'm on railroad tracks atop a small levee. Flattening myself next to the tracks, I aim my weapon down the tracks to where Clyde should be, the marsh to my left now. Slowly, the clouds part and the moon beams through. To my right, beyond the levee, is a line of live oaks dripping Spanish moss. Beyond is a wide cypress swamp. In the distance I see the black water of what must be the Mississippi River Gulf Outlet intra-coastal waterway and Lake St. Catherine, Lake Borgne beyond, shimmering in silver moonlight.

As the tracks take form, I know I can't stay here so I crawl across the levee to the oaks where I can stand, wipe sweat from my eyes again. I slowly steal my way toward where Clyde must have crossed the levee. The moonlight seems brighter as it streams through the canopy above me.

Rounding an oak I spot Clyde's footprints heading away from me. I watch for any hint of ambush and I follow the prints through the trees until they turn left and head back toward the levee.

What did I tell Angie? "You may not believe this, but I'm always careful."

As I slip through the trees, I sharpen every sense. Directly ahead, the levee seems to have a hole in it. I go down on my belly and crawl forward. Stopping behind another oak, I peer around the trunk. It's not a hole in the levee, it's a railroad trestle, a small bridge across one of the ribbons of water which falls away into a pond to my right.

Clyde's footprints head directly for the trestle. Did he cross back to the marsh? Is he hurrying back to the Chef? No.

He's waiting to bushwack me. The footprints are too easy to follow.

In the dappled moonlight, the oak's gnarled branches hover over me like tarantula arms. Without even a breath of air, the moss dangles lifelessly around me. The drone of insects echoes, like distant waves rolling to shore. Humidity, like lukewarm steam, presses against my face and sweat drips from my chin to my wet shirt.

I back away from the tree and crawl all the way to the end of the tree line. I'll circle the pond, cross the levee and come up from the other side. Moving as quickly as I can in the bog, I make good time to the pond. I scoop up fresh mud and reapply it to my arms, neck and face. I cover my exposed skin, blackening myself, painting myself like a good Sioux warrior.

As I round the pond, a splash freezes me, but only momentarily. I am one with the swamp. In case it was a gator, however, I pick up my pace. I tip-toe to the levee and crawl over it to lay on the grass on the marsh side focus my senses again.

To my right, the marsh is lit in moonlight and there is no blot crossing it. Slowly, I inch forward, flat on my belly. It takes a while to cross the distance to the trestle. I reach the edge of the steel bridge and stop and listen.

My skin tingles and my heartbeat rises. He's there. I can *feel* him. He's under the trestle waiting for me in the blackness. Peeking up, I see a thick cloud cover the moon. A minute later, a blanket of darkness falls over us.

I close my mind to any thought and direct my senses ahead. There's a soft sound in front of me, as if he's repositioning himself. And slowly, I hear raspy breathing.

Moving my Glock forward, I aim in the direction of the sound and wait.

The sound fades. Is he moving away from me? Does he know I'm here? Is he getting into a better firing position?

Stop thinking!

Concentrate your senses. Harden yourself. Steel yourself. Deny the enemy a place to wound you. The seconds drag into minutes. I blink perspiration from my eyes, not daring to move my hands. My vision becomes blurred, then clear, then blurred again. Gradually, the moonlight returns. I see something. High, beneath the trestle up close to the tracks. It's shiny.

We both fire. Squeezing off three rounds, I roll down the levee to the high marsh grass. I'm not hit but the bright flashes from Clyde's magnum revolver has me seeing yellow dots.

Clyde fires again. Three shots striking the marsh grass around me. I aim for the flashes and squeeze off three more rounds. Jumping up, I scatter the remaining nine hollow points toward Clyde as I race back up the levee.

I reach the tracks, drop my empty magazine, and reload the Glock, chambering a round. I start to cross to the other side of the levee, but turn and crawl back the way I came. He won't expect me to come back this way.

The ensuing silence is complete. The air reeks of cordite. Another cloud passes in front of the moon, then moves away. Eventually, the cicadas start up again. A mockingbird, rousted from its nest, begins it long litany of calls. And I hear a cough. He's under the trestle.

There's another cough.

"Pretty good shootin', ass-hole!" Clyde's voice is scratchy.

I move up the levee a few feet.

"You fuckin' hit me, you bastard!"

That was the fuckin' point.

Clyde coughs again. "Did I get you?"

His voice has a slight echo to it. He's on the same side of the trestle as I.

"Why don't you come and get me?" He coughs again. "If you're waiting for me to pass out, think again. It's just a nick."

The insects buzz in response. A minute passes, then another. I remain motionless.

"What you waitin' for? Come and get me, you gutless fuck."

He's close, all right.

"Ain't you supposed to call out 'Police'? Ask me to surrender?"

Clyde coughs again, louder and lets out a moan.

As more minutes slip by, I hear Jodie's voice in the back of my brain reminding me we have to capture them, have to get the whole story. Then I see Mullet's ugly face grinning at me, telling me he'll be king of parish prison. King of the cop killers. I squeeze the Glock's grips and keep the sights aimed forward.

Harden yourself. Steel yourself.

"I surrender! You hear me. I give up!" Two seconds later, he snarls, "Answer me, you fuck!"

Good, he's losing it. And suffering. Very good.

"I'm comin' out! You hear me?" Two seconds later – "*Answer me!*"

I don't.

"I know you ain't dead. I heard you creeping back. I been hearing you since you started after me, you lucky fuckin' bastard. What the fuck are you, some ex-Green Beret or somethin'?"

Concentrate. Don't let him distract you.

"I'm crawling out, you fuck. I surrender!"

He comes out not ten feet from me, dragging his right leg, his revolver still in hand. I keep my sights trained on him.

"Get me outta here. Get me to a fuckin' hospital!"

Clyde pulls himself into a sitting position and drops his revolver. Holding his right leg with both hands he looks right at me. A dark stain on his pants shows he's lost blood. Good.

"*Get me to a fuckin' hospital!*"

I rise slowly on weary legs and step down the levee, still keeping myself a good fifteen feet from him. He leans forward to get a better look at me. I can see his eyes clearly in the moonlight as he focuses on me. There's a slight twitch as he sees this mud-covered man pointing a Glock between his eyes.

"You gonna say something, fuck head?"

I start squeezing the trigger, very slowly.

Clyde grimaces and shouts, "Come on. Get me outta here!"

"You're not going anywhere."

"*Fuck you!* Get me to a hospital!" His voice echoes over the marsh. Only the mockingbird responds, chirping angrily.

"You know the old saying," I tell him. "Kill a cop. You die."

I wait for the realization to register in Clyde's eyes. It doesn't. He coughs again. I go down on one knee. This is a better angle for an entry wound.

"Who – ," Clyde says in a harsh whisper. "Who the fuck are you?"

"I am Sharp Eyes of the Oglala Sioux. And you killed of my tribe. So you die."

It finally registers in Clyde's eyes, the realization. I smile coldly and see my hands are rock steady as I squeeze off a round which strikes Clyde in the forehead, snapping his head. He falls straight back, his hand conveniently close to his revolver.

Good. When they get here, they won't see any of my footprints near him. He and his revolver will get me through another Grand Jury. I sink down on the levee as the air in my lungs finally exhales. My breathing eventually returns to normal. Holstering my weapon, I lean back on both hands and look up at the beaming moon.

"When I came on the job," I tell the moon. "I swore to uphold the law to the best of my ability, didn't I?" I look at Clyde's body. "This is the best of my ability."

I sink back on the levee and lay there, staring at the sky above. My weary eyes close and I rest, let the tension float away, let the hardening and steeling soften until I feel almost light-headed.

In the waning moments of The Battle of the Little Bighorn, a battle we Sioux call 'The Battle at the Greasy Grass' because of the oily grass surrounding the Little Bighorn River, a warrior came upon a Sioux woman standing over a wounded soldier. The soldier was begging for his life. Before killing the soldier, the woman, known as Eagle Robe, called out to him, "If you did not want to be killed, why did you not stay home where you belong and come to attack us?"

As I lay on the levee in this thick Louisiana marsh, my mind drifts back to that dusty Montana plain where my ancestors, Sitting Bull, Crazy Horse and his brother Little Hawk, killed those who had killed of our tribe.

I feel a deep peace inside.

Chapter 20
I WAS CAREFUL

The sun rises along the flat, eastern horizon, eerily illuminating the vast swampland around me. Marsh fog hugs the ground, like steam from a boiling kettle, until the sun is completely above the horizon and burns away the warm fog.

The cackling of gulls behind me turns me around. Moving in from Lake Catherine, laughing gulls float above and past me. One at a time, they swoop down to the marsh for their breakfast of cock-a-hoe minnows. Snowy egrets, their white plumes gleaming under the bright sun, stand in the ribbons of water dotting the marsh.

I peel the dried mud from my face and arms as I sit on the levee. Facing the marsh I'd crossed in the darkness, I'm surprised how far I'd crawled. The tree line along the Chef is a good two miles away, at least. The hot sun makes me want to lie back and go to sleep. Someone'll find us sooner or later. No way I'm leaving Clyde and his gun until the crime lab arrives to process this scene.

When I was a rookie homicide detective we thought we had a murder on the river batture, when we found a body with a bullet wound in the head. Checking the wound we found unmistakable evidence of a contact wound to the temple – powder burns, blow-back and stippling. We were immediately confused when we discovered the victim's car parked nearby with a suicide note in it.

It took us a while to put the pieces together. Some brazen street thug had come upon the body and snatched the victim's gun. The last thing I need is Clyde's gun disappearing. Guess those bloodhounds weren't so good after all. I'll bet they're all still on the other side of Chef Menteur Highway, dodging spiders and cottonmouths.

I lean back on my elbows and close my eyes. You'd think that someone would look over here. Maybe a train will come along slow enough for me to flag it down or get a message out. The tracks look in pretty good shape.

I keep checking the tracks. An hour later, I spot two figures moving my way along the tracks. My legs ache as I rise and stretch. The knee I tore up at LSU creaks as I climb to the top of the levee. The figures stop about a hundred yards away, two men, one carrying a pump shotgun.

I wave my arms, then wave them forward. The man with the shotgun pulls it off his shoulder and points it at the ground as the two come slowly toward me. The taller is black and wears a shoulder holster rig. The man with the shotgun, a pudgy white boy, looks young. Both have small silver badges clipped to their khaki shirts.

When they are within earshot, I put my hands around my mouth and shout, "Police! I'm a police officer!"

The men pause a moment, but continue cautiously. I turn my side to them and pull my ID folder, with my badge clipped to the outside, and hold it open above my head.

"NOPD!"

The black man raise a friendly hand, then shouts back, "Railroad Detectives!"

Fuckin' A! The muddy dirt on my face cracks as I smile. As soon as they reach the trestle, I hold my ID folder out front. They cross the trestle easily.

"I'm Detective John Raven Beau. Homicide. Y'all have a radio?"

The black man, who's darker-complected than Merten, pulls a small radio from his pants pocket, then stops and says, "You're Beau?"

"Yeah."

"Jesus. We all been looking for you."

I point down the levee to Clyde's body. "Thought y'all might be looking for him."

The pudgy man steps over, looks down and whistles.

"He's dead," I tell them. "Can y'all call in and get NOPD out here?"

The black man reaches a hand out and tells me he's Sam Martinez. His partner is Irvin Martinez. Irvin runs a hand through his carrot red hair and says, in a serious voice, "We're not related."

Ah, humor. Nice. Sam asks if I'm all right.

"Just tired and muddy."

"Is that blood on your leg?"

Damn palmetto. My jeans are ripped and coagulated blood is clustered around the tear.

"Can y'all call in?"

"Sure." Sam calls his headquarters. I return to my original position on the levee, sitting cross legged like a good Indian. I have to tell Irvin to stay away from the crime scene.

"Just sit here with me." I nod toward the Chef. "They'll be coming soon."

"Damn right," Sam says. "You got a passel of cops out searching for you."

Irvin passes me his canteen and the water is sweet and cool.

I thank him as the mockingbird starts chattering behind us. I can't spot it in the oaks, but it fusses us through a long series of calls. Hell, maybe it isn't fussing at us. Maybe it's just advertising for a mate.

Sam points across the marsh. A long line of blue moves out of the trees toward us. Shielding my eyes with both hands above my brows, I watch their slow progress. I spot Jodie's white-blonde hair near the center of the line. A dark, hulking form seems to be out front. He's moving quickest. It's Merten, in another dark brown suit, coat flapping as he tries to jog through the mire.

"That's my lieutenant out front," I tell Sam.

"From the way he moves, he looks mad."

"Naw. He's just ornery."

Someone helps Jodie across one of the waterways. "See that Elmer Fudd looking guy next to the blonde woman?"

Sam squints and nods.

"Don't let him talk to you."

"Why not?"

"He'll never stop." Turning to Irvin, I ask if I can have more water.

"Sure." He passes the canteen back to me. "Can you tell us how you killed him?"

I shake my head. "Have to tell my lieutenant first."

"Cool!" Irvin bobs his head. "I never met anyone who killed someone before. I mean right after and all." Sam tells him to keep quiet. And we watch the cavalry approach.

Merten nearly falls climbing out of the last ribbon of water. Pulling himself up, he hurries forward. A second line of people stream out of the trees. Most of these are in civilian clothes. Several are carrying cases. Crime Lab and FBI probably. The men in white are probably from the coroner's office.

As Merten closes in, a rail car approaches and Sam and Irvin get up and move to it. I watch my lieutenant slow down and turn towards Clyde's body. He stops twenty feet from it, gives it a long look, then turns to me. His face glistens with sweat. He's breathing heavily and to my surprise, the normally present scowl is gone. He stops in front of me and goes down on one knee, his yellow-brown eyes staring into mine.

"Are you all right, son?"

"I'm OK."

He plops heavily and wipes the sweat away from his face with both hands. Covering his face with his hands, he lets out what could be mistaken for a cry, followed by a nervous laugh. He clears his throat. "Beau," his voice wavers with emotion. "You don't know how much you worry me."

A dog's howl echoes over the swamp. Looking across the marsh, I see the bloodhounds have finally made it. The first line of uniformed officers closes in on me.

Merten directs two to guard the area around Clyde's body. "Don't let anyone within thirty feet until I start processing the scene. And I mean anyone, I don't give a fuck what rank they are!"

Four other officers continue toward me. They stare at me as if I'm from Mars. I suddenly feel like a wild animal in a cage. When one of the officers speaks, I realize it's Gonzales, the brim of his dark blue NOPD hat nearly hiding his eyes.

"You got mud all over your face, Crazy Horse," he tells me.

His dark blue uniform pants are caked with mud. He wears black rubber boots that slosh as he tries to climb the levee. They're full of water.

"You got demoted or something?" I ask back.

"No! Just didn't want anyone shooting me by mistake."

Merten stands and tells Gonzales to go secure the scene. "I need Homicide there until I'm finished with Beau." He reaches a hand down to help me up. I grab it and he pulls me up on my achy legs. My lieutenant leads me up to the trestle, away from everyone and asks me to run it down to him, quickly. As I tell him, my voice scratches with exhaustion. I tell him about the tracks in the mud and the trek which led us to this trestle in the middle of last night.

"I finally cornered him," I say. "He tried to bushwack me. We exchanged gunfire. That's it." I withdraw my Glock to hand it to him.

"Save it for the Crime Lab," he tells me. "You're going to the office. You know the routine."

He leaves me up on the trestle. I close my eyes to the relentless sun, now hot on my head. A lightheaded feeling of floating makes me waver as I stand, so I sit on a cross-tie, arms folded and wait.

Channard's voice booms from below, something about how this is the most incredible case. Whistles and chirps, followed by zoom sounds and a loud pop tell me Tony Dunn is down there too. Footsteps approach, lightly. Someone leans over me, blocking out the sun momentarily. A hand touches my shoulder and I catch a whiff of Jodie's perfume.

"My God," she says, brushing my hair off my forehead. "I'm getting a doctor."

"I don't need a doctor." My voice almost cracks. "I just need water." I'm famished, but I know I need water immediately. I blink up at her. Her blonde hair dangles in front of her face, as she leans forward.

"You need a stretcher. I'll get a helicopter."

"No! I'm walking outta here." It takes all my strength to stand. Jodie takes my arm as my legs quiver.

"I could use some water," I say with a rasp.

"Somebody bring a canteen up here!" Jodie shouts.

Channard hustles up, pulling a large plastic canteen out of the knapsack on his back. I take one look at the hat on his head and almost fall down. He's in khakis and looks *exactly* like Elmer Fudd.

Laughing, I lean on Jodie. I can't stop. I point at him and laugh even louder, which causes Channard to pull the canteen back. Jodie snatches it out of his hand, opens it and pours water over my head.

It's chilled and sends a shiver through me. I grab it and press it to my mouth. For the next several minutes, I down as much as I can. Jodie pulls the canteen away and douses my head again.

I have to bend over to catch my breath. As soon as I do, I thank Channard.

"Can you do me another favor?"

"Sure."

"Give me just one 'Oh, you waskally wabbit.'."

Standing straight I hold tight to Jodie's arm and look Channard in the eyes that seem hurt. "Can you two help walk me outta here?" To his credit, Elvis 'Elmer Fudd' Channard sees it in my eyes and grabs my other arm. We three descend the levee.

"Wait." I stop and dig my car keys from my pocket and call out to Gonzales. When he looks up from taking notes for the crime lab technician processing the scene, I toss them to him.

"See if you can bring my car home, OK partner?"

He smiles and misses the keys, but digs them out of the muck immediately. Holding them up he says sure, he'll get the T-Bird home.

We move through the small army of law enforcement officers who stare at me as if I'm some exotic predator at the Audubon Zoo. Crossing the wide marsh takes a long time. I'm moving fine now that I'm not so stiff. Jodie flags down an EMT who dresses my leg. They're several scratches, but none are deep enough for stitches.

Chef Menteur Highway is partially closed, lined with dozens of police cars as well as TV vans. Jodie waves several wild-eyed patrol officers forward and asks them to help me to her car. She rushes ahead.

Off to my right, I spot a flash of blonde hair. Abby Grange, microphone in hand, hurries through the maze of cars, a cameraman trying to keep up. She wears a flowery red skirt with a black top and high heels.

"Detective Beau!" She has to slow to let her cameraman catch up.

I pull away from the officers holding my arms and continue away on my own power.

"Detective Beau! Did you kill another?"

Jodie waves us forward as she stands next to the open front passenger door of her car. When I get close, she hurries around me and heads for Abby who's not far behind now. I climb in. The sun, shining through the front windshield temporarily blinds me. I rub my eyes and let them water.

Loud voices and shouting breaks out in front of the car. I blink and focus my eyes in time to see Jodie heading for the car, a flash of red in her left hand. The cops who'd escorted me are laughing a few feet beyond, the cameraman beating a hasty retreat. I don't see Abby.

When Jodie climbs in, she tosses Abby's flowery skirt on my lap.

"It got this caught on my watch," She says as she cranks up the engine. "Stupid bitch," she adds as we pull away. "Next time, she'll wear panties under her pantyhose."

I laugh, close my eyes and lean my head back against the head rest. Sirens echo in front of us. I peek and can't fuckin' believe it. We have a motorcycle escort.

"Is the Pope behind us or something?"

•

Jodie doesn't say a word the rest of the way to headquarters. She doesn't even look at me, but I know what she's thinking. We're supposed to catch them, build a case, bring them to court, put 'em away. I know. I'm an aberration. I want to tell her I know that, know I'll never fit in. Hell, I don't want to anymore. I'm Sharp Eyes of the Oglala Sioux. Fuck 'em all if they don't understand.

Pulling in the police garage, Jodie parks and shuts off the engine, but doesn't move. Staring straight ahead, she has a white-knuckled grip on the steering wheel.

"Damn," she says in a throaty voice.

I wait.

Eventually, she pulls her right hand off the steering wheel and reaches for my hand. I grab hers and she squeezes my hand hard. Two deep breaths later, she pulls away, climbs out and we go in. Thankfully, the Homicide Squad Room is empty.

"I have to make a call."

"Make it quick. This place'll be swarming in a minute."
She heads for the water cooler.

I don't dare sit. Leaning my butt against my desk, I pick
up the phone and punch in my home number. Angie answers
after the first ring.

"Hello there."

"John!"

"I was careful."

"Where are you? Are you all right?"

"Sure." Then I realize. "You've been watching the
news."

"You're all over T.V."

"Do yourself a favor and switch to the SciFi Channel. It's
more realistic."

Then I tell her, if she wants, she can go home. I'll still be
a few hours. I'm at headquarters.

"No. I'll wait here for you, if that's OK."

"Sure. I'll see you soon."

"Good." She doesn't hang up. I wait, listening to her
breathing on the other end. Two-L follows Jodie back across
the squad room. He heads for the coffee pot and starts fixing
a pot of coffee. Jodie, tape recorder in one hand, a wet rag for
my dirty face in the other hand, pauses next to the first
interview room and looks at me.

"I have to go," I tell Angie.

"OK. I'll see you soon."

I hang up. The tone of her voice tells volumes about how
she feels. My Daddy used to say a man doesn't make his own
luck, it just finds him like a nice surprise. I guess found it in
the swamp this morning. With Angie, it's found me, big time.

Darlene Wilson enters the squad room and heads straight for me. I wait. Stopping next to me, she gives me the angry, black woman's head-bob.

"We'll never get the names of who else raped Felice."

She's right, of course, but I don't feel like discussing it, so I walk away. She won't let it rest, so I turn and tell her, "There's no such thing as a perfect case, Darlene. Show me one and I'll show you a made-for-TV movie."

I cross to the interview room as Two-L arrives with two cups of coffee. He hands one to Jodie and one to me. He looks at me as if he's never seen me before and gives me a cold, mortician's smile.

"All right," I tell Jodie as we step into the room. "Let's get this over with."

•

Buck's out on deck, wagging his tail like a maniac as I approach the gate. He barks, then throws back his head and tries to howl, only it gets caught in his throat and fades. Angie opens the houseboat door and hurries out on deck. As soon as she sees the mud still covering my clothes, she stops.

"How about that supper?" I ask as I step up, put my hands on her shoulders and lean forward to kiss her lips softly. She presses against me and I feel her tongue. We're at it big time, our tongue moving against each. I'm awake now.

Eventually we come up for air.

She kisses my lips again as she's still pressed against me. Then she pulls her mouth away and hugs me, her arms under mine. I'm *very* glad I had Gonzales stop for breath mints on my way home.

"Angie, right?" he had to ask when I climbed back in the car.

I didn't respond.

"It's about goddamn time," he'd said.

I didn't respond.

"I was about to put a move on her myself since you've been too fuckin' busy to put – "

"Shut the fuck up! Just get my T-Bird back later."

To my shock, he actually shut-up.

"You must be famished," she says.

"Actually, I am."

"I'll cook – "

"No," I cut her off. "I'm taking you to dinner. Someplace where we need reservations. Someplace where I have to wear a coat and tie."

She pulls back and looks into my eyes. "You in a coat and tie? This I have to see," Angie says.

"I think I could use a shower too." I take her hand and lead her back into the houseboat.

"You telling me?"

I laugh as I pull away.

"I need to go home and change, too." Angie pulls me back and wraps her arms around me again. She takes her time hugging me. I close my eyes and hug her back tightly.

Chapter 21
THE PROMISE

I can't keep my eyes open.

Sitting on Angie's sofa, my charcoal-gray suit coat draped across an easy chair, I loosen my silver tie, kick off my black loafers and lay back. The brisk, air-conditioned air feels so good. I drift ... into a deep sleep.

Her voice wakes me. She's calling John. I blink open my eyes and Angie stands smiling at me. In a sleeveless, dark red mini-dress, she does a slow pirouette. The dress is triple-tiered and her legs look so fine in stockings and red high heels. I sit up immediately.

When she finishes her pirouette, I stare at her face. Mocha lipstick makes her lips look fuller and her eyes are radiant with only a hint of beige eye-shadow.

I stand and let out a long, breathy, "Wow!"

She smiles broadly and says, "That's the reaction I was looking for."

Of course, she's driving. I have to push the passenger seat as far back as I can in her little white Geo Storm. Soon we're parking at the edge of the French Quarter on South Rampart Street. Stepping out, I readjust my off-duty, compact nine-millimeter Smith and Wesson Model 669, which I've tucked in the waistband of my suit pants, along my back.

Hand in hand, we stroll down narrow St. Louis Street, passing Creole cottages, nestled between masonry buildings built right up against the banquette. Passing beneath black, wrought iron balconies, I notice how most of the buildings have natural gas lamps outside their doors.

Soon the electric streetlights will flicker on in the fading light.

Angie squeezes my hand and says, "For over two centuries men have walked their ladies along here."

She's right. The Quarter is like a time-machine back to the days when people walked everywhere, ladies and young men, arm-in-arm, on their way to fine restaurants beneath a beaming summer moon. As we approach our destination, Antoine's Restaurant, I ask Angie, "Wasn't there a book called *Supper at Antoine's?*"

"Actually, it's *Dinner at Antoine's.*" She tucks both arms around my left arm as we walk. "It's such a cliché now. The books so dated. About how so and so spent the morning and how so and so spent the afternoon and how they all had dinner at Antoine's."

Stopping in front of the glass window of Antoine's, beneath yet another wrought iron balcony, I notice the gas lamps attached to the building. The lamps give off an amber glow, reflecting off the beveled glass front doors. Except for the electric lights inside, I'm sure Antoine's looked exactly like this a hundred years ago.

The main dining room in front is packed and smells wonderfully of cooked foods I can't identify, but want immediately. Angie leads the way to the prim maitre d' standing behind his podium. He finds our reservations and waves to a thin waiter with cafe-au-lait skin.

"Hello, I'm Marcel," the waiter announces as he leads us to an even larger back room with no windows. Instead, the room is lined with photographs. Most are autographed and almost all of well-known people.

We are led past pictures of Tyrone Power and Jimmy Carter, Aretha Franklin and a series of black and white photos of pretty women movie stars from the 1940s, including Lauren Bacall. Stopping at a table nestled into a corner, Marcel asks if this would be fine.

"I thought you two would prefer a more private dinner." None of the tables around us are occupied.

"Thought you were tucking the working class people in a corner," Angie says in a pleasant voice.

He holds her chair for her. "Oh no, this room is for locals only. We put the tourists out front where it's noisy. They like all the glass and the view. We've seen the city before, haven't we?"

The table is round and we sit with our backs to the room, a little uneasy for me. Cops like to see what's coming. But the view of Angie's face is more than enough tonight. Beneath the warm light, her aquamarine eyes seem a shade darker, like the ocean water just above a coral reef. I've never seen that color, except in pictures of the Caribbean, until I saw her eyes.

Marcel returns with ice water and warm bread and menus.

"Good, they used to be in French only," Angie says, studying the menu.

"You've been here."

"Once, when I was ten."

She orders trout amandine. I order the baby veal and wonder aloud what kind of wine to drink. Red or white.

"According to wine experts, it really doesn't matter," Angie tells me.

"Could you order for us?"

Marcel brings a wine list and Angie orders a bottle of Médoc Bordeaux. While the bottle breathes, we nibble on the bread and butter. I ask Angie how her classes are going.

She tries not to laugh. "It's summer. The semester's over."

"So you passed."

"Silly."

I wave Marcel over and ask for coffee and chicory. Strong. He returns with a silver tray carrying a silver coffee pot, two cups and saucers, a silver creamer and matching sugar bowl. I need all the caffeine I can get.

"Seriously, how'd you do this semester?"

"I made the Dean's List, but only for the second time."

"American Literature, right?"

She smiles again and tells me about Poe, about discovering some of his lesser known stories, about his four mysteries, how he invented the detective story. She's animated and I watch her, listening as closely as I can. I don't want to think about ... the case.

Angie keeps talking, using her hands, tilted her head to the side. She's a vision. I pour myself a second cup of strong coffee. Marcel returns with her trout and my veal, which is tangy and succulent. I don't realize how hungry I am. I have to force myself to eat slowly. Marcel brings fresh bread without us asking. At first, I pay no attention to the steady beating in the background. When thunder rolls through the old building, I realize it's raining outside.

I try not to think of that wet May night, the evening of the great flood, when Cassandra Smith lay dead in a pool of her blood. I try not to think of the exploding gunfire in Exchange Alley and the deep silence after the echo died. I try not to think of Felice's scarred face and Sandie's frightened face, the fear I put in Mullet's evil eyes when my knife drew blood from his forehead, Clyde Pailet's face when the realization hit him just before my bullet struck.

I try not to think of the pain I bring to Jodie's eyes, or Merten's face without the scowl as he tells me how much I worry him. I don't even want to think of my Daddy's face or the great plains warriors of my people. Not tonight.

I focus on Angie, on this delightful woman sitting next to me. She's very smart. I like that. I don't want to think of the pain I will probably bring to those mesmerizing aquamarines – one day. I won't think of that tonight, no matter how tired I become. It's our first night together. We have a right to this evening, without all the baggage I tow around.

We take our time at dinner and dessert after, then leave this *grande dame* of New Orleans restaurants. Angie wraps her hands around my arm as we step into the night air that still smells of rain. The places I hardened inside during the long night in the swamp feel softer now. I pull Angie close and smell her light perfume. We cross Dauphine Street and a sharp noise explodes behind us.

Angie jumps.

"Car backfire," I tell her, wrapping my arm around her.

She looks back. "You sure?"

"Count on it."

Pulling her close, we walk off into the promise of a beautiful, south Louisiana evening.

THE END

•

ALSO BY THE AUTHOR
Novels
Grim Reaper
The Big Kiss
Blue Orleans
Crescent City Kills
The Big Show
Mafia Aphrodite
Slick Time
Short Story Collections
LaStanza: New Orleans Police Stories
Hollow Point & The Mystery of Rochelle Marais
New Orleans Irresistible
New Orleans Mysteries
New Orleans Nocturnal
New Orleans Confidential
Screenplay
Waiting for Alaina
Non-Fiction
Specific Intent
A Short Guide to Writing and Selling Fiction

•

COVER PHOTO *JOHN RAVEN BEAU* by O'Neil De Noux
Copyright 2011 © O'Neil De Noux

For more information about the author go to
http://www.oneildenoux.net

"O'Neil De Noux ... No one writes New Orleans as well as
he does." James Sallis

" ... the author knows his stuff when it comes to the Big
Easy." *Publisher's Weekly*, 3/13/06

NEW BOOKS by De Noux
http://www.oneildenoux.net

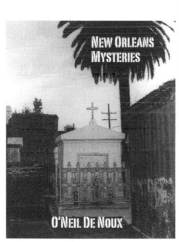

Made in the USA
Charleston, SC
21 March 2011